Scandal TAKES A Holiday

Scandal TAKES A Holiday

DEBORAH HALE

ISBN 978-0-9940693-4-4

Dedication

To Sue and The Girls, who so deserve
their Happily Ever After

Chapter One

"DASH IT ALL! What is that wretched pirate doing at an earl's country house?"

Her twin sister's vexed outburst made Lily Crawford glance toward the frosted window where Iris stood, gazing outward.

"Pirate?" Lily shook her head. "What are you talking about? Lady Killoran invited us here for a house party, not a Christmas pantomime."

"Precisely!" Iris pointed down at the front courtyard of Beckwith Abbey in a dramatic gesture of disdain. "The countess assured Aunt Althea that all her male guests would be of the finest pedigree, with no wretched fortune hunters to plague us. Yet there is that incorrigible Captain Turner descending as if he owned the place. Everyone knows he hasn't a drop of noble blood."

"Neither have we," Lily gently reminded her sister as she joined Iris at the window of their guest chamber. "How can you snub Captain Turner for his lack of pedigree when you resent the titled ladies who turn up their noses at us?"

"That is different," Iris insisted in a sharp tone. She was not accustomed to having her opinions questioned by her meek, retiring sister. "We have accomplishments and deportment to equal any lady in the *ton*. Captain Turner positively enjoys shocking everyone in Society with his rough, blunt manner."

Ordinarily, her sister's vehement response would have

been enough to silence Lily on the subject, but for some reason she could not hold her tongue. "A privateer is not the same thing as a pirate, though I expect the captain has been accustomed to taking a firm hand with his crew. As for being a fortune hunter, I hear he has considerable wealth of his own. He does not need to marry an heiress to feather his nest."

Iris gave a contemptuous sniff, but did not try to contradict her sister. "I do not care if he has ten thousand a year! No amount of money could induce me to accept such an ill-bred creature. I want a husband I can be proud of."

During the last fortnight of London's *Little Season*, Lily had frequently heard her sister heap abuse on Captain Aaron Turner. The captain did not seem to be discouraged by Iris's rebuffs, but instead redoubled his efforts to win her regard. Lily was anxious to discover if Captain Turner looked as much a blackguard as her sister had made him sound.

Peering down at the courtyard, she spied three men engaged in conversation. Though she had never met Captain Turner in person, Lily had no difficulty picking him out of the trio. His rugged, chiselled features had clearly been bronzed by relentless sun and wind. His wide stance and thrust-back shoulders gave him an unmistakable air of confidence and command. His thick dark hair hung almost to his shoulders. The man might not be a pirate, but Lily could not deny he looked the way she imagined a pirate might. The sight of him provoked a quiver of alarm, but also an unexpected flicker of fascination.

"Perhaps Captain Turner has not come to stay," Lily made a belated effort to pacify her sister. "He may only have brought the other gentlemen from London on his way to spend Christmas elsewhere."

Iris considered her sister's suggestion. "I hope you are right. I cannot abide the thought of that scoundrel lurking about, intimidating more worthy suitors to keep their distance, the way he did in London. Why, I might have been engaged to Lord Parrsborough by now if not for his interference."

Lily could not hold that offense against Captain Turner. She had been desperately alarmed that her sister might make a match with the Earl of Onslow's feckless heir. If the captain had managed to prevent that calamity, he had done her a service.

As she mulled over that notion, Captain Turner suddenly turned to survey the gracious sandstone façade of Beckwith Abbey. His gaze rose at once to the window through which the Crawford sisters were watching him.

A sharp stab of panic struck Lily, as if they had been caught doing something illicit. But the captain did not seem to mind their scrutiny. His mouth stretched into a broad grin that was visible even from a distance. Then he doffed his hat and made an extravagant bow.

"Presumptuous beast!" Iris cried and spun away from the window.

Lily knew she should follow her sister's example. From earliest childhood, her personality had been as reserved and bashful as Iris's was vivacious. The mere prospect of being regarded by a gentleman had long filled her with dismay — especially one of such imposing presence as Captain Turner.

And yet, some bewildering force rooted her to the spot, unable to move or look away. Her cheeks flushed with heat, as if she were standing in front of a roaring fire rather than an icy window. To her further confusion, her hand seemed to rise of its own accord and acknowledge the captain's gesture with a cheerful wave.

"Lily!" her sister shrieked. "What on earth has got into you?"

As she staggered back from the window, Lily wondered that as well. She usually avoided social gatherings whenever possible. When forced out of comfortable isolation, she cultivated an air of silent disdain to mask her timidity. What could have possessed her to behave in such a forward manner toward a man she knew only by reputation — and a very unfavorable reputation at that?

"For pity sake, do not encourage that odious creature!" Iris's full lower lip thrust out and her fine brows drew together over the bridge of her delicate nose. "What if he mistook you for me from a distance? I might never be able to get rid of him."

Mistaken for Iris? In spite of Lily's consternation, the idea almost made her laugh. Although they were twins and their features identical in every respect, their opposite natures made them appear quite dissimilar. No one ever had the slightest difficulty telling which Crawford sister was which.

Lily always wore her hair in a simple, subdued style. According to their aunt, it made her look several years older than Iris with her girlish froth of curls. A sickly childhood had left Lily pale and slender, while her sister possessed a fine figure and brilliant complexion.

Lily shook her head. "I'm certain you do not have to worry about the captain making that mistake, unless he is half-blind."

Even as she muttered those words in an apologetic tone, Lily wondered if her sister's unlikely suggestion might explain her strange behaviour. The captain had been too far away to require conversation, which she found so awkward and unsettling. The distance, and possibility of being mistaken for Iris, might have overcome the worst of her timidity.

Iris seemed to realize how unfounded her worry was. "I suppose you are right. But if Captain Turner ends up staying at Beckwith Abbey, I shall waste no time making certain he knows the truth."

A choking lump of dismay leapt into Lily's throat. "Please don't, Iris! It would be so humiliating. I could never hold up my head for the rest of our visit."

"You hardly do that anyway." Iris turned toward the glass above the dressing table and fluffed her hair. "Except when you are pretending to be too haughty to speak. I do not see why your embarrassment should signify more than my dislike of that detestable man."

Before Lily could come up with a satisfactory response, a

brief, insistent rap sounded on the door of their guest chamber, making her jump.

Without waiting to be invited, their aunt swept in. A widow of comfortable means, Althea Henderson had once been a great beauty. Even in her mid-forties, she was still a handsome woman with sharp blue eyes and golden brown hair, which she watched anxiously for any threads of silver.

"My dears, are you ready?" Mrs. Henderson swept a scrutinizing glance over her nieces and seemed satisfied with their appearance. "You must come at once to greet the gentlemen. They have just arrived from London!"

"We know, Aunt Althea." Iris gave each of her cheeks a little pinch to summon a becoming blush. "We saw them down in the courtyard. You will never guess what Lily did, the little goose."

Lily's cheeks tingled with embarrassment as, if she had been pinching them hard for an hour.

Fortunately their aunt took little interest in her doings, good or ill. "You may tell me all about it later, my love. Now you must come and make the best possible impression before the other ladies beat you to it."

Lily bit back a protest she knew would be useless. Her beautiful, vivacious sister would be an immediate favourite with the gentlemen, no matter how many other pretty faces they encountered first. She on the other hand could not hope to find favour, nor did she wish to. Already she was heartily sick of the marriage market, where eligible men made it clear they only admired the size of her fortune. The sooner she could protect her future by finding her sister an honest, responsible husband, the sooner she could settle down and enjoy the tranquil spinsterhood she craved.

"Welcome to Beckwith Abbey, Captain Turner." The Earl of Killoran exchanged polite bows with Aaron. "How fortunate my brother was able to prevail upon you to join our party."

Aaron bit back a mocking grin at the earl's courteous duplicity. Rory Fitzwalter had not "prevailed upon him" to spend the holidays at Beckwith Abbey. Aaron had procured the invitation in payment of a rather large gambling debt the earl's brother owed him. In general, Aaron preferred to call a spade a spade, but if Lord Killoran wanted to pretend he was a welcome guest, he would play along. Anything to permit him a fortnight in private company with the divine Miss Crawford!

"I am grateful for your hospitality, Lord Killoran." Aaron scanned the richly appointed Great Parlor with approval.

The dark panelled walls rose to a lofty white and gilded ceiling. They were hung with an array of portraits from past centuries. Fine carpets covered most of the intricate parquet floor. The vast hearth was a showpiece, carved from snow-white chalk.

"This will be the first year in many that I have not spent Christmas at sea," he continued. "It will be a most welcome change, I assure you."

At times, he missed the pitch and sway of the deck beneath his feet, the rhythmic roll of the ocean waves and the briny tang of the spray. But it would be a welcome change to dine on festive fare that was not salted, smoked, dried or pickled until barely edible. Ready access to company of the fair sex would be an even more precious boon — one lady in particular.

He had not made as much headway as he would have liked in courting Miss Crawford during their acquaintance in London. Aaron blamed the formal atmosphere and the distraction of so many other suitors vying for her attention. As vibrantly beautiful as her namesake flower, Iris Crawford had been the most sought after debutante of the *Little Season*. Aaron had made no secret of his determination to win the lady's hand, going so far as to make a number of wagers with those who doubted him. In the more intimate setting of a winter house party, he had no doubt he would prevail.

That thought was still fresh in his mind when a group of

ladies entered the room. Aaron could scarcely contain his delight at finding Miss Crawford among them. It had amused him to catch her spying on his arrival at Beckwith Abbey with Rory Fitzwalter and Lord Gabriel Stanford. Such behaviour betrayed greater interest than she had shown him previously. It buoyed his confidence.

"I see the gentlemen have arrived," remarked a refined-looking lady whom Aaron guessed must be the countess. "How kind of dear Rory not to keep us waiting."

Rory Fitzwalter laughed heartily, as if he had not detected a subtle sting in her quip. "I cannot take the credit for that, Regina. Captain Turner offered us the use of his carriage for the journey. When I heard he would be on his own for Christmas, I insisted he must join our party. I know an extra bachelor never goes astray on these occasions."

"How thoughtful of you." Lady Killoran glared at her brother-in-law with a smile that might have curdled milk. Her bristling tone belied the proper courtesy of her words. "I am certain the captain will be a marvellous addition to our company."

She seemed determined to waste no further time on Aaron. "Gentlemen, allow me to introduce Mrs. Henderson and her nieces, Miss Iris Crawford and Miss Lily. My dears, it is my pleasure to present my husband's brother, Rory Fitzwalter and his particular friend Lord Gabriel Stanford, son of the Duke of Cheviot."

"*A* son," Lord Gabriel muttered, as if self-conscious about his lofty connections. "The youngest of several."

He and Rory bowed to the ladies. Mrs. Henderson and Miss Crawford smiled warmly and swept the gentlemen deep curtsies. Miss Lily made a barely civil bob.

Aaron tried to catch Iris Crawford's eye and include himself in her smile, but she looked past him as if he were quite invisible. He resented the enthusiastic way she greeted his aristocratic companions. Stanford and Fitzwalter were decent enough fellows, in spite of their titled relations, but they would be the first to admit he had more to offer a wife than both of them put together.

He caught Rory Fitzwalter's eye and made subtle nod toward Iris Crawford.

The earl's brother needed no further prompting. "Now that we have been introduced, ladies, it is my pleasure to present my new friend, Captain Aaron Turner. I am certain he will make an excellent addition to our party. He has led a far more exciting life than Lord Gabriel and I. Wait until you hear some of his stories."

Iris Crawford regarded Aaron as if he had suddenly appeared out of nowhere. "My aunt and I are already acquainted with the captain, though I had no idea he would be celebrating Christmas at Beckwith Abbey."

The surprise did not appear to please her, judging by the way her blue-violet eyes flashed. Aaron welcomed the challenge to improve her opinion of him. He executed a bow that would equal the grace of any nobleman. "Mrs. Henderson, Miss Crawford, it is a pleasant surprise to meet you again under such agreeable circumstances, and to make the acquaintance of your charming sister."

He directed his warmest smile at Miss Lily. Though not nearly as vivacious as her sister, she possessed a subdued beauty he could not help but admire. It occurred to him that the lady might be able to provide him with helpful information about her sister's interests and habits. He would be wise to cultivate her acquaintance.

"One would suppose you and Lily were old friends, Captain," Iris Crawford's merry tone and dazzling smile quite bewitched Aaron, though he sensed her remark was directed more at her sister than him, "the way she greeted your arrival with such a display of enthusiasm."

Miss Lily did not acknowledge her sister's words but turned away sharply. "What a fine house you have, Lady Killoran. Pray, who is the lady in the picture beside the mantel?"

"I'm certain Lord Gabriel could tell you better than I."

The countess beckoned the young nobleman forward. "He is quite an authority on art and history. Rory, perhaps you could show Miss Crawford ... something of interest. I must confer with my husband about the arrangements for Captain Turner, if you will excuse us."

No doubt the earl was about to get an earful from his wife for failing to send their unexpected guest packing. Aaron hoped his presence would not cause too much inconvenience at Beckwith Abbey. From what he had seen of the sprawling old mansion, he doubted it would be difficult to accommodate one more guest. If he succeeded in winning Iris Crawford, he would do everything in his power to repay the Killorans' hospitality ten times over.

Lord Gabriel approached Miss Lily as the countess had bidden him. She regarded him with sullen silence, quite unlike the animated greeting she'd given Aaron upon his arrival.

Meanwhile Iris Crawford and her aunt descended on Rory Fitzwalter, peppering him with questions about Beckwith Abbey and his family. The Irishman responded with his usual wry charm, which seemed directed more toward Mrs. Henderson than her enchanting niece. Aaron could not deny she was a striking woman, though she radiated severe disapproval of him.

Tempted as he was to join the threesome and bask in Iris Crawford's lively company, Aaron decided it might be wise to learn more about her from the person who knew her best. Besides, he sensed that Miss Lily might need to be rescued from Lord Gabriel ... or vice versa. When she showed little interest in the young nobleman's remarks about the painting, he had lapsed into offended silence.

Now he glanced toward Aaron with an unmistakable plea in his eyes.

Aaron approached the pair. "I beg your pardon, Lord Gabriel, but I should like a word with Miss Lily."

"By all means, Captain!" The young man's eagerness to foist his unsatisfactory companion upon someone else was so obvious; Aaron could not stifle a pang of sympathy for the lady. He remembered all too well the sting of having one's company shunned. Though he had grown a thick hide and come to regard such coolness as a challenge, he suspected a woman might be more sensitive to such slights.

"Miss Lily." He bowed again. "I wish to thank you for your warm greeting when I arrived. Though unexpected, it was flattering and most welcome."

Aaron hoped his appreciative words might ingratiate him with Iris Crawford's sister. Instead, her alabaster complexion paled further and her tense bearing grew positively rigid. The lady seemed to freeze into a statue of ice, which he feared might chill him to the bone.

———— • • ————

Lily wished she could sink through the elaborate carpet in the Killorans' great parlor and disappear until the torment of this house party was over!

Had it not been bad enough for Iris to shame her by mentioning her earlier lapse in propriety? If Captain Turner possessed a single gentlemanly impulse, he would have ignored the subject altogether. Instead, he seemed bent on further humiliating her. Clearly he must be as great a scoundrel as Iris had described him!

Masking her mortification behind a façade of icy hauteur, Lily tried to look down her nose at the captain. But he was so tall she could not manage it without tilting her head at an awkward angle.

She settled for adopting a chilly tone. "There is no need to be grateful, sir. It was a foolish mistake on my part. I thought you were someone else."

Lily's conscience chided her for telling a falsehood, but her pride insisted it was necessary.

She assumed Captain Turner would reply in a gruff tone, befitting his formidable presence. Or perhaps he would be stung into affronted silence by her prickly manner. Instead he gave a cheerful shrug, accompanied by a dangerously endearing grin. For an instant, she glimpsed the cheeky cabin boy beneath the intrepid commander.

"Mistake or not, I thank you just the same. As a last-minute guest, invited thanks to Mr. Fitzwalter's charity, I was uncertain what sort of reception might await me. Your enthusiastic welcome reassured me that at least one person was pleased to see me. But I must apologize for disappointing you. The gentleman for whom you mistook me is most fortunate to have secured such warm regard."

The roguish twinkle in Captain Turner's dark eyes appealed to Lily far more than she wished, considering the irony of his words. Anyone overhearing them might have believed he was perfectly sincere, but she knew better.

How often, as a child, had she overheard the servants comparing her unfavourably to her engaging, outgoing sister? Iris would have her pick of beaux when she grew up, they had confidently predicted, while her sickly twin would be lucky to snare a husband who wanted her fortune.

The first time she'd heard such tattle, Lily had privately vowed she would never marry a man like that. As the years passed and she encountered a number of grasping fortune hunters, her resolve had hardened to the point where she refused to consider marrying at all.

Now here was a far-too-attractive man, taunting her about having an admirer. Captain Turner might not be an obvious fortune hunter, like some gentlemen of their party, but that did not mean he could be trusted.

Lily shot him a frosty glare. "I will thank you not to amuse yourself at my expense, Captain Turner. I know very well it is my sister, not I, who draws gentlemen like moths to a candle. I have no doubt you pursued her here. Tell me, how did you secure your invitation from Mr. Fitzwalter — with a bribe or a threat?"

If she had pulled out a loaded duelling pistol and aimed it

at his head, Lily doubted Captain Turner could have looked more confounded. His mouth fell open and every twinkle of levity fled from dark his eyes as they widened.

"Y-you are quite mistaken, I assure you" he stammered, though his denial only confirmed her suspicions.

The timid part of Lily, which hid behind her mask of cool disdain, urged her to take advantage of the captain's confusion and stage a strategic retreat. But his bewilderment gave her a surge of unexpected confidence. "I may not possess my sister's vivacity, sir, but I am not a fool. I know what you are doing here and I am inclined to approve. If you are as shrewd a man as I hoped, you might recognize how valuable an ally I could be to you and treat me with a little respect."

If she thought the captain had been taken aback before, it was nothing to his present reaction. His firm, resolute mouth opened and closed, but no reply emerged. Lily sensed this was an uncommon state for him. She doubted he could have become a successful privateer if he'd allowed his composure to be easily shaken.

Once again her self-protective instincts warned Lily to extricate herself from their conversation while she had the opportunity. Who knew how such a man might lash out once he'd collected his wits? Yet somehow, her legs refused to cooperate.

Fortunately, a welcome distraction arrived just then. The earl and countess returned, accompanied by the rest of their guests. One was a stocky middle-aged man with dark, bushy brows. His rough, weathered features did not match his well-tailored attire. The other two, a younger man and woman, were both very attractive — perhaps too much for their own good.

Conversation in the room fell silent and all attention turned to the newcomers.

Nodding toward the fair-haired young gentleman, Lady Killoran addressed the rest of the company. "I am delighted to present my dear brother, Sidney, Viscount Uvedale."

As everyone greeted Lord Uvedale with bows and curt-sies, Lily noticed her sister giving the viscount an encouraging smile. Clearly Iris was in her glory, with three handsome young noblemen from whom to choose.

"It is also our pleasure," said the earl, "to welcome Mr. Brennan and his daughter, Miss Moira Brennan, to spend Christmas with us."

Mr. Brennan regarded his fellow guests with an engaging grin, as if he had been waiting all his life to meet them. For an instant, Lily let her armor of reserve slip to greet him with a fleeting smile. It remained in place long enough to reach his daughter as well. Lily could not help but admire Moira Brennan's rich auburn hair and luminous complexion. Her green eyes seemed to sparkle with innocent merriment.

"Mr. Brennan made his fortune in shipping," the earl continued in a tone that betrayed none of the disdain for *trade* which Lily had encountered from others of his rank. "It is something you have in common with the Crawford family, sir. Allow me to present Miss Iris Crawford, her sister Miss Lily and their aunt, Mrs. Henderson."

As Lord Killoran gestured toward each of them in turn, Lily noticed her sister did not look pleased by the arrival of Miss Brennan.

"And Captain Turner, of course," the earl added, as if the privateer was a less-than-pleasant afterthought.

Lily recalled what the captain had said about being uncer-tain of his welcome at Beckwith Abbey. It seemed he might be right to have expected a cool reception. The thought roused her sympathy, in spite of her recent antagonism toward him. Aaron Turner must have exercised some resourcefulness to secure a place at the Killorans' house party, so he would have an opportunity to court the lady he admired. Was that so wrong?

A qualm of dismay gripped Lily as she wondered whether she might have misjudged the captain's earlier remarks. Could he have been sincerely grateful for the brazen manner in which she'd greeted his arrival? Might he truly believe she had a beau?

She stole a glance in his direction only to discover his bold features clenched in a fierce scowl. Had she offended him so much that he might abandon his pursuit of her sister?

Lily pondered that unsettling possibility as Lord Killoran continued his round of introductions. Once they had concluded, the guests began to mingle and get acquainted. Lily retreated to a quiet corner, pretending to admire a painting of a gentleman holding the bridle of a black horse. The presence of two such spirited beauties as Iris and Miss Brennan insured that no one paid her the least attention, which was just what she preferred.

Unnoticed, she took the opportunity to listen in on the other guests' conversations. Nothing she overheard disposed her to approve of Rory Fitzwalter, Lord Uvedale or Lord Gabriel Stanford as a prospective brother-in-law. Iris needed a husband who could safeguard their fortunes by making their late father's business prosper. None of the attractive, well-spoken noblemen seemed to possess the slightest spark of ambition. By comparison, Captain Turner had demonstrated considerable initiative and resolve.

Besides, Lily wanted to see her sister happily wed for more than a year or two. From all she had observed of aristocratic gentlemen, fidelity was not a virtue they made any effort to cultivate. She sensed Captain Turner would not be quick to cast aside a prize he had worked so hard to win.

She must persuade him not to give up his pursuit of Iris on her account. But was it already too late?

Chapter Two

HOW HAD HE managed to aggravate Iris Crawford's sister, when he'd wanted nothing more than to make a favourable impression on her? Aaron puzzled over that question as he dressed for his first dinner at Beckwith Abbey that evening.

Had his years at sea in the company of rough sailors left him at an insurmountable disadvantage when it came to engaging the fair sex? He could not deny the possibility, yet for the life of him he could not fathom why Miss Lily had been so deeply offended by his efforts to ingratiate himself. Could it be the same reason her sister resisted his attempts to court her? If so, he must identify his flaws as a suitor and set about correcting them.

With three other gentlemen competing for Iris Crawford's affections, Aaron knew he had no time to waste. Since it would not do to inquire of the lady herself about his deficiencies, there could only be one source for that vital information.

He cast a critical glance at his reflection in the glass, hoping his appearance would pass muster, at least. Although he had invested in a fine new wardrobe from the most fashionable tailor on Bond Street, Aaron feared he might never acquire the air of effortless refinement that Stanford and Fitzwalter achieved with far more limited means. The fierce dark appearance that had served him so well in the past now marked him as an interloper in polite society.

Never mind about that. Aaron stood tall and thrust out his chest. He would not apologize for looking more like a wolf than a pampered lapdog. He would compel Society to accept him without conforming to its dictates.

With that objective firmly in mind, he strode off to the drawing room, where he'd been informed the guests would gather before dinner. Finding the chamber deserted, Aaron wondered whether he had got the location wrong. Or perhaps Rory Fitzwalter had steered him amiss on purpose, to beat him to the march with Iris Crawford! Aaron cursed under his breath and stormed back out the door.

In his haste, he collided with someone trying to enter the room.

Miss Lily? Aaron almost spit out another curse. Knocking the lady over was not likely to mend a bad first impression.

"I beg your pardon!' he cried, seizing her in his arms to prevent her from falling.

A faint scent wafted up from her severely braided hair to beguile him. The subtle floral fragrance put him in mind of a dew-kissed country garden. Somehow it addled his wits, making him cling to Miss Lily longer than he intended — far longer than she cared to endure, no doubt. He would be lucky if she did not strike him for his pains!

Once he made certain she had regained her balance, Aaron released her and backed out of reach. "Forgive me, Miss Lily! I hope I have not injured you, charging about like that. You will never have a good opinion of me now I fear."

"Do not fret, Captain," she assured him, though her breathless, high-pitched tone betrayed the shock she had suffered. "We collided by accident and your quick reflexes prevented me from taking any harm to my person or dignity."

A wave of gratitude washed over Aaron as her words sank in. He would not have blamed the lady for being vexed with him.

"I believe I will sit for a moment," she continued, making her way to a window seat in the far corner of the room with a rather unsteady gait. "The surprise did take my breath a little."

Aaron followed, wanting to offer her his arm for support but fearing the gesture might be one liberty too many. Spying a decanter and glasses clustered on a side table, he asked, "Can I fetch you a restorative?"

Miss Lily shook her head, making the loops of braided hair over her ears waggle. "There is no need. I shall be right in a moment."

"I should have watched where I was going and not made so much haste." Aaron felt compelled to explain as Miss Lily sank onto the window seat. "When I found no one else here, I thought the guests must be gathering elsewhere and I did not wish to be late. The fact is I had hoped for a word with you before dinner ... though not under these circumstances."

His words betrayed less assurance than he usually tried to project. Yet somehow he did not feel so anxious to act that way around Iris Crawford's sister.

The lady opened her fan and fluttered it before her face, which had acquired a becoming flush. "What a fortunate coincidence, Captain. I came down early, hoping I might speak with you. Upon reflection, I believe I misjudged you and spoke unkindly. If we are to spend this season of peace and goodwill in each other's company, surely we should try to behave accordingly. Don't you agree?"

"I do indeed." Aaron's features relaxed unto a smile of relief. This was a far better outcome than he had dared to hope. "If you suspected me of being impertinent earlier, I am grateful for your tolerance. I swear I did not mean to mock you or underestimate your intelligence. You were correct about my admiration for your sister. I should not have tried to conceal from you the measures I was prepared to take to get closer to her."

As he spoke, Lily Crawford nodded. The flickering radiance cast by the candles and the hearth fire illuminated her delicate features to much better advantage than the cool light of day. "I thought so. Tell me, how *did* you manage to secure an invitation to Lady Killoran's house party?"

"Not by bribe or threat," Aaron insisted, though his conscience suggested it might have been a bit of both. "I merely offered to discharge a debt of honor Rory Fitzwalter owed me. I might have suggested he could express his gratitude by availing me of his brother's hospitality …"

Would his confession make Lily Crawford reconsider the olive branch she'd extended to him? Aaron braced for a rebuke.

To his surprise, the lady's lips arched and a spark of merriment danced in her blue-violet eyes. "How determined and resourceful you are, Captain! Those happen to be two qualities I require in a brother-in-law."

"B-brother?" Aaron's jaw fell slack.

The lady had a rare knack for catching him off-guard.

"What else?" Her earlier coolness seemed to have thawed considerably. "Did I not tell you I was disposed to approve of you as a suitor for Iris?"

He had hoped to secure her cooperation, but he had never supposed she would yield it so easily. Now, if only her incomparable sister would do the same, it would be the best Christmas gift he could imagine!

Suddenly Aaron felt uncomfortable towering over Miss Lily. He sank onto the window seat beside her. "May I ask why you would favour me over the other gentlemen, when I have received so little encouragement from your sister?"

He hoped she would not consider his question too blunt.

If she did, the lady gave no sign of it, but replied with refreshing candor. "Iris has a fancy to be a fine lady and take her place in Society. I am not convinced that will make her happy, especially if the nobleman she weds is more interested in her fortune than her company."

"A very sound opinion." Aaron contemplated another advantage to be gained by winning Iris Crawford. In doing so, he would acquire a sister worthy of his respect. "As you may know, I have secured a comfortable fortune of my own. I would wish to marry your sister even if she did not have a penny to her name."

Was that entirely true? His conscience demanded. He had

not gone looking for a wife at some small rural assembly but among the cream of London Society, where Iris Crawford shone as a diamond of the first water.

Miss Lily's gaze fell before his admiring scrutiny. "I must confess my motives are not altogether selfless, Captain. Since I have no desire to wed, *my* security as well as my sister's will depend upon her choice of husband. I would prefer to see our father's business in the hands of a man who knows how to earn and keep money rather than squander it."

Aaron gave an approving nod. "You have every right to consider how your sister's choice of husband will affect you, Miss Lily. I do not think less of you for being more sensible than sentimental in your view of matrimony."

But why did she not wish to wed? Aaron dared not pose the question that puzzled him so greatly. Though he could not deny the lady suffered in comparison to her dazzling sister, she possessed an elusive charm all her own. As he had discovered, her manner could be aloof, even testy. Was that the *cause* for her to be so much less admired than her sister ... or the result of it?

As his curiosity struggled against discretion, another lady darted into the drawing room. Though dressed with almost severe simplicity, she possessed a vivid raven beauty that almost rivalled Iris Crawford's golden loveliness.

The newcomer started at the sight of the couple on the window seat. "Pray excuse me for intruding! I was told Lady Killoran's guests were to gather here before dinner."

Aaron and Lily scrambled to their feet in a way that might have appeared furtive. It was clear the other lady believed she had interrupted some sort of romantic tryst. The idea almost made Aaron laugh.

He and Lily Crawford had only one thing in common — the desire to promote a match between him and her glorious sister.

A surge of embarrassment engulfed Lily at being discovered alone with Captain Turner. What must the other woman think of her and the handsome captain conversing together in the shadowy alcove?

The way Captain Turner shot to his feet made it clear he disliked being caught with her in a somewhat compromising situation.

"Do not trouble yourself!" he cried. "You are not interrupting anything of consequence. It appears the three of us have arrived early ... or perhaps the others are late."

Their conversation meant nothing of consequence to him? Lily bristled ... on her sister's behalf, of course.

Captain Turner did not redeem himself by immediately striding toward the lovely newcomer. "I do not believe we have been presented. In the absence of our hosts I suppose it is not improper to introduce ourselves. I am Aaron Turner, a last-minute addition to the party."

The lady responded to his polite bow with a curtsey. "A pleasure to meet you, sir. I believe I owe my invitation to dinner to your presence. I am Lady Killoran's companion, Kitty Delany. Ordinarily I do not dine with the family when they entertain, but the countess did not want her table to be put out."

Lily stifled an impatient sigh. Did it really matter so much if the number ladies and gentlemen at the countess's table were not precisely equal?

Miss Delany caught her lower lip between her teeth. "I should not have told you that! Please do not mention it to Lady Killoran. She would not wish you to think your presence is an imposition."

The captain chuckled. "You may depend upon my discretion, Miss Delany. If my arrival has been of benefit to you, I am pleased. Now that we are acquainted, allow me to present Miss Lily Crawford. She, her sister and her aunt are proper Christmas guests of the Killorans."

"Of course." The lady glanced toward Lily as if having

forgotten her presence. "The countess has spoken of you often of late. Welcome to Beckwith Abbey. I hope you will enjoy your holiday here."

"Miss Delany." Lily curtsied, but did not make an effort to engage her in conversation.

Something in the other woman's manner suggested that she might once have been more than a hired companion to the countess.

The trio were soon joined by the rest of the party. There followed a half hour of lively conversation, which felt more like torment to Lily. She stuck close to her aunt, hovering on the edge of the group, hoping no one would single her out by addressing her directly. She cast a glance toward the captain and Miss Delany, who chatted like old friends with Rory Fitzwalter and Lord Uvedale. How did Captain Turner expect to win Iris if he never spoke a word to her? Lily quietly fumed.

At last their hostess paired the ladies and gentlemen of the party to go in to dinner. Lily found herself on the arm of Lord Gabriel Stanford, who looked as though he expected her to bite his head off at any moment. Captain Turner was chosen to escort Miss Delany, a duty he appeared to undertake with considerable pleasure. Did it not trouble him how delighted Iris looked to be in the company of Lord Uvedale?

Lily did not have long to fret about that, for she soon found herself at the Killorans' long dining table, splendidly decked with greenery and towers of fruit.

Lord Gabriel sat to her right and Captain Turner to her left. She would rather have been tucked away in a far corner, where she might have avoided notice as much as possible.

Fortunately Lord Gabriel did not seem inclined to trouble her with conversation. Instead he turned his attention to Miss Brennan who was seated on his other side.

"So that's how it is." Captain Turner leaned toward Lily and made his comment in a low murmur that was lost amid the general conversation and serving of the soup.

"I beg your pardon?" she replied just as quietly.

Deborah Hale

He gave a soft rustling chuckle that Lily found difficult to resist. "I only wished to observe that Lady Killoran's match-making plans are quite plain."

"Indeed?" Lily tried to remain cool. She had not approved of the captain paying so much attention to a lady other than her sister. "And what do you suppose those plans to be?"

Since their conversation was not one she cared to have overheard, she was obliged to lean closer to the captain and lower her voice. The captain's nearness made her anxious. Her heart fluttered like the wings of a trapped moth and she could only breathe in swift, shallow gulps. Her flesh tingled too. She could not recall that happening before.

Captain Turner's dark eyes twinkled with roguish mischief. "Notice the seating arrangements and think of how her ladyship paired us to come in. Lord Uvedale is meant for your sister, Miss Brennan for Rory Fitzwalter and you for Lord Gabriel Stanford."

Lily's stomach twisted in a painful knot. Lord Gabriel was very good looking and he seemed to possess a certain boyish charm. But it was clear that any attention he paid her was only at the urging of Lady Killoran. He was precisely the kind of suitor she wished to avoid. She would gain nothing from such a union but worry, humiliation and perhaps heartbreak.

"What about my aunt?" she asked, in an effort to distract herself from such troubling thoughts. "Is she meant to make a match with Mr. Brennan? And you with Miss Delany?"

The latter dismayed her almost as much as the thought of herself with Lord Gabriel.

"A matter of convenience, I suspect." The captain's husky whisper sent a ripple of agitation down Lily's neck. "Or perhaps the countess wishes to provide a distraction for me, so I will not upset her plans for your sister and her brother. If she knew me at all, she would realize how futile such tactics are. Once my mind is made up, I will not be thwarted."

A warm ripple of relief swept through Lily. She was growing more and more certain that Captain Aaron Turner would make an excellent husband for her sister. She had feared the presence of the lovely Miss Delany might upset her plans. But if the captain could remain constant to Iris without any encouragement, Lily felt certain he would remain faithful after they were wed.

She regarded him with a smile of warm approval, which he returned in equal measure. Lily's earlier anxiety eased and an unaccustomed sense of satisfaction stole over her.

Then, from across the table, Iris's voice broke in upon her confidential exchange with the Aaron Turner. "I vow, Captain, you have accomplished a miracle, coaxing my sister to converse in company. As a rule, she disdains such frivolity. You must be quite a gentleman of information to have engaged her interest."

Lily's cheeks blazed. How she detested being made the center of attention! The only time it ever seemed to occur was when someone made her a figure of fun. This was the second time today that her sister had held her up to ridicule.

If only she could make some light-hearted quip to cover her confusion and deflect the quizzical gazes fixed upon her. But her vocal organs felt paralyzed.

Then Captain Turner spoke in a bantering tone Lily wished she'd been able to adopt. "Much as I would like to merit your praise, Miss Crawford, it was your sister who engaged *my* attention. I cannot recall when I have enjoyed a conversation more."

"With Lily?" Iris gave a trill of mischievous laughter, while their aunt shook her head in disbelief. "Oh Captain, surely you jest."

"I assure you," he insisted. "I am in perfect earnest."

Rory Fitzwalter must have sensed an undercurrent of friction among the party and sought to smooth it out.

"I say, Charles," he called down the table to his brother, "what manner of amusement do you have planned for us after we dine?"

Lord Killoran pulled a droll face. "I fear our party would

languish in boredom if such arrangements were left up to me. Fortunately, such matters are in the far more capable hands of my dear wife. You must appeal to her for information."

Most of the guests chuckled and any tension quickly eased — except that within Lily. As the countess spoke of the diversions she had planned for their time at Beckwith Abbey, Lily kept her gaze fixed on her brimming bowl of oxtail soup. She consumed the clear, savory liquid with single-minded attention, as if she had been fasting for days before this meal.

If she concentrated very hard on bringing the spoon to her lips without spilling a drop, she might be able to ignore the suffocating lump in her throat and the furious tingling of her eyes. Over the years she had mastered many such tricks to conceal her distress from others.

"I beg your pardon, Miss Lily," the captain murmured when the table conversation around them had resumed. "I hope I did not say anything to offend you just now?"

The sincere concern in his tone taxed Lily's composure worse than her sister's teasing. She shook her head vigorously, hoping he would be content with that answer and not expect her to speak.

How could she deny her emotions were roused when she could scarcely contain them? Even if she could bring herself to confess the truth, how could she expect a man like Captain Turner to understand that she had been moved nearly to tears by the gallant way he'd stood up for her.

Iris Crawford's sister was the most baffling lady Aaron had ever encountered! One minute she bristled with frigid hostility, the next she overwhelmed him with unexpected support. Now she seemed afflicted with mute dismay, for no reason he could fathom.

He found himself wanting to cajole her into a better humor, the way he'd once done with his own beloved sister, but he feared he might only upset her worse. He could not afford to do that after she had offered to help him win her sister's heart and hand.

He would need all the assistance he could get, judging by the progress Lord Uvedale appeared to be making with Iris Crawford. Could Miss Crawford not see that the viscount's smooth flattery was all a charade? Even as the young coxcomb paid her an extravagant compliment, his glance strayed down the table toward his sister's companion, Miss Delany. Aaron had seen the gleam of lust often enough in the eyes of his crew on shore leave to recognize it at a Society house party.

Was Miss Delany often bothered by such lewd interest from the Killorans' male guests? Rory Fitzwalter had greeted her in rather too familiar a manner this evening, though she did not seem to mind. Privately Aaron resolved to keep an eye out for the countess's companion during the coming fortnight, to make certain none of the other men tried to impose upon her.

Since Lily Crawford seemed reluctant to converse with him now, he turned toward Miss Delany. "Have you been Lady Killoran's companion for long?"

Miss Delany had been staring toward the foot of the table, where the countess sat. When Aaron spoke, she ducked her head and muttered a barely audible reply. "Three years, sir."

Had he said something he shouldn't? Aaron had never been one to doubt his abilities, but his exchanges with the Crawford sisters and now Miss Delany undermined that certainty. "I beg your pardon for my ignorance, but I am not certain precisely what a companion is or does. Perhaps you would be so kind as to enlighten me."

Miss Delany cast a furtive glance toward the earl, who sat on her left, at the head of the table. He was currently absorbed in a discussion of Irish politics with Mr. Brennan and Iris Crawford's aunt.

Keeping her voice low, Miss Delany answered Aaron's question. "It varies from one situation to another. But in general a companion is something between a poor relation and a lady's maid with certain privileges."

She did not make it sound like an enviable position to occupy.

"How did you become her ladyship's companion?" Aaron could not stifle the question, though he sensed it might not be welcome.

After a long pause Miss Delany murmured. "The countess was a friend of my family when we lived in Ireland. After my mother and stepfather died, Lady Killoran invited me to come and live with her. She has been very kind to me. I owe her a greater debt than I could ever repay."

Aaron sensed there was more to her story than the lady cared to confide. What little she had told him reminded Aaron of his own youth. Only, there had been no titled benefactor to assist him and his sister. If there had been, perhaps he would not feel this nagging animosity toward members of the *ton*, and an urgent desire to make them accept him on his own terms.

Finding that thought too uncomfortable, Aaron focussed his attention on the one person he could rely upon to divert him — Iris Crawford.

At the moment, she was regaling Lord Uvedale and Rory Fitzwalter with a story of her misadventures in trying to purchase a new hat. Her blue-violet eyes sparkled in a bewitching manner as she spoke. Her features looked more attractive than ever for being so delightfully animated. The lively inflection of her voice and the lilting music of her laughter captivated Aaron, as they had from the first moment he'd set eyes upon her. How could he abide it, if she fell in love with some other man, especially one as patently unworthy of her as that swaggering puppy, Uvedale?

The viscount did not improve in Aaron's estimation when Lord Killoran and his male guests lingered over brandy after the ladies had excused themselves from the table.

"My stables have had a vile run of luck this year," he complained to Rory and Lord Gabriel. "Merrylegs went lame a week before Ascot and Pocketwatch finished well out of the prize money at Newmarket, for which I blame her jockey. Papa threatens to make me sell my stable to settle my debts, but I'd sooner lose a mistress than a good mare."

While the others laughed at Lord Uvedale's quip, Aaron had to bite his tongue to stifle a very rude remark.

"Horses are an expense, to be sure," Mr. Brennan commiserated.

Lord Uvedale did not even bother to glance in the older man's direction, but kept on talking as if he had not heard. "Speaking of mistresses, did either of you see the item in *Town and Country* about me and Madame Reynard? Her favors are well worth the price, though she might be a bit young for your taste, Rory."

Lord Gabriel sputtered with laughter. "Rory is not inclined to pay for what he can be well compensated to receive."

Aaron knew what that meant. It was no secret that Lord Killoran's personable younger brother admired women of more mature years, who could be very generous. Yet the noblemen's banter set his teeth on edge. How could Uvedale brag about some strumpet, no matter how coveted, when he had recently enjoyed the company of a respectable enchantress like Miss Crawford?

If he paid any more heed to the coxcomb, Aaron knew he risked saying or doing something that might offend his hosts. He could not afford to make himself any more unpopular with the earl and countess.

Since Viscount Uvedale seemed determined to ignore him and Mr. Brennan, Aaron saw no reason why they should provide him with an audience.

He caught the older man's eye and offered a comradely smile. "A fleet of ships can cost a great deal more than a stable of horses and get into far worse trouble. I'm sure you know a thing or two about that, Mr. Brennan."

Lord Uvedale shot Aaron an indignant glare for having the presumption to speak.

Mr. Brennan appeared as pleased with Aaron's remark as Lord Uvedale was annoyed. "Quite right you are, Captain. Between weather, winds and hostilities at sea, every voyage can be a different sort of gamble."

Uvedale returned to his conversation, raising the volume of his voice. Aaron and Mr. Brennan cheerfully ignored him, and had a pleasant discussion about the caprices of the sea. Before long, Lord Gabriel joined their conversation. Perhaps he sensed he would have more opportunity to get a word in than would be possible with Lord Uvedale.

When the viscount responded by raising his voice almost to a shout, Lord Killoran rose from his chair and cleared his throat. "Gentlemen, I believe we have lingered over our brandy long enough when such congenial company awaits us. Shall we join the ladies and discover what entertainment my wife has in store for us?"

The other men responded with eager agreement. They practically raced one another to the door and down the wide candlelit passage. Following the lure of sweet music, they flocked to the Great Parlor. A merry fire crackled in the vast chalk hearth, while the windowsills were decked with festive greenery.

They found Iris Crawford and her sister playing a duet on the pianoforte. Miss Lily supplied the lower part with understated skill, while her sister played the melody in a graceful, animated manner that was as much a pleasure to watch as to hear.

When Miss Crawford concluded with a playful flourish, Aaron and Lord Uvedale competed to offer the most enthusiastic applause. She acknowledged their accolades with a bright, confident smile while Miss Lily bowed her head and blushed as if such attention was the last thing she desired.

"Well done, indeed!" cried the countess. "How very accomplished you are, ladies."

Though she clearly intended to praise the Crawford sisters, Aaron sensed her surprise that daughters of a tradesman had acquired such skill.

"I hope you will favor us with many more performances during your stay at Beckwith Abbey," Lady Killoran continued. "But now that the gentlemen have rejoined us, we must take advantage of their presence to enjoy some dancing."

"What a marvellous idea!" Iris Crawford sprang from her seat at the pianoforte. She beamed at Lord Uvedale as if the suggestion had been his rather than his sister's. "I love to dance."

Rory Fitzwalter turned to Mrs. Henderson with an invitation, which earned him a vexed look from the countess.

Meanwhile Lily Crawford began to play a pleasant melody of moderate tempo.

"How obliging of you, my dear," Lady Killoran swooped down on her, "but we must not deprive the gentlemen of such a charming partner. Miss Delany would be happy to play for us, wouldn't you, Kitty?"

"Of course." The countess' companion hurried to take the seat Miss Lily had vacated with such obvious reluctance. She began to play a more spritely air.

Lady Killoran practically dragged Lily Crawford toward Lord Gabriel. "Here is a gentleman I believe would be delighted to have you for a partner."

But the young nobleman already had Miss Brennan on his arm.

"I would indeed for the next dance," he said, though he did not sound eager.

"Do not trouble yourself, sir," Miss Lily replied in a cool tone which Aaron was beginning to sense might mask more vulnerable feelings. "I have neither my sister's relish for dancing nor her skill."

Some impulse Aaron did not understand propelled him toward the lady. "I believe you are being too modest, Miss Lily. Pray do not disappoint me by refusing my invitation."

For the first time since his arrival, Lady Killoran regarded Aaron with something approaching approval.

Miss Lily hesitated. Was she vexed with him for placing her in an awkward position or grateful that he had rescued her from the humiliation of being unsought? Aaron could not tell.

He caught her skittish gaze and gave a subtle nod toward her sister. Country dances involved so much toing and froing that he would have many opportunities to grasp Iris's hand and be near her, even if she was not his chosen partner. But to avail himself of such delights, he needed to take the floor with someone.

Miss Lily must have understood, for she responded with a little curtsey. "It would be an honor, Captain."

As she took his arm, her pale cheeks blossomed with a faint rosy glow and the corners of her mouth arched in a fleeting smile that quite transformed her features. For an instant Aaron almost forgot that he was only getting close to Lily Crawford in hopes of getting even closer to her enchanting sister.

Chapter Three

FROM THE MOMENT she'd first ventured out in Society, Lily had hated dancing and avoided it at all costs. Perhaps if she had learned at a young age, like her sister, it might have been different. By the time she was considered strong enough for such exertions, she had become too self-conscious about making mistakes to relax and enjoy herself. Yet that night in the Killorans' festively decorated parlor, she quickly forgot her dislike of such frivolity.

Perhaps it was the music. Miss Delany played very well and favored rollicking, spirited tunes. Perhaps it was the wine. Lily seldom indulged in spirits, having too often seen the unpleasant results of inebriation among the servants when her father was absent from home. But tonight the exertion of dancing whetted her thirst. The excellent vintages from Lord Killoran's cellar made her less unsure of herself, more easily inclined to smile and laugh.

Captain Turner's courteous attention might have played a part as well, Lily had to admit. Though she knew he was only being kind to her so she would help him win Iris, no one else in the party was aware of that. It was a rather heady sensation to have such an attractive, personable man show particular interest in her.

Of course, propriety would not permit her to dance with the captain exclusively. The other gentlemen each took their turns with her as the evening wore on. Yet Lily sensed they were less reluctant to ask than they might have been other-wise — even Lord Gabriel. Still, Captain Turner claimed the greatest share of her company.

"Where did you learn to dance so well, Captain?" Lily whispered to him behind the screen of her fan. "I would not have thought a privateer would have many opportunities to practice such social accomplishments."

"You are most generous in your praise, Miss Lily." His husky chuckle sent a warm ripple through her. "It is true that there is little dancing at sea, apart from the occasional hornpipe. But I have not been a privateer all my life."

Somehow his remark, begun on a light-hearted note, ended with a puzzling sigh.

Lily had no time to reflect on it, for Miss Delany began to play the liveliest tune yet. Captain Turner whisked her onto the floor and she was soon caught up in the sheer exuberance of the music and movement. When the captain grasped her hand and spun her about, a bubble of laughter rose within her and burst from her lips.

"You seem to be enjoying yourself this evening," he observed in a somewhat breathless voice once the set had concluded. "May I take that as a compliment to my company?"

"I suppose you may." Lily fanned her warm cheeks. Then, seeing the captain looked rather flushed, she waved her fan in front of his face as well. "I do not doubt you *will*, being so confident. It is a trait you share with my sister — one I envy you both a great deal."

Captain Turner replied with a roguish wink. "It is not a quality in which I can take pride, for I never took pains to acquire it. As far back as I can recall, it has been part of my character, for good or ill."

"How can it possibly be ill?" Lily asked, genuinely puzzled.

The captain gave a self-deprecating shrug. "Like anything positive, I suppose. An overabundance can have the opposite effect. My confidence sometimes makes me underestimate difficulties. Or if I find it is *possible* to pursue a particular course of action, I do not always stop to consider whether it is advisable."

He nodded toward the fan she was fluttering in his direction at a rather frantic pace. "Now and then I wish I had a voice of caution I could trust, to cool my enthusiasm when confidence runs away with me."

Suddenly conscious of how flirtatious her behavior might look, Lily snapped her fan shut and hid it behind her back. Fortunately a swift glance around the room reassured her that no one else had noticed. Was it foolish of her to fret so much that others might be watching — ready to criticize her slightest misdeed?

"Surely you have no reason to lack confidence, Miss Lily," Captain Turner remarked almost as if he could overhear her thoughts. "A woman of your beauty, accomplishments and good sense would be well justified to hold her head high in any company."

When a footman offered them more wine, Lily accepted eagerly. "You need not flatter me, Captain, to secure my assistance with Iris. I told you how I feel about your suitability for my sister. Everything I have learned about you this evening confirms my impression that the two of you would make an excellent match."

"I assure you I am quite sincere," the captain insisted. "As we become better acquainted, you will discover that flattery is not one of my talents. More the contrary. I cannot understand what makes you doubt my good opinion of you."

"The same reason my confidence has suffered, I expect." Lily nodded toward her sister, who had most of the gentlemen and some of the other ladies hanging on her every word. "It is not easy living up to such a paragon. One is bound to suffer by comparison."

Captain Turner looked as if he was about to reply when Lord Killoran called for another dance and asked Lily to do him the honor.

The party broke up at a much later hour than Lily was accustomed to. Fighting back a yawn, she promised the captain she would speak favorably to Iris about him.

He bowed over her hand. "I shall be forever in your debt if you can persuade her to give me a chance. I look forward to becoming better acquainted with you, also. Sleep well, Miss Lily, and sweet dreams."

A strange tingle quivered through Lily. She bid the captain good night in a halting, tongue-tied fashion and fled to her room.

———◆———

"Have you made any progress with your sister at all?" Aaron asked Lily Crawford over breakfast two days later, on the morning of Christmas Eve.

It was one meal the Killorans' guests did not eat together. A toothsome buffet was laid out in the breakfast room for whoever wished to partake when they rose for the day. The other ladies took trays in their rooms, while Miss Delany attended to her duties on behalf of the countess. None of the gentlemen rose as early as Aaron, so he was pleased to have Miss Lily's company. It gave the two of them an opportunity to compare notes and plan strategy in relative privacy, while still maintaining propriety.

"Yesterday she avoided me worse than ever." He sighed. "It provokes me to see Uvedale worming his way into her affections, while I sit by and do nothing. It goes against my nature. I should take more decisive action to win her!"

He speared a crispy fried sausage and tore a bite off roughly with his teeth. It did nothing to relieve his mounting frustration.

"Please be patient!" Lily begged him. "I know that must be difficult for a man of action, but you need to trust me. I know my sister and she is not the kind of woman to be won by force. It will only make her dig her heels in — like that old fable about the wind and the sun wagering which one could make a traveller lose his cloak and hat."

Aaron gave a reluctant nod. "I recall reading that story

many times to my sister. Her favourite book was an illustrated volume of Aesop's fables. Ella enjoyed the stories because so many were about animals. But I was old enough to grasp the valuable lessons they were meant to teach. Those morals stayed with me."

"I did not know you had a sister." Miss Lily brightened. "Where does she live now? I should like to meet her."

Something about her eager inquiry tore at Aaron's heart. Perhaps it was hearing her refer to Ella as if his sister were still living.

"I am certain she would have liked to make your acquaintance as well," he responded gently. "But I fear that is impossible."

"Oh dear!" A stricken look flooded Lily Crawford's gentle eyes. It mirrored the feeling in Aaron's heart.

She fumbled for his hand and gave it a sympathetic squeeze which reminded him of his sister even more vividly than her words had done. "I am so very sorry, Captain! I should have realized. I beg your pardon for stirring up unhappy memories at this festive time of year."

When she snatched back her hand with an air of self-conscious confusion, Aaron found himself dismayed to lose the comforting contact.

"Do not fret, Miss Lily." He shook his head. "Ella has been gone for many a year. Memories of her are more pleasant than otherwise. I meant it sincerely when I said she would have been happy to meet you. You remind me of my sister in many ways. That is one of the reasons I hope to have you for a sister one day, when I succeed in winning the hand of a lady who is very dear to both of us."

Lily Crawford continued to look troubled. Had he not said the right thing to ease her regret over mentioning Ella?

"Like you, my sister had a delicate constitution and a retiring nature," he continued. Perhaps if he spoke more of his sister, Lily would see that memories of Ella did not distress him. "Only in my company was she able to speak and laugh freely."

From what he had seen so far at the Killorans' house party, Lily Crawford was far more at ease in his company than that of the other gentlemen. Perhaps it was only because she knew he had no designs on her. Yet Aaron hoped there might be more to it. A budding sense of trust, perhaps? Or recognition that he did not compare her unfavorably with her sister. Who could expect one family to produce two such paragons as Iris Crawford?

"Your sister was younger than you, I take it?" Miss Lily returned her attention to her breakfast, though with little evidence of appetite.

Aaron nodded and began to eat again. "By ten years. Our father died before Ella was old enough to remember him. After that, I tried to fill the role of both brother and father to her."

"It cannot have been an easy task, when you were scarcely more than a child yourself." The mixture of sympathy and admiration in Lily Crawford's voice kindled a soft, sweet ache in his heart. Aaron had known little of either in his life.

He gave a self-deprecating shrug with which he had often met reverses of fortune. "Ella is the reason I joined the crew of a privateer rather than seek a more respectable place in the Royal Navy. I knew there would be opportunities for prize money and I wanted to make my fortune quickly, for her sake. I wanted to provide her with every comfort and the best care money could buy."

He failed to mention that he had been driven to rescue his sister from the grudging charity of their stepfather, though he sensed Lily Crawford might understand.

"A most commendable intention!" she cried. The glow in her eyes made Aaron's chin tilt upward as his chest seemed to swell. "Once I tell Iris, I am certain it will dispel her ... unease about your ... nautical activities."

Though he appreciated the lady's kind effort to spare his feelings, Aaron threw back his head and laughed. "Your sister thinks I am a pirate!"

"No!" Lily Crawford's furious blush contradicted her protest.

When his continued chuckling made it clear he did not believe her, she sputtered, "Iris *might* have said something like that, but it was all in jest I assure you."

Aaron tried to ignore the implied criticism, as he had so often in the past. However, considering the source, it troubled him more than he cared to admit. "I see nothing dishonorable about attacking my country's enemies at sea. If my crew and I could make our fortunes from it, that only induced us to succeed. England benefited from our efforts, at no cost to the Treasury. We bore all the risks in return for the opportunity to reap a rich profit."

Miss Lily followed his reasoning with thoughtful attention. "That makes excellent sense, Captain. I shall be certain to tell my sister what you said. I wish Iris did not set so much store by what others think of her. It is all very well when everyone showers her with acclaim. Yet I fear admiration can be a liability, when a person allows their conduct to be influenced by the desire for it ... or the fear of losing it."

"I had not considered that." Aaron mulled over her words. "You talk excellent sense, Miss Lily. I have always prided myself on being a man of action rather than reflection. Now I wonder whether greater understanding of human nature might not be an asset at times."

His praise appeared to fluster the lady, rather than flatter her, as he'd intended.

"I fear I have spent too much of my life watching and reflecting," she murmured. "My sister may wish to keep the admiration of others, but I fear I am too anxious to avoid drawing their notice. We could both learn a valuable lesson from you about being indifferent to the opinions of others."

"Not altogether *indifferent*," Aaron corrected her. "I do care very much about the regard of the few people who matter to me. Your sister in particular, but you as well."

Again his compliment seemed to unsettle her, but now

Aaron had an idea why.

"What about *your* sister?" Miss Lily avoided his gaze by staring down at her plate and moving the last morsels of food around with restless motions of her fork. "She must have been very proud of you and grateful for your endeavors on her behalf."

"So she always claimed in her letters." A disconcerting idea occurred to Aaron. "Though I wonder if Ella might have preferred more of my company, even if it meant fewer comforts or an even shorter life."

It was too uncomfortable a thought on which to dwell. He had been right to avoid the subtle dangers of reflection. Whatever advantage he might gain from it would come only at an intolerable cost in regret.

Aaron shot to his feet. "I failed in my mission to keep my sister alive. It made me all the more determined to accomplish any future tasks I set myself. If you will excuse me, Miss Lily, I have had enough of thinking and talking. Now it is time for me to take action."

Without waiting for her to reply, he strode away to the stables, ordered his horse saddled and embarked on a hard ride in the cold air.

He returned to Beckwith Abbey with renewed determination to win Iris Crawford by whatever means necessary.

Lily woke on Christmas morning with a compelling urge to go down for breakfast. It had been the most enjoyable part of the past two days, sipping coffee and sharing a quiet meal with only Captain Turner for company. Since she knew he had eyes for no one but her sister, Lily found she was able to relax in his presence without worrying that he might either criticize or pursue her. She had no need to fear him finding her conversation tiresome. As long as she talked about Iris, the captain would be most attentive.

But there was no use going down this morning, Lily reminded herself, burrowing deeper under the bedclothes. Captain Turner would much rather have her spend time with Iris and use the opportunity to praise his many good qualities.

Not that Iris seemed prepared to heed her. Much like the captain, she had made up her very determined mind about the sort of beau she was prepared to encourage. Any suitor who could not boast a noble title had better not waste her time, no matter how great his fortune or how fine his character. It was difficult for Lily to make much headway against such stubborn prejudice, especially since she was reluctant to antagonize her strong-willed sister.

Lily had almost fallen back to sleep when Iris stretched and yawned.

"Heavens." She regarded Lily with surprise. "What are you still doing in bed at this hour?"

Lily rubbed the sleep out of her eyes and affected a light-hearted tone. "I thought on Christmas morning I might lie in a little longer and enjoy a bite of breakfast with my sister before we dress for church."

"I suppose." Iris grasped the bell pull and gave it a vigorous tug to summon her lady's maid with the breakfast tray. "As long as you are not going to start on about Captain Turner again. You have gotten quite tedious on the subject."

She plumped her pillows and sat up with an air of having settled the matter to her satisfaction.

"I'm sorry." Lily sat up beside her sister. "I do not mean to be tiresome. I care about you and want to see you happy with a husband who is worthy of you."

Her words seemed to melt Iris's animosity. She turned toward Lily and caught her in a warm embrace. "Dear heart, of course you do! I did not mean to be short with you, but you must see there is no hope of my being happy with a man I think so ill of."

Lily hesitated. Iris had ordered her not to mention Captain Turner. But surely now that her sister had raised the subject, it might be permissible to respond.

"Perhaps," she ventured. "I only thought if you got to know him better, your opinion might improve as mine has."

Before Iris could forbid her to say anything more, Lily told her how Captain Turner had only become a privateer to support his invalid sister. Then she repeated his clever explanation of how his dubious endeavours had actually benefitted the nation.

"That is all very well," A doubtful frown creased Iris's pretty features. "But I have no interest in getting to know him better. Besides, I cannot see that you have made any effort to become acquainted with Viscount Uvedale or Lord Gabriel Stanford. You seem to hold it against them for coming from titled families."

Lily was tempted to answer back that she did not fault the gentlemen for their aristocratic birth, only their lack of ambition. Then she caught herself. This might be a way to work around her sister's intractable opposition. "You make a fair point, Iris. I should not dismiss Lord Gabriel and Lord Uvedale without getting to know them better."

"Excellent!" Iris broke into a delighted smile that no gentleman could resist. "Then you will be more agreeable and keep an open mind about them?"

As Lily considered, there was a rustle at the door and Miss Ingledew entered with Iris's breakfast tray.

The maid spied Lily and heaved the sort of put-upon sigh with which she was all too familiar. "I didn't think you would still be here, Miss. Shall I fetch you a tray as well? It may take a while."

Lily shook her head. "Do not trouble yourself, Ingledew. I can wait until luncheon."

"Nonsense," Iris insisted. "You can share my breakfast. Lady Killoran's cook is more than generous with portions and I do not have much of an appetite this morning. No doubt I am still full from that sumptuous dinner last night. The countess has a perfect genius for entertaining. We must learn from her example."

Though Lily could scarcely imagine anything that appealed to her less than learning how to be a grand hostess, she refrained from antagonising her sister by saying so. Instead she thanked Iris and helped herself to a piece of buttered bread from the tray. Iris nibbled a few bites then contented herself with sipping tea.

Meanwhile, Miss Ingledew set to work laying out their church clothes.

"Iris," said Lily, "if I do as you suggest and try to be more agreeable to Lord Gabriel and the viscount, would you be willing to do the same for Captain Turner?"

For a moment Iris looked as if she meant to refuse. Then perhaps she considered the advantages if her sister could also secure a well-born husband.

"Very well." She took another sip of tea. "We have a bargain. Though you will have a pleasanter time of it, I assure you."

Lily had grave doubts about that.

She pondered them as she and Iris dressed for church. Even if Viscount Uvedale and Lord Gabriel were better men than she believed, she knew that trying to converse with them would be an ordeal. But if it meant Iris would give Captain Turner a fair chance, Lily knew she must try.

For Christmas morning worship, the Crawford sisters donned warmer dresses, trim little spencer jackets and pretty bonnets. Iris's spencer was a festive cherry red, which the ribbons and trim of her bonnet matched. Lily's was a dark green the shade of holly leaves. Together they looked very well suited to the season.

Their fellow guest Miss Brennan complimented them when they arrived in the entry hall. "Upon my word, what a Christmassy pair you make with your sister, Miss Crawford!"

Even when Lily and her sister wore similar outfits and had most of their hair hidden, Moira Brennan had no difficulty telling the twins apart. Lily wondered how easy a time Miss Brennan might have had if *she* wore the cheerful red and Iris the dark, sombre green. There was no danger of that, she reflected. The last thing she wanted was to draw attention to herself by wearing bright colors.

Miss Brennan was dressed in a long green pelisse, a lighter shade than Lily's which looked most becoming with her vibrant auburn hair. From what Lily had observed, the Irish heiress had childlike high spirits that were quite engaging, though she lacked Iris's vibrant confidence. Lily suspected a frosty rebuff or a harsh word might easily injure Moira Brennan's cheerful temperament.

As the other guests drifted in, Lily watched anxiously for Captain Turner to appear, half fearing he might choose not to attend the Christmas service. That would add another black mark against him in Iris's opinion. Though not devout by any means, she would want a husband who kept up the appearance of respectable piety.

When he strode into the hall behind Lord Gabriel and Mr. Fitzwalter, Lily's heart swelled with relief. At least that's what she thought it must be. It pleased her to see how handsome he looked in a dark grey coat with silver buttons and snowy white linen of Spartan simplicity. His garb accentuated the captain's tall, erect bearing and broad shoulders. Iris might disdain his former occupation and his forthright manner, but surely she must admire his bold, masculine good looks if she gave him a second glance.

"I believe we are all assembled." The countess regarded her party with an approving smile, as if she believed they would do her credit with her country neighbours. "Let us set out so we do not need to hurry."

"It is not worth the bother of taking carriages," said Lord Killoran as they set off. "St. Fremund's is less than a mile away and the weather is mild enough for a stroll."

Lily edged toward Captain Turner, anxious to inform him of the bargain she had struck with her sister. Though she did not look forward to keeping up her end of it, she eagerly anticipated the captain's reaction to her good news.

But before she could reach him, he strode past her to accost her sister.

"Miss Crawford." He lavished Iris with a smile of fawning admiration. "You personify the spirit of Christmas. A single glance at you would be enough to put the sourest old Puritan in a festive mood."

Iris stiffened and looked as though she intended to rebuff him. Then she caught Lily's eye.

"Thank you, Captain," she replied in a tone that was at least civil, if not cordial. "I cannot take credit for my apparel since my maid chose it. No doubt she had the season in mind."

Lily shot her sister a little smile, though her lips seemed to resist — perhaps because she would soon be obliged to extend the same courtesy to Lord Gabriel and Viscount Uvedale. Not only that, but she would need to approach the gentlemen and strike up a conversation, something that went against her reserved nature.

Clearly encouraged by Iris's courteous response, the captain stuck close to her as they walked to church. Lily sidled toward Lord Gabriel only to find him engaged in a lively conversation with Miss Brennan. Intruding on such a pleasant tête-à-tête was more than she could bring herself to do, even to further Captain Turner's chances with Iris.

Instead she turned her attention to Viscount Uvedale, who strode along beside her sister and the captain, clearly trying to insinuate himself into their conversation. Though Lily would rather have emptied chamber pots than chat with the viscount, she knew it would assist Captain Turner in two ways. It would show Iris that she meant to keep her end of their bargain and it might prevent Lord Uvedale from intruding on Iris and the captain.

Bracing herself for the ordeal, Lily quickened her pace and fell into step beside the viscount.

"Merry Christmas, Lord Uvedale." She forced her unco-operative vocal organs to produce the greeting.

The viscount gave a visible start and glanced toward her

as if she were some sort of distasteful curiosity that had materialized out of nowhere. "The same to you, Miss Lily."

He gave her no opening to continue, but a grateful glance from Captain Turner strengthened Lily's resolve. "Do you often celebrate Christmas at Beckwith Abbey?"

Lord Uvedale frowned, making Lily wonder if he would ignore her query. Then perhaps it occurred to him that rebuffing her might offend Iris.

"Not very often," he replied in the tone of someone who fancied himself a wit, "Only when I do not receive a more tempting invitation."

Lily forced a lame chuckle as the viscount quivered with mirth at his own jest. She racked her brains for another question to keep him talking.

To her surprise, Lord Uvedale continued without further prompting. "I spent last Christmas at Pelswick at the invitation of the Duchess of Bolton. A most amusing party, indeed. Marvelous hunting."

He went on to name his fellow guests, all of whom boasted fine titles or elevated connections. His manner conveyed the impression that his sister's party was inferior to Lady Bolton's in every respect. Meanwhile Lily overheard Aaron Turner asking Iris all sorts of questions about herself.

Doing her best not to appear offended or bored, Lily let the viscount's words flow in one ear and out the other. She hoped Captain Turner appreciated the Christmas gift she was giving him today!

Chapter Four

AARON COULD SCARCELY imagine a better Christmas Day than this one was turning out to be!

The surroundings, food and weather were all ideal. Best of all, Iris Crawford was responding to his bold, direct pursuit.

The lady permitted him to walk beside her all the way to church and even chatted with him after a fashion, which was to say, she gave civil replies to his litany of questions about her. Of course, she did not reciprocate by asking questions about him, but no doubt that would come in time now that they had begun to talk.

At first he feared Lord Uvedale might interrupt and divert Miss Crawford's attention. But a Christmas angel in the shape of Miss Lily had intervened on his behalf. She'd approached the viscount and engaged him in conversation, a feat Aaron guessed must be quite daunting for a lady of her retiring nature. His heart swelled with gratitude for her timely assistance.

He had even more reason to thank her when they reached the church. Somehow she contrived to delay Lord Uvedale so that Aaron was able to sit beside her sister. He savored every moment next to Iris Crawford, sharing a prayer book, listening with keen appreciation to her high clear voice as they sang the familiar Christmas carols. When they knelt together on the cushioned prayer bench, her elbow once brushed lightly against his, filling him with an intoxicating sense of hope.

He glanced over at Miss Lily who knelt on his left hand side and gave her a warm smile which he hoped would begin to convey his gratitude. He thought she looked pleased with how matters were progressing.

However, Lord Uvedale was not prepared to let Aaron have all his own way on that mild, sunny Christmas morning. When worship concluded and the Killorans' guests filed out with the rest of the congregation, the viscount lingered in the aisle, ignoring Miss Lily's attempts to distract him. He practically pounced on Iris Crawford when she emerged from the pew.

"What a delightful voice you have, my dear Miss Crawford." Lord Uvedale managed to insinuate himself between the lady and Aaron. "Listening to you sing was all that made that interminable service bearable."

Aaron had quite enjoyed the service with its uplifting seasonal message of peace, joy and the elevation of virtuous lowly folk. Privately, he considered Lily Crawford's singing voice even better than her sister's, though he did not wish to offend the lady by saying so.

"I agree with Lord Uvedale." Aaron refused to relinquish Miss Crawford's company, but walked along on her other side. "Your singing voice is very fine. Did you take lessons?"

Iris Crawford gave a melodic little laugh. "You gentlemen are very gallant, I vow. I did receive lessons in music from an excellent teacher at the ladies' academy where Papa sent me to be educated. It was one of my favorite subjects. I fear I have no head for figures or natural history."

"Nor should you fill such a pretty head with that tiresome stuff." Lord Uvedale's lip curled in disdain.

No doubt he preferred ladies to be less informed than he on any subject. Aaron had no objection to learning a thing or two from an accomplished, well-read lady.

He chuckled as if the viscount had made an intentional jest. "Come, sir. Surely you do not mistake Miss Crawford's modesty for the strict truth. I suspect she could run mathematical rings around us both."

The viscount's sneer deepened into a dark scowl that did

not show his aristocratic profile to its best advantage.

But Aaron would not have cared if his rival's head exploded like a barrel of gunpowder, for Iris Crawford rewarded him with a perfectly divine smile. "You are very kind, Captain. But truly you flatter me. My sister is the scholar of the family."

Miss Crawford's generous praise of her quiet sister further endeared her to Aaron. It also reminded him to look for Miss Lily who walked a little ways behind them, solitary and neglected.

"Is that true, Miss Lily?" Aaron sacrificed his coveted place at Iris Crawford's side to make room for her sister to join them. "Were you the prize pupil of the ladies' academy?"

Lily Crawford shook her head, while her sister laughed merrily at Aaron's suggestion. "Lily did not go to school, Captain. She was tutored at home because she was so delicate. She is a voracious reader, though. Some days it is a perfect ordeal to coax her nose out of a book."

Her sister's cheerful quip made Lily Crawford blush as red as a holly berry, though Aaron could not think why. Surely learning was an accomplishment of which any sensible person ought to be proud — particularly ladies, who had fewer opportunities to cultivate their intelligence.

Their conversation drew the attention of Lord Killoran who was walking a little way behind with the countess and Miss Delany. "If you enjoy reading, Miss Lily, feel free to avail yourself of our library. My grandfather was an avid book collector. There is something for every taste and a number of rare volumes."

Lily Crawford's eyes lit up like those of a privateer who had made an unexpectedly rich capture. "Thank you, sir! I shall be delighted to sample the treasures of your collection."

Was it only the notion of losing herself in a good book that appealed to the lady? Aaron wondered. Or did she relish the prospect of slipping away from the party to a quiet spot where she would not be expected to make amusing conversation or listen with flattering attention to one of the gentlemen?

A party like this, with so obvious a matchmaking aim, must be especially taxing for a diffident person like her, especially when she felt so conscious of being compared unfavorably with her sister. Aaron's heart went out to her, as it did to anyone who was put upon or made to feel like an outsider.

By now the party had made their way back to Beckwith Abbey where a pleasant luncheon awaited them. This was followed by an afternoon of singing around the pianoforte and a few boisterous games that took Aaron back to the carefree years of his early childhood.

Even in these light-hearted amusements, he was conscious of a competitive undercurrent between him and Lord Uvedale. It galled him that the viscount seemed to feel his elevated station entitled him to win at everything he tried. That obnoxious attitude spurred Aaron to best his lordship as often as possible. He also wanted Iris Crawford to see him excel, even if it was only being the first to find a hidden slipper.

Yet somehow the day that had begun on such a promising note seemed to grow less satisfactory as it progressed. Aaron seized every opportunity to be near Miss Crawford. He complimented her on every merit she possessed and continually tried to engage her in conversation. Though she did not ignore him, as she had in past days, her responses became briefer and cooler as Christmas Day wore on. Besides that, his staunch ally, Miss Lily, seemed annoyed with him for reasons Aaron could not fathom.

At dinner that evening, he made several unsuccessful bids to converse with Iris Crawford, leaving him frustrated and out of sorts. After his last failed attempt, he felt something strike him on the shin. He glanced at Miss Lily and found himself the target of a fierce amethyst glare.

Had she just kicked him under the table? Aaron found it hard to imagine and even more difficult to guess why.

Women! Would he ever understand them?

Aaron Turner was the most obstinate man she had ever met! Lily fumed as she took refuge in Lord Killoran's library two days after Christmas.

Ordinarily it was a room in which she might have wiled away many hours in blissful solitude, pouring over atlases and wonderfully illustrated volumes of natural history. She might have lost herself in the pages of a rollicking novel by Henry Fielding, thrilled to the exquisite poetry of Dryden or sought to improve her understanding by contemplating the philosophy of Erasmus.

Today, not even the romantic comedy of Goldsmith or Sheridan could hold her attention for long. Instead she found herself recalling Christmas and St. Stephen's Day, when she had watched in helpless frustration as Captain Turner relentlessly pursued her sister. Why could he not see that his efforts were having exactly the opposite result to the one he desired? If she'd believed it would do any good, Lily might have tried to shake some sense into him.

As she imagined doing precisely that, her breath hastened and her loins began to tingle in a most improper fashion. It suddenly occurred to her that she might have trouble letting go of the handsome privateer if she dared lay hands on him!

At that moment the library door flew open and Aaron Turner strode in.

"I thought I might find you here, Miss Lily." His words had the sharp ring of accusation.

Lily gave a violent start. Her cheeks blazed as if Captain Turner could tell what she'd been thinking. A brew of powerful conflicting emotions boiled over, sweeping away her accustomed reticence.

She shot to her feet, sending a heavy leather-bound volume thumping to the floor. "Yes, you have found me. Now be so good as to lose me again. If I cannot have an hour of peace and quiet I fear I shall run mad!"

The captain froze in his tracks and recoiled at her hostile response. But he did not turn and stalk away. Lily could not decide whether to be vexed or grateful.

"Forgive me for disturbing your solitude, but I am at my wits end and I need your assistance." His words tumbled over one another in their emphatic haste, fairly throbbing with frustration. "You promised you would help me to win your sister, yet I find you hiding in the library when you could be with her, persuading her of what a fine match we would make."

"I am *not* hiding!" Lily protested though she knew it was not true. "And I have done far more to assist you than you seem to realize."

She told him about the bargain she had made with Iris on Christmas morning. "I have had to endure the self-important prattle of Lord Uvedale in order to keep my sister from ignoring you, only to have you behave in a fashion that is certain to drive her away."

"Drive her away? Nonsense!" Captain Turner seemed genuinely unable to understand what Lily was trying to tell him. "I praise her. I try to be near her as often as I can. I endeavor to express my regard for her. Why should any of that drive her away?"

"I tried to tell you." Lily heaved an exasperated sigh. The captain had many excellent qualities but she feared that heedfulness might not be among them. "Iris cannot stand to be forced into anything. The harder you push, the harder she will resist. Remember what I told you about the sun and the wind from Aesop's fable."

"Of course I remember." The captain seemed to take her reminder as an insult. "I'm not a fool! I have not behaved like the wind. I have been as pleasant and agreeable as I can short of turning into a lap dog. Perhaps if you were doing more to influence her in my favor, my efforts would not be in vain."

Lily gave a barely-stifled shriek. Though irritated by her sister's stubborn rejection of a man who possessed ten times the merit of that insufferable Lord Uvedale, she could not blame Iris for growing impatient with a suitor who refused to accept her choice in the matter.

"You may not be a fool, Aaron Turner, but you are a stubborn ass and an ingrate! If I have not praised you to my sister every time I open my mouth, it is because I know it would do your cause far more harm than good. Instead I persuaded her to give you a chance, for which I paid a far higher price than you seem to appreciate."

Lily had never spoken to anyone in that tone, especially not anyone as physically imposing as the rugged privateer. Nor to anyone she liked so well.

At the moment she was not entirely certain she *did* like him, which might be why she dared permit her tightly leashed anger to burst its bonds for the first time. While such intense feelings frightened her, their release also brought an unexpected surge of elation.

Her outburst rocked Captain Turner back on his heels. His dark eyes flashed with answering rage that made Lily quail. Yet a subtle tilt of his black brows put her in mind of a child who'd been harshly and unjustly scolded.

Perhaps that was what made her eyes begin to sting so furiously. If there was one thing she'd find more unbearable than losing her temper at Captain Turner, it would be bursting into tears before him. She must get away with her dignity intact.

"If you cannot appreciate my efforts on your behalf or heed my advice about how best to win my sister ..." Lily willed her voice not to break and her tears to keep from falling for just a moment more. "... then perhaps you are not the right man for Iris after all!"

With that, she bolted for the door.

She had no idea what she might do if the captain tried to hinder her departure. Fall into his arms and weep like a wet goose? The possibility horrified Lily even as it made her knees grow weak.

For good or ill, Aaron Turner was enough of a gentleman not to detain her. Instead he fell back a step as she dashed past him.

Not wanting any of the other guests might see her in such

a state, Lily rushed toward the back stairs and flew up them as fast as she dared. Fortunately this was a time of day when most of the servants remained below stairs, unless specifically summoned. Lily was able to reach the guest chamber she shared with Iris, unseen by anyone in the Killorans' household.

There she hurled herself onto the bed and gave way to a storm of tears so passionate they shocked her.

She had known Captain Turner for less than a week, yet the man was playing havoc with her emotions. He was definitely not someone she could afford to have in her life, not even as Iris's husband.

———— ◆ ————

As Lily Crawford's swift footsteps retreated down the thickly carpeted passage, Aaron sank onto the nearest chair. Their encounter had left him shaken in a way he had not been for many years.

At a young age, he had learned to let ridicule and criticism roll off his heart as harmlessly as drops of water off the feathers of a duck. When a person had no other recourse, a persuasive show of indifference was the best way to strike back, for it deprived the persecutor of the response they desired.

If Viscount Uvedale had called him an ass and an ingrate, he would have paid the insults no more heed than the vaguely annoying buzz of an insect. Those same words out of Lily's Crawford's mouth had attacked like a swarm of angry wasps. Aaron reacted as if he had been stung.

How could Miss Lily turn on him like that? She was supposed to be his ally. She had pledged to help him win her sister. If there was more merit to her charges than he could bring himself to admit at the moment, she might have brought them to his attention in a manner that was not so harsh. He'd only been trying to follow her advice after all, by being the attentive, flattering sun to Iris Crawford rather than the blustering wind. How could he expect to woo the lady if he left her in any doubt of his admiration?

All the scathing rebuttals he might have hurled at Miss Lily ran through Aaron's mind, fast and shrill. The accusations she'd flung at him echoed in his thoughts as well, continuing to batter him long after she had fled. How dare she rile him up like this only to run off, leaving him to stew?

Worst of all, his own damnable conscience began to insist that Lily Crawford might be right. Perhaps he was a stubborn, ungrateful ass of no account, unworthy to covet a rare jewel like Iris, let alone fancy he could win her.

It took some time for Aaron to get his churning emotions under a measure of control. The chiming of a tall pedestal clock in the corner of the earl's library warned him it would soon be time for tea.

He rose from the chair, about to hurry away when he spotted the book Miss Lily had dropped on the floor earlier. He strode over to pick it up when the library door swung open and Lord Killoran peered in.

"Oh, it's you, Captain Turner." The earl sounded as if Aaron were the last of his guests he expected to find there. "I thought I heard someone."

He glanced at the fallen book with a stern frown. "Most of the volumes in our collection are old and quite valuable. I would appreciate your handling them with proper care."

Lord Killoran's rebuke made Aaron feel like a wayward schoolboy. He considered informing the earl that Lily Crawford was the offender who had mishandled his precious book.

Instead he retrieved it from the floor with exaggerated care. "Of course, sir. Rest assured I shall not let it happen again."

Spying an empty space on a nearby shelf, he replaced the volume, glancing at the title as he did so.

Why was Lily Crawford reading a collection of plays? Aaron had seen some of them performed at Drury Lane and Covent Garden. Sentimental love stories presented in a comic manner — was that where Miss Lily had acquired her ideas about how a courtship ought to be conducted?

When Aaron turned back toward the door, he found the earl had slipped away. The exasperation that had gripped him earlier seemed to have fled as well. It left him in a more sensible frame of mind to consider his heated exchange with Lily Crawford.

By the sound of it, she *had* been trying to assist him, even if it was not in the way he would have preferred. Aaron could not deny that the bargain she'd struck with her sister must have been a sacrifice for someone of her temperament. How might he have reacted if he's been making a strenuous effort on someone else's behalf, only to be accused of not doing enough? *Ingrate* and *ass* would be the mildest insults he might heap upon them.

In an unusually chastened mood, he joined the other members of the party for tea, only to find Miss Lily absent from the group.

"My sister is feeling a little unwell," Iris Crawford replied to Aaron's query. "I doubt it is anything serious. Lily is not accustomed to keeping so much company. She finds it tiring. A little quiet time will soon set her right."

The lady made it sound as if her sister's aversion to the constant society of a group of strangers was perverse. Perhaps it seemed so to someone like her, who thrived on the company of others.

Aaron retreated into silence for the remainder of tea time. Consuming toasted muffins and slices of cake with scant attention, he let the surrounding conversation swirl around him, unheeded.

By that evening, he was ready to excuse the things Miss Lily had said to him earlier and refocus on their common goal. The lady clearly felt otherwise.

Joining the party at the very last moment before dinner, she answered Aaron's inquiries about her health with brevity that was barely civil. During dinner, she joined in conversation with Lord Gabriel and Miss Brennan as if they were long lost friends. Not once during the meal did she glance in

Aaron's direction.

He hoped to have a word with her later in the evening, only to find her playing cards with her aunt, Mr. Brennan and Rory Fitzwalter. Her determination to avoid him seemed to echo her final words in the library. Clearly Lily Crawford had decided that he was not the right man for her sister after all.

Chapter Five

HOW ON EARTH would she survive the remaining week of Lady Killoran's house party?

Lily found herself exhausted after a single evening spent trying to avoid Aaron Turner, for it meant she must join in with the other guests to a greater degree than she had before. Lurking on the fringes of the group with the captain had been much less taxing. In his company, she had felt as comfortable as when she was off by herself, yet without the nagging sense of loneliness.

This evening, she felt painfully isolated even while surrounded by other people.

She would need to speak with Captain Turner at some point and work out a truce. But tonight her emotions were still too raw. Besides, she was afraid of how he might respond when she told him she could no longer help him to win Iris.

Once he had retired for the night, along with some of the other guests, Lily decided it was safe to slip off to bed herself.

She had almost reached the main staircase when Captain Turner emerged from a small sitting room to intercept her. "Please, Miss Lily, all I ask is two minutes to make my apologies to you."

He wanted to beg *her* pardon, when she was the one who had hurled insults at him?

"Can it not wait until tomorrow?" Lily heaved a weary sigh. The intense emotions of the day had worn her out. She might be better able to deal with them after a good night's sleep.

The Captain shook his head as he beckoned her into the

empty room from which he'd come. "I cannot bear to have a whole night pass with you continuing to think ill of me. I fear I have given you good reason."

His air of humble repentance disarmed Lily.

"Very well, then." She entered the room, but only a few steps, as it was dimly lit.

The captain followed her. He must have thought she would only allow him the two minutes he'd requested, for he wasted no time coming to the point. "Dear Miss Lily, I can scarcely express how much I regret the things I said earlier. They were ungenerous and untrue. I believe you have done everything in your power to assist me, both by appealing to your sister on my behalf and by advising me about the best way to approach her. I was wrong to blame you for my failure of understanding. I plead frustration, not as an excuse for my behaviour, but so you know it was that rather than ingratitude which prompted my ill-chosen words."

Lily did not know what to say. Never in her life had she dared speak to anyone as she had to him. Deep down, she'd been certain it would lead to punishment or perhaps abandonment. She was not prepared for what she was hearing — especially not from such a strong, confident man. Somehow it made her feel a little more powerful, even as she struggled to produce a reply.

Not that she needed to, since the captain clearly had more to add. "I was wrong to doubt your efforts on my behalf. I promise I never will again, and I will do anything in my power to make amends to you, if you can find it in your heart to forgive me."

How could she refuse such an appeal, or resist the anxious look which made his rugged features appear much younger?

"The only amends I need is your pardon in return, Captain. I spoke in haste and out of frustration as well. I wish I could find the proper words to explain how you should approach Iris. I fear my example from Aesop's fable only confused you. What I meant to convey is that my sister enjoys a challenge. She does not want what comes to her too easily, and she detests anything that is forced upon her. Does that make any sense?"

"All the sense in the world, dear lady!" A flash of understanding lit Captain Turner's dark eyes with a radiance that seemed to brighten the whole room. "I am the same way — hankering for what is difficult to attain. I believe it is what separates ambitious folk from everyone else. We are not too easily contented."

"Precisely so!" she cried, catching his enthusiasm. "I knew you would understand if only I could explain it properly."

"You explained it brilliantly. Now I know what I must do and I have a whole week to do it. Thank you, Miss Lily. You are a true gem!"

To Lily's astonishment, the captain threw his arms around her like the most affectionate brother and pressed a fond kiss upon her cheek.

The sensations that swept through her in response to his sudden embrace were anything but sisterly. Her heart galloped out of control even as she forgot how to breathe. A fevered blush suffused not only her cheeks, but every scrap of flesh that covered her body.

"Good night and God bless you!" the captain murmured as he released her from his impulsive embrace and hurried away.

A moment later Lily followed, one hand pressed to her cheek where Aaron Turner had kissed her. Why in heaven's name had she given him further encouragement to continue his pursuit of her sister? More than ever, prudence warned her that it was not a good idea.

Preoccupied with such thoughts, she drifted up the main staircase and down the passage. She was just about to enter the guest room she shared with Iris when the sound of hushed voices and half-smothered laughter drew her toward a dim alcove near the servant's stairs. Was a randy footman trying to steal a kiss from one of the housemaids?

"Lily?" Her sister's voice emerged from the shadows. "Why are you prowling about at this hour? I thought you went to bed."

Iris stepped from the alcove, her golden curls tousled and one sleeve of her dress pulled down to expose her bare shoulder. Behind her sister, Lily glimpsed the shape of a man. Lord Uvedale's features came into focus, his lips curled in a smirk of lecherous triumph.

If anyone else had caught them together in such a compromising position, Iris's reputation might be ruined. Then she would have no choice but to wed the viscount, even if she changed her mind about liking him.

"I lost my way and I am not feeling at all well." Lily seized her sister by the wrist and pulled her away from Lord Uvedale. "You must show me to our room, before I retch all over Lady Killoran's carpet!"

"Oh, you mustn't!" Iris squealed. "We would be disgraced!"

Worse than by *her* scandalous impropriety? Lily was tempted to demand, but she held her tongue. What mattered was that her claim of illness seemed to be working to draw Iris out of danger. Not that it was entirely fabricated. The sight of Lord Uvedale's predatory grin had truly nauseated her.

"Come along, then." Iris cast a regretful glance back at her paramour. Then she took Lily by the arm and hustled her down the passage. "Our room is this way. You walked right past it."

She sounded vexed at having her tryst interrupted, yet still concerned about her sister's wellbeing. "I do hope you haven't caught some dreadful illness. My maid was complaining of a sore throat this morning. Now sit down and take a few deep breaths while I fetch you a basin."

Lily sank onto the chair as her sister bid her. "I am feeling a good deal better already."

"I am glad to hear it." Iris glanced at her reflection in the looking glass and tugged up the sleeve of her dress. "Now get to bed and you should be fine in the morning."

As Iris started for the door, Lily reached out and grasped her hand. "You should come to bed as well. Please be careful of Lord Uvedale. I do not trust him."

"Nonsense!" Iris scowled. "His lordship is perfectly charming — a good deal more so than that dreadful Captain Turner."

"At least the captain is not a fortune hunter," Lily shot back, all her earlier doubts about Aaron Turner and her sister dispelled. It might be a bit awkward at first, having him for a brother-in-law, but he would be a hundred times better than Viscount Uvedale. "The two of you are more alike than you may realize. I believe you would get along very well if you would give him a chance."

"I get along very well with Lord Uvedale." Iris shook off her sister's grasp. "And he can make me a countess one day."

"A penniless countess, when he has run through your fortune." Lily could scarcely believe such quarrelsome words were coming out of her mouth. Had her earlier confrontation with Captain Turner emboldened her?

Iris glared at her. "I am certain you are fretting about nothing. Besides, my life is my own to live in whatever way will make me happy. Perhaps if you made some effort to secure your own happiness, you would not be so determined to spoil mine."

Lily had never seen the wisdom in pressing an argument with her strong-willed sister. But there was too much at stake now for her to simply give up. "Please, Iris, I am not trying to spoil your happiness! Captain Turner admires you so much. I believe he would do anything that might bring you comfort or pleasure. I do not like the way Lord Uvedale leers at Miss Delany behind your back."

"That is not true!" Iris stormed, yet Lily sensed she would have been less indignant if she'd sincerely doubted it. "You have some foolish prejudice against his lordship. As for Captain Turner, if you like him so well perhaps you ought to set your cap for him!"

At that moment Miss Ingledew appeared to help get them ready for bed. The maid's face looked flushed and her voice sounded very hoarse, but Iris seemed not to notice. Instead she changed into her nightclothes and retired to bed in frosty silence.

Lily soon followed, equally quiet but for different reasons. She was shaken by her quarrel with Iris and even more by the disturbing idea of herself in pursuit of the dashing privateer.

She could not deny Aaron Turner was the sort of man she had never expected to find — one who cared nothing about fortune when it came to choosing a wife. He had so many fine qualities it was difficult to enumerate them all. If she permitted herself, Lily sensed she could easily develop feelings for Captain Turner that trespassed far beyond proper sisterly fondness.

But what did that signify?

Captain Turner had set his heart on the witty, vivacious, confident twin, as any sensible man would. Lily knew better than to suppose he could easily change his affections. Even if he could, such a man would never be content with a backward, unsociable creature like her.

There was no sense hoping otherwise, for it would only make her miserable. Instead she must emulate the captain's dogged tenacity and stick with her original plan to play matchmaker for her sister.

———•◆•———

What had possessed him to embrace Miss Lily last night? Aaron chided himself the next day.

The weather had turned foul, making hunting and shooting impossible, so the party had gathered in the earl's billiard room to while away the dark, rainy afternoon.

Lily Crawford was not among them, which troubled Aaron. He'd been relieved when she failed to appear at breakfast, for he could not decide whether he ought to apologize for his behavior or pretend nothing had happened. How he wished that were true!

He had never intended to put his arms around the lady, much less kiss her on the cheek. But her willingness to forgive him and acknowledge her part in their quarrel had stirred something in him. When she'd been able to make him see how he had gone wrong with her sister, it had brought him a powerful surge of hope. Like a rising wave, that feeling had swept him along, not fully in control of his actions.

Suddenly Lily Crawford seemed to fill the place in his heart once reserved for his sister as supporter, confidante and admirer. He could no more resist the urge to offer her a brotherly hug than if Ella had returned to be with him again.

He had not expected the brief, chaste contact with Miss Lily to affect him any differently than an embrace from his own sister. But it *had* ... most decidedly.

Lily Crawford was not a child, but a young lady of undeniable attraction. Out of her sister's shadow, she might have outshone most of the Season's debutantes. Aaron could not help but react to her sudden nearness, the scent of her hair and the softness of her skin against his lips the way any man might. All the sensation in his body seemed to concentrate in his loins. His flesh roused, aching with desire. Even as he pulled away from her and fled, a primitive part of him demanded more. It craved passionate kisses where lips melted together and tongues mingled. It yearned to hold her closer and longer, in a foretaste of the way their naked bodies might fit together.

Those forbidden desires had haunted Aaron's dreams. Now, in the cold light of day, they plagued his conscience. He had no business entertaining such carnal thoughts about Lily Crawford. She was his friend and ally. If his conquest of Iris concluded in the way he hoped, he would be delighted to have Lily for a sister — nothing more!

"I beg your pardon, Captain." Miss Delany's voice interrupted Aaron's turbulent thoughts. "I hope you are not unwell. I was told that one of the servants has fallen ill."

"I am sorry to hear that," Aaron responded, grateful for the distraction. "I am quite well, I assure you, only a little preoccupied."

"With thoughts of a certain lady?" Miss Delany cast a

significant glance toward Iris Crawford, who was applauding a skillful billiard shot that Lord Uvedale had just made.

"Is it that obvious?" Aaron pulled a droll face.

Kitty Delany grinned. "It is not difficult to discern your admiration for Miss Crawford, nor hers for Lord Uvedale. No wonder you look pensive."

"So you believe it is impossible that I will prevail?" For an instant Aaron's confidence flagged. Perhaps he did not deserve Iris Crawford after the way he had responded to her sister.

Miss Delany's cheerful air grew more subdued. "I hope not, for her sake. I have been acquainted with Lord Uvedale long enough to be certain he cares for no one but himself."

From her tone, Aaron sensed there might be some history between her and the viscount. "You told me your families were friends in Ireland."

After the Act of Union had abolished Ireland's Parliament, nearly ten years ago, Irish peers had been brought into the House of Lords in London. Some, like the Earl of Killoran, had settled here and seldom even visited their Irish estates.

"That is true." The lady sounded sorry she had disclosed even that much, yet with her next breath she revealed more. "The Fitzwalters, the Nolans and the Barrymores were all neighbors in County Carlow for generations."

Aaron knew that Nolan was the family name of Lord Uvedale and Lady Killoran. But who were the Barrymores?

Miss Delany did not leave him guessing. "Charles Barrymore, Baron Carlow is my stepbrother. He did not approve of his father's remarriage to my mother. While my stepfather lived, I was treated as a daughter of the house. But after he died, my mother and I were left all but destitute. If it had not been for Lady Killoran ..."

Aaron knew all too well how such injustice came to pass. "Pardon me for asking, Miss Delany, but if your stepfather cared for you and your mother, why did he not make some provision for you?"

"That I cannot say." The lady lowered her voice until Aaron

could scarcely hear it over the clacking of the billiard balls and other conversations in the room. "My mother believed he had made a will that included us. Yet when the time came, all that could be found was an older document that left everything to his son."

Perhaps she sensed Aaron's particular sympathy with her situation, for she added, "Mama suspected my stepbrother of underhanded dealings but we were powerless to act against someone of his influence."

Aaron had no doubt her late mother's suspicions were correct. He knew how such families treated those they considered interlopers. "I am very sorry for your situation, Miss Delany. If I can ever be of service, I hope you will look on me as a friend."

His gaze strayed toward Iris Crawford only to collide with a proprietary glare from Lord Uvedale. What reason could the viscount have for being vexed with him now? Did he disapprove of Aaron speaking with *any* of the other ladies at the party?

If by some miracle he could secure Iris Crawford, Aaron vowed he would not grudge any other couple their happiness.

But would it take a miracle to win the lady now?

She must do something soon! But what?

Lily paced the perimeter of Lord Killoran's library, muttering to herself. If she stopped doing either, she feared her mind would be flooded with images of her sister in the arms of lecherous Lord Uvedale. Or of Aaron Turner so deep in conversation with Miss Delany that he did not even notice Iris . . . or anyone else.

The previous afternoon, Lily had overcome her reluctance enough to look in on the rest of the party in the billiard room. She regretted her decision the moment she spied the captain and Miss Delany talking quietly together. It was clear from their demeanor that they were exchanging confidences, oblivious to Iris who flirted with Lord Uvedale barely ten feet away.

Recalling the sight made Lily's cheeks flush and her stomach clench. Unless something drastically altered the situation soon, Iris would end up betrothed to the odious viscount. Meanwhile, Captain Turner would turn his attention to a lady sensible enough to recognize an excellent prospect and give him proper encouragement.

But what could prompt so drastic a change at this stage? As Lily pondered that baffling question, the clock in the corner of the library chimed, startling a gasp of dismay from her.

That feeling intensified when she realized she had only half an hour to dress for dinner. Her toilette never took as long as Iris's, but today she felt anxious to look her best.

Dashing from the library, Lily burst into the hallway, startling a couple who were talking quietly together. Miss Delany blushed to a fierce shade of scarlet and fled in the direction of the servant's stairs, but Rory Fitzwalter did not appear discomposed in the least.

Regarding Lily with his usual sardonic grin, he gave a slight bow. "Miss Lily, we have been deprived of your company too often of late. We must make a greater effort to compete with the information and amusement you find in my brother's books."

Iris would have had some charming quip by way of reply, but Lily found herself quite tongue-tied. She settled for a smile that she feared must look perfectly insipid. No wonder any worthy gentleman would not give her a second look.

Mr. Fitzwalter was too gallant to let her awkwardness fluster him. He took his leave with a deeper bow. "Until dinner. Adieu."

Lily tried not to let him see how relieved she was to conclude their brief encounter. Now she had even less time to prepare for dinner. She hurried back to the guest chamber only to encounter one of the Killorans' servants in the passage.

"Beg pardon, Miss Crawford." The girl bobbed a hasty

curtsey. "But your lady's maid has been taken ill. The house-keeper thinks it might be the quinsy and ordered her quarantined to one of the sick rooms so she doesn't spread it about. I'm Hannah Jackson. Mrs. Walter said I should look after you and your sister until Miss Ingledew is well again."

The girl had clearly mistaken her for Iris. It surprised Lily to be reminded how much she and her sister looked alike. Most people of their acquaintance had no difficulty telling the twins apart by their opposite temperaments and styles of dress.

"Poor Miss Ingledew!" Lily cried. Though she had never been on very cordial terms with her sister's maid, she recalled more than one bout of quinsy she had suffered as a child. She would not wish the pain and fever on her worst enemy. "I hope she is better soon. If there is any medicine that might hasten her recovery or make her more comfortable, we should be happy to pay for it."

"That is kind of you, Miss." The girl seemed surprised by her concern for the welfare of a servant. "I'll tell Mrs. Walter you said so. Now, may I help you and your sister dress for dinner?"

Lily doubted her sister would welcome the ministrations of an untrained maid. It was a wonder Iris had not rung the bell to pieces trying to summon Miss Ingledew. Lily decided she had better break the news to her sister and beg her to be patient with the replacement.

Approaching the door to their room, she advised the maid. "If you will wait out here for a moment, I shall inform my sister of the new arrangements."

The girl gave an obliging nod.

Lily slipped into the guest room, expecting to find Iris at the dressing table, fretting over her maid's unaccustomed tardiness. Instead, at first glance, the room appeared empty.

Then a hoarse moan erupted from the bed.

"Iris?" Lily rushed toward the shivering figure huddled there. "Are you ill?"

The fiery heat of Iris's brow confirmed her fear.

"Is it your throat?" Lily wondered why she had not contracted the illness instead of her sister, who'd always enjoyed a more robust constitution.

Iris gave a listless nod.

"It must be the quinsy." Lily pushed back the damp wilted curls from her sister's face. "Miss Ingledew is ill with it as well. I shall send for a doctor."

Though it worried her to see her sister ill, Lily consoled herself that it might prevent Iris from making an ill-considered match with Lord Uvedale.

The doctor arrived very quickly and examined the patient with a grave countenance. Iris's throat seemed too painful for her to speak. She nodded, shook her head or pointed in answer to the doctor's questions. Afterward, he beckoned Lily toward the door and conferred with her in a hushed voice.

"It does appear to be the quinsy, Miss Crawford," the doctor informed Lily, using the address that properly belonged to her elder sister.

She was too concerned about Iris to correct him. "What can I do to make her more comfortable?"

The doctor shook his head. "What she needs most is rest and to be kept away from others in the house so the illness does not spread. Her ladyship will not thank us if more of her guests are laid low with it. Your sister must be taken to one of the sick rooms where she can be properly tended."

Lily was about to protest that it would be no hardship for her to join Iris in quarantine rather than endure the festivities. But if she did that, who would encourage Captain Turner to remain constant until Iris recovered?

At that moment Lily was struck by a notion so audacious she could scarcely believe it had occurred to her. Might there be a way to turn this unfortunate situation to their advantage and ensure Iris made a match that would benefit them both?

The Killorans' housemaid and the doctor had each mistaken Lily for her sister. What if she took Iris's place and did everything she wanted her sister to do?

She could snub Viscount Uvedale until he gave up any thought of proposing to Iris. Meanwhile she could give Captain Turner all the encouragement he needed to stay the course. This was precisely the sort of drastic action she'd known was needed, but had not been able to imagine. Now that a solution had presented itself, Lily knew she must seize the opportunity.

Once Iris had been whisked off by litter to the quarantine rooms, Lily looked through her sister's gowns and chose one of periwinkle blue with a low-cut bodice she would never have dared to wear. Then she put herself in the hands of the Killorans' eager little housemaid to complete her transformation.

Fortune smiled on her in that regard, for the girl proved a skilful hair dresser. With an application of tongs, comb and a solution of sugar water, she was able to coax Lily's severely braided locks into a delightful confection of curls.

"You are a wonder!" Lily cried at the sight of Iris staring back from her reflection in the glass. "I never looked so well in all my life. You should not be wasted laying fires and beating carpets when you possess such talents!"

"Thank you, Miss." The girl blushed with obvious pleasure. "I want more than anything to be a proper lady's maid. I used to dress my sisters' hair all the time. But I cannot take much credit for making you look lovely, Miss. Your maid said you were the toast of London Society and no wonder."

It was more than the dress and hair, Lily realized as she continued to stare in amazement at her reflection. Delight in her appearance and enthusiasm for her plan had kindled a rosy glow in her cheeks and a brilliant sparkle in her eyes.

She cast the maid a grateful smile. "We shall have to see what can be done to further your ambition, Miss Jackson. I could use ... that is ... I believe *my sister* would benefit from having her own lady's maid when we return to London."

"You would do that for me, Miss Crawford?" Hannah Jackson grinned so broadly that her freckled cheeks looked ready to burst. "Then you are as kind as you are beautiful!"

"Tush." Lilly tried to shrug off the compliment but found she could not. Its effect was oddly intoxicating. "But now I must get down to dinner before everyone thinks I have fallen ill, too."

She hurried off at a speed that was not quite proper for a lady of her position. Only when she entered the dining room and everyone turned to stare at her did Lily question what she had gotten herself into.

Chapter Six

WHILE THE PARTY dined that evening, Aaron found himself all too aware of a pair of empty places at Lord Killoran's table — one immediately beside him.

"Lily has fallen ill again," her aunt announced with a sigh that suggested more impatience than sympathy. "She was such a sickly child my poor brother often despaired of her living to grow up. I understand the doctor has placed her in seclusion and advised Iris to keep her distance so she does not catch whatever ails her sister. I hope she will listen. It would be too bad if both my nieces missed out on the festivities."

It was clear Mrs. Henderson did not intend to let Lily's illness spoil her enjoyment of the party. Aaron cast a dark scowl in the lady's direction to no avail. She hardly ever glanced toward him, her attention being divided between Mr. Brennan and Rory Fitzwalter.

Meanwhile Aaron's mind was divided over Iris Crawford's absence from the party. On one hand, he missed having the object of his affection nearby. Even when she did not give him as much encouragement as he'd hoped, the lively cadence of her voice still delighted his ears and his eyes were free to feast upon her beauty as often as he pleased. Without her, the whole party lost its zest.

Yet, much as he yearned for her company, the lady's concern for her ailing sister endeared her to him more than ever. Until now he had not seen much evidence of her affection for Lily. That had troubled him, especially since her sister clearly cared a great deal for her. Aaron was heartened to discover that, when it mattered most, Iris Crawford could rise to the occasion.

"Is there anything that can be done to speed Miss Lily's recovery?" he asked. "May she have visitors?"

It surprised him to realize how much he missed Lily Crawford's company. In spite of their recent disagreement, he sensed she was the only other guest who genuinely welcomed his presence in the party. Miss Delany was willing to converse with him now and then, but she often seemed preoccupied. This evening, she'd seldom replied until he had repeated himself at least once.

"Visitors?" Mrs. Henderson regarded Aaron as if he were a troublesome imbecile. "Surely that would defeat the purpose of quarantine, unless you wish to see us all sickened. Besides, Lily does not care much for company even when she is well."

Lady Killoran spoke up. "Your concern for Miss Lily is commendable, Captain. Be assured, she will receive the best possible care at Beckwith Abbey. It is our hope she may be well enough to rejoin the party very soon."

Though he suspected their hostess was more concerned with the symmetry of her dining arrangements than in Lily Crawford's health, Aaron nodded. "If there is anything needed to make her more comfortable, it would be my pleasure to provide it."

The reply to his offer came not from the countess, but from Iris Crawford, who breezed into the dining room like a gust of fragrant spring air. "That is very generous of you, Captain Turner. My sister is resting as comfortably as possible under the circumstances. I am sure she would wish us all to make merry until she is able to rejoin the party. I shall make certain she knows you inquired after her so kindly."

"Forgive my tardiness," she begged the countess sweetly, casting a smile around at the gentlemen who had scrambled to their feet when she entered. "I was anxious to speak with the doctor and make certain my sister is in no danger."

Lord Uvedale held the chair beside his for Miss Crawford

to be seated, a duty Aaron envied him intensely. But the lady did not favor his lordship with any special word or look of gratitude.

Instead she continued to relay news about her sister in a manner that seemed directed at Aaron. "I have been assured Lily will come to no harm as long as she is careful not to exert herself. In particular, she must not aggravate the inflammation of her throat by trying to speak. Fortunately that is not so great a hardship for my sister as it would be for me."

Iris Crawford concluded with a bright melodic chuckle, in which several of the other guests joined, including Aaron.

He thought her voice sounded subtly different than usual. He hoped she was not coming down with the illness that had banished her sister from the party.

"It would be a great misfortune if both your voices were stilled," Aaron addressed Miss Crawford directly, before Lord Uvedale could engage her in conversation.

He hoped she might find his compliments more acceptable if they included her sister. Until now, she had bristled as if his attempts at flattery were somehow insulting.

To his relief, Iris beamed at him. "How gallant of you, Captain Turner. No wonder my sister is so insistent in her praise of your kindness."

A warm glow kindled in Aaron's heart and spread rapidly through his whole chest. How could he have doubted Miss Lily's promise to exert herself on his behalf with her sister? Here was indisputable evidence that her efforts had borne fruit. He only hoped the poor lady had not talked herself hoarse or fretted herself ill on his account.

Aaron gave a self-deprecating shrug. "I cannot claim any special merit in showing kindness to so agreeable a person as your sister. It pleases me to know she felt I treated her as she deserved."

"Just so." The countess inserted herself into their exchange with an air of being anxious to end it. "We all regret Miss Lily's illness and hope she will soon be recovered. Until then, we must endeavor to entertain ourselves in her absence."

He and Iris had been rather monopolizing the conversation, Aaron admitted to himself, mildly chastened. He cast a rueful grin at her, pleased to discover she was looking in his direction and paying no heed to Lord Uvedale.

Could Lily Crawford's matchmaking efforts finally be having the desired effect? Aaron only wished his dear ally was on hand to witness her success.

Everyone believed she was Iris — even Aunt Althea! As the ladies gathered in the drawing room after dinner, Lily could scarcely contain her amazement. Which surprised her more, the fact that no one saw through her audacious charade or the bewildering ease with which she had taken on the light-hearted confidence of her twin sister?

There had been a moment of paralyzing doubt when she first entered the dining room. Hearing Captain Turner inquire so anxiously after *Lily* had given her the courage to speak. When she did, it astonished her to hear Iris's spirited voice emerging from her lips.

No one in the party seemed to suspect the truth. They all regarded her with the admiration usually reserved for her sister. That set something free within her that had long been hiding in a prison of its own making.

The warm glow in Aaron Turner's dark eyes liberated Lily from her fear that she might say or do the wrong thing. Clearly he would approve of her no matter what. No one else's opinion mattered. Throughout the meal, they exchanged several amused glances and a number of flirtatious smiles.

It was clear he had no more idea than the others that she was not Iris. Lily told herself that was precisely what she wanted. Her plan could not begin to succeed if the captain had any doubt about her identity. Yet she could not suppress an irrational wish that he might see through the bright clothes, bouncing curls and feigned high spirits to recognize her true self.

Now, as she and the other ladies waited for the gentlemen to rejoin them, Lily ordered herself not to be so foolish. Aaron Turner had made her acquaintance only a week ago. How could she expect him to see through a ruse that her own aunt could not?

"Are *you* feeling quite well, Iris?" Aunt Althea's sudden question made Lily start. "You have been unusually quiet since dinner."

So she had, Lily realized. Somehow it was easier to keep up the charade of being Iris when the gentlemen were present — particularly Captain Turner.

"Never fear." She affected Iris's sparkling laugh. "I am not feeling ill in the least. If I seem distracted, it is because I have been thinking about my poor sister. I pity her missing all the amusement."

Her aunt dismissed the sentiment with a flick of her fan. "Do not let that spoil your enjoyment, my dear. You know Lily does not relish company the way we do. Once the first discomfort of her illness is past, I am certain she will be perfectly content in the peace and quiet of the sick room."

Was that true? Lily wondered, as she nodded and smiled at her aunt's remark. Would she have changed places with Iris if she could? While the thought of tranquil solitude appealed to her, she knew she would worry about Iris and miss the company of Captain Turner.

Fortunately the gentlemen arrived just then, rescuing Lily from her aunt's questions. She rose from the settee and greeted them with a welcoming smile.

To her dismay, Captain Turner did not come and speak to her, but strolled over to the pianoforte, where Miss Delany was playing quietly. Was it already too late for her to revive the captain's interest in Iris? The surge of alarm that engulfed Lily was more intense than she would have expected on her sister's behalf.

Viscount Uvedale sidled up to her. "How pleasant it is to rejoin you, Miss Crawford. Have you missed my company as much as I have missed yours?"

Much as she longed to answer that question truthfully, Lily did not dare. For one thing, it might rouse suspicion about her identity. For another, she had always dreaded giving offense to others, fearing they might retaliate against her in some way. Only with Captain Turner had she been able to speak her mind.

Forcing her lips into a bright smile, she answered Lord Uvedale in the flirtatious tone she had often heard Iris use. "I am certain you can guess the answer to that question for yourself, sir."

"Indeed I can!" The viscount gave a gratified chuckle, which proved he had no idea of her true thoughts. "Segregating the party after dinner is the most tedious custom. My brother-in-law provides excellent brandy, but the company leaves much to be desired. Ill-bred fellows like Turner and Brennan have no idea of proper subjects for gentlemanly conversation."

Did Lord Uvedale not realize that, by his standards, her father would have been considered equally *ill-bred*? Yet the viscount seemed to have no scruples about acquiring the fortune of such a man by wedding his daughter.

"Pray what do you consider proper subjects for gentlemanly conversation?" Lily strove to imitate the teasing tone in which her sister might have posed such a question. "I fear you will find me every bit as ignorant of them, and my company equally tiresome."

As she spoke, she kept one eye on the captain and Miss Delany, who seemed on far too friendly terms for her liking.

The rest of the party had divided up to pursue their preferred amusements. Aunt Althea had joined the Killorans and Mr. Brennan at the card table, while Rory Fitzwalter hovered nearby, advising her on how to wager. Miss Brennan and Lord Gabriel pretended to play chess, but spent far more time conversing quietly together than moving the pieces.

"I could never find such beauty as yours tiresome, Miss Crawford." Lord Uvedale's eyes ranged over Lily as if he could see through her gown and undergarments. He lowered his voice. "What a pity your sister interrupted us the other night. Her timing was most unfortunate."

If she stayed there another instant, Lily feared she might pluck off her slipper and strike the viscount with it.

Instead she forced a chuckle that held not a trace of merriment. "I believe my sister would say her timing was perfect. If you will excuse me, sir, I must speak with Captain Turner. Lily wished me to give him a message from her."

She did not wait for Lord Uvedale to reply but flounced off toward the pianoforte, in what she hoped was a perfect imitation of Iris. As she approached the captain, she wracked her brains to think what sort of message from *Lily* might distract him from the charms of Kitty Delany.

She need not have worried.

When she drew near, Aaron Turner turned toward her with a sparkle of admiration in the depths of his dark eyes that took her breath away. "Miss Crawford, can I prevail upon you to give your sister a message from me?"

He nodded toward the window in the far corner of the room, where they had sat together a week ago, discussing his plan to court Iris.

Several conflicting emotions flooded Lily as she thought of her sister, lying feverish and in pain. She did not wish Iris to be ill, of course. But if it could not be prevented, she hoped her sister's ailment would last long enough for her to carry out her plans. Though it felt disloyal to wish Iris a single moment of additional discomfort, Lily reminded herself that her sister's future happiness was at stake. Once Iris realized what a fine husband Aaron Turner would make, surely she would not regret her illness nor Lily's well-intentioned meddling.

"Of course, Captain," Lily replied, falling in step beside him. "The countess and Aunt Althea may discourage me from visiting my sister, but I am certain they exaggerate the danger. If

I am not allowed to see her, I shall write her a note. You and ... Lily seem to have struck up a very friendly acquaintance."

Her tongue tripped in the unaccustomed effort to refer to herself by name. "She sings your praises so constantly that I cannot help but look upon you with greater favor than I did before."

Having reached the far corner of the drawing room, they gazed out the bay window into the darkness of the midwinter night. All Lily could see was their faint reflection in the glass, which gave her an uncanny sense of watching Iris and the captain.

"Miss Lily is very kind." Captain Turner spoke in a reflective tone as if his thoughts were focused more on the absent invalid than the present object of his admiration. "I feared *she* did not have a good opinion of me at first. I must admit, on first acquaintance I considered her rather haughty. Yet we both improved to the other since then. I have become extremely fond of your sister."

Extremely fond? The sincere tone of affection with which he uttered those words made Lily's heart quiver in her chest. Her conscience sternly reminded her that she was posing as her twin sister in order to promote a match between Iris and Captain Turner.

"Should I inquire what intentions you have toward Lily?" Hard as she tried to pass off her question in the casual bantering way her sister would, Lily could not subdue an anxious flutter to hear the captain's answer.

She found herself short of breath yet could not inhale as deeply as needed. The music from the pianoforte and the conversation of the other guests seemed distant and muted. It felt as if she and the captain were quite alone in the room.

She turned toward him and gazed up into his dark eyes. A warm glow emanated from them, like a candle in the window on a cold dark night. It promised welcome and sanctuary for the lost, lonely wayfarer.

With an indulgent smile, the captain shook his head. "I

have no *intentions* toward your estimable sister. I like her better than any other lady of my acquaintance ... except one. I believe you can guess the identity of that one, my dear Miss Crawford."

Indeed she could and it should come as no surprise. Even before she'd met Aaron Turner, Lily knew from Iris's reports he was smitten with her vivacious sister. He had never for a moment pretended otherwise.

Then why did his words bring her such a crushing sense of disappointment, even as his nearness made her simmer with anticipation?

Had he spoiled his chance? Aaron held his breath as he awaited Iris Crawford's reply. Surely the lady could have no doubt of his feelings. The sudden thawing of her manner toward him suggested that she had become more receptive to his attentions.

Yet he feared his declaration had not achieved its desired effect. Miss Crawford's slender frame tensed, like a delicate blossom frozen by an icy blast. She averted her eyes, though not before he glimpsed a baffling shadow in their blue-violet depths. Had he disappointed her by failing to provide the romantic challenge she craved?

The next instant, he wondered if he had only imagined those subtle signs of distress. Miss Crawford tossed her golden curls and favored him with a smile of breathtaking sweetness. "I believe I *can* guess that person's identity, Captain. If my speculation is correct, it brings me great pleasure and relief."

Even as her reply elated Aaron, concern for her ailing sister nagged at him. It felt wrong to be so happy while his faithful ally suffered in solitude. He told himself it was nonsense to let such ideas interfere with his romantic conquest. Lily wanted him to woo, win and wed her sister. Reports of his success might help her get well all the sooner. Yet he could not escape the feeling that he was letting her down.

"Nothing could please me more than to bring you pleasure, Miss Crawford. But why should my words bring you relief?"

"Surely you can guess, Captain. I was afraid that you might have been offended by my foolish indifference earlier and decided you wanted nothing more to do with me. I could not have blamed you for feeling that way."

This was a side of the lady Aaron had not seen before. "Surely the celebrated Miss Crawford cannot doubt her ability to sustain the fancy of her admirers. You would not be the first lady to enhance her appeal by refusing to be won too easily."

Miss Lily had tried to explain to him how her sister craved such a romantic challenge. Aaron wished he had not been so slow to understand.

"Have I spoiled that challenge for you?" Iris Crawford's bantering tone could not entirely mask a quiver of misgiving. "Would you prefer me to remain aloof?"

It surprised him to catch these unexpected glimpses of vulnerability from Iris Crawford. One of the qualities he had most admired was her supreme confidence. Yet this new insight did not diminish her in his eyes. On the contrary, it made him feel closer to her, as if they shared a secret that she hid so carefully from all but a trusted, intimate few. She was not as different from Lily as she would have most people believe.

"Remain aloof? Hardly!" Aaron gave an affectionate chuckle to show that he'd only meant to tease her. "I reckon you have an instinct for the perfect moment to offer your suitor the sweet mead of encouragement, so he does not despair."

His attempt to flatter her did not succeed as he'd hoped. The intrepid set of Iris Crawford's chin faltered and her gaze fell. "You make me sound like the most calculating flirt, Captain. I assure you it is not my intention to toy with the feelings of any man — least of all you."

"No, indeed!" Her protest drove Aaron to grasp her slender hands in his, relishing their cool delicacy. "I beg your pardon if I have given offense. That was never my intent. I only wanted to rally you a little and express my admiration for the skilful way you navigate the perilous waters of courtship. I have always had great faith in my abilities, but lately I have begun to doubt myself on that score. Had it not been for Miss Lily's advice and support, I fear I might have failed where I most long to succeed!"

Had he made the mistake of appearing too easy a conquest? Aaron wished he could have a few moments with Lily to ask her opinion.

Miss Crawford cast an anxious glance toward the card table, clearly apprehensive that her aunt might notice the minor liberty Aaron had taken. With an air of regret, she withdrew her hands from his grasp. "My sister has very particular ideas about the type of suitor I should encourage. I must admit, I have resisted her guidance in the matter. We are so opposite in a great many respects. Over the years I became accustomed to getting my way, while she has always complied with my wishes. Yet I do not doubt she has my best interest at heart."

"She does, indeed." Moments from his conversations with Lily Crawford ran through Aaron's mind so clearly that he felt as if she could hear him now, all the way from her sick room. "I envy you the affectionate, clear-sighted regard of such a sister. I only wish I had shown more gratitude for the assistance she gave me this week. I fear she may have exerted herself too much on my account and fallen ill as a consequence."

Even before he finished speaking, Iris Crawford began to shake her head vigorously, making her curls sway in a most beguiling manner. Aaron longed to take her in his arms, press his cheek against those silken locks and plant a kiss on the crown of her head.

"Do not blame yourself, captain! My sister has always been delicate and her ... that is *our* lady's maid is laid low with the same symptoms. I have no doubt Lily caught it from her. I will tell her that you appreciate her match-making efforts on your behalf. I assume that was the message you wished me to pass along to her."

"It was." Aaron chided himself. He had been enjoying

Iris Crawford's unexpected favor so much that he had almost forgotten the point of their conversation. "Also, please tell her I miss her company for its own sake. If I could spare her this illness by taking her place, I would do it gladly."

"I am certain she would not want that." Miss Crawford insisted, though she seemed touched by his concern for her sister. "If Lily were here now, I know she would tell us to stop talking about her and make the most of this opportunity to become acquainted. Do tell me about your life at sea. Being a privateer must be so exciting."

Clearly Miss Lily must have succeeded in persuading her sister that privateering was not the same as piracy, after all. Further gratitude to his loyal ally welled up in Aaron's heart, as well as pleasure over Miss Crawford's approving interest. She looked at him the way Moira Brennan looked at Lord Gabriel — as if he were the only man in the world whose acquaintance was worth cultivating.

Much as he wished to impress her, Aaron could not lie. Instead he gave a wry chuckle. "If by *exciting* you mean weeks of tedium broken by hours of terror, then privateering qualifies for your description."

The lady did not seem disappointed, but responded with a delightful chuckle that reminded Aaron of a slender Caribbean waterfall trickling through lush palm fronds. "You do not seem like a man who has ever been afraid of anything. I am certain you keep a cool head even in the midst of the fiercest battle. Did you capture many valuable prizes over the years?"

Coming from any other woman, such a remark might have made Aaron suspect she was trying to size up his fortune. But he knew an heiress like Iris Crawford had no reason for such mercenary motives. If she liked him, it must be for his character and his achievements. She would measure his success not in pounds and pence but in the courage and cleverness it took to amass his fortune. With her, he did not need to prove himself, the way he did with the rest of the world. He sensed that she and her sister held him in even higher esteem than he was determined to win from others.

"There is a tale or two worth telling," he admitted. The lady's obvious partiality rendered him unaccountably modest. "Like the time we captured both a French merchant ship and the pirate sloop that was attacking her."

He told of how his ship had come upon the desperate sea battle and held back until he judged both of the others were weakened enough to be defeated by a third.

"Mind you," he concluded, "that was a matter of luck rather than skill or cunning."

Miss Crawford shook her head, making her froth of curls dance once again. "It took both skill *and* cunning to turn a bit of luck so thoroughly to your advantage. It must have taken some hard fighting to subdue two foes, no matter how weakened. Your sister must have been so proud when you wrote her with the news!"

Indeed Ella had been. The memory made Aaron glow. He had taken immense satisfaction in capturing so rich a prize to secure his sister's comfort. But his pleasure in being able to entertain her with a written account of the skirmish had been almost as great.

A sudden quiver of unease ran through him. "How do you know about my sister, Miss Crawford? I do not recall ever mentioning her to you."

The color drained from Iris Crawford's face. For an instant, her resemblance to Lily was stronger than Aaron had ever noticed.

"I ... er ... surely you must ..." The look in her eyes was nothing short of panic — an excessive reaction that puzzled Aaron.

Then, just as quickly, she recovered her composure, making him wonder if he had only imagined her alarm.

"*My* sister must have told me about yours," she cried in what sounded like a rush of relief. "When she extolled your brotherly affection, I must admit it made me view you in a far more favourable light."

"Of course." Aaron reproached himself for casting a shadow over their pleasant conversation. "I seldom speak of Ella, but there is something about Miss Lily that made me feel I could confide in her. I am grateful that she told you about our conversation."

Might the protective concern they had felt for their ailing sisters create a bond between Miss Crawford and him? Much as Aaron wished it, he did not sense as strong or tender a connection on her part.

Before they could explore the subject, Miss Crawford glanced past him, toward the card table. "I believe Aunt Althea wants a word, if you will excuse me, Captain. It has been most enjoyable getting to know you better."

Aaron scarcely had a chance to mutter a reply before she hurried away, leaving him bewildered by her abrupt departure.

Had he said something amiss? Did Miss Crawford still disapprove of his privateering past? Or did she resent him sharing confidences with her sister instead of her? Neither explanation made much sense, yet he could not dismiss his finely-honed instinct that something was not right.

Chapter Seven

Dᴵᴰ Aᴀʀᴏɴ Tᴜʀɴᴇʀ suspect she was not who she claimed to be?

Lily spent the rest of the evening trying to avoid the captain without appearing to. That was not easy when she felt so powerfully drawn to him. Part of her would have liked nothing better than to find a secluded spot and devote many pleasant hours to discovering everything there was to know about him. Not only so she could relay the information to Iris, but for her own sake.

Yet she could not risk having him discover her ruse. In some ways, pretending to be Iris was easier than she'd anticipated. In other ways, it was much more difficult. Not only did she have to speak and behave as her sister would, she must also remember to avoid mentioning things Iris might not know. It was true that she'd told Iris about Captain Turner's sister, but his suspicious-sounding question had shaken her assurance.

It also troubled her conscience to mislead him this way. He clearly trusted her. Was it a betrayal of that trust to misrepresent herself?

By the time the Killorans' guests began to retire for the night, Lily could hardly wait to make her escape even though she knew her sister was usually one of the last to leave. A good night's rest and some precious solitude might calm her nerves and help her decide how to proceed.

But first she had to endure an inquisition from her aunt, who caught up with her on the stairs.

"What on earth were you playing at, Iris, spending so

much time with *that man*?" Aunt Althea gave a loud sniff, as if she smelled some offensive odor.

An emphatic defense of Aaron Turner tingled on Lily's tongue, but she reluctantly swallowed it. She could not afford to rouse her aunt's suspicion as well as the captain's by behaving in ways her sister never would.

Instead she affected Iris's petulant response to any sort of criticism. "I could ask the same thing about your flirtation with Rory Fitzwalter, Auntie. The man is half your age and has nothing but debts to his name."

How liberating it felt to say something so shockingly forthright!

"Half my age? Nonsense!" Aunt Althea blushed fiercely. "A year or two perhaps. No more than ten. Mr. Fitzwalter is very amusing and gentlemanly, which is a great deal more than one can say for Captain Turner. I thought you wanted nothing to do with such a vulgar scoundrel."

Lily forced a chuckle, as if her aunt had made an amusing quip. "The captain is more civilized than I first assumed. Besides, nothing fans the flames of a gentleman's ardor more than having a rival. Did you not tell me that?"

It was one of several ploys for catching a husband that Aunt Althea had impressed upon her nieces. Talk of such calculating wiles had done nothing to encourage Lily's interest in courting. Now she found herself relieved and rather surprised that she recalled her aunt's unwelcome advice.

"Ah!" Aunt Althea's eyes widened and her lips arched in a sly smile. "I should have known you had some cunning motive, my dear Iris. Only, do not discourage Lord Uvedale too much, or he may decide to look elsewhere for a wife."

Lily fervently hoped the viscount would do just that. "Never fear. I know what I am about. I will do nothing to jeopardize my campaign."

"I rather wish your sister had not fallen ill," her aunt sighed.

"Oh?" The unexpected remark took Lily aback. Did Aunt Althea truly care about her well-being? Like Father, she had always seemed to consider Lily a distant afterthought behind Iris.

 Her aunt nodded. "Lily kept the captain occupied. I hoped he might turn his attention to her and leave you alone. Not that a man like him could sustain an interest in such a milk-and-water miss as your sister for more than a few days."

Her aunt's off-hand slight stung more than usual. Between Captain Turner's impulsive kiss and his obvious concern about *Lily's* condition, the real Lily had begun to wonder if his feelings for her might be more than friendly. Aunt Althea was right, of course, which was fortunate. It was Iris who needed a strong, resourceful, constant husband.

Lily's aunt did not seem inclined to linger and lecture her further.

"Good night, Iris." Aunt Althea gave her a glancing peck on the cheek. "Get your beauty sleep and think on what I said about your suitors."

With that, she slipped into her bedchamber and firmly closed the door.

Lily hesitated a moment. Much as she longed for some time alone to think, she knew she would not be able to rest until she made certain Iris was resting comfortably.

She slipped down to the far end of the east wing where she found her sister asleep in a sparsely furnished sick room, watched over by an older serving woman.

The servant shook her head and waved Lily out of the room. "You shouldn't be here, Miss. The physician said your sister's not in any danger, though she must keep to her bed for a few days after the fever breaks. She's been asleep the whole evening. That'll do her more good than any apothecary's draft."

"I expect you're right." Lily gazed past the woman at her sister, who looked strangely childlike and vulnerable in slumber. "Thank you for looking after her. May I sit with her for a moment ... please?"

The woman looked torn. She glanced from Lily to Iris

and back. "I have my orders from Lady Killoran. She'll have my head if she hears of it."

"I will not breathe a word, I promise." Lily assured her. "I'm certain there is no danger of me falling ill. My sister and I have shared a room this whole week. Surely if I was going to catch what she has, I would have done so by now, don't you think?"

"I s'pose so, Miss. I need to go fetch my mending basket, so you can keep watch over her until I get back, but not a minute longer."

"Agreed," Lily replied.

The sound of their voices must have roused the patient. No sooner had the waiting woman departed than Iris's eyes fluttered open. She fixed Lily with a puzzled look. The poor thing must wonder if she was seeing her own reflection in the glass.

"I'm sorry I woke you." Lily perched on the edge of her sister's bed and took her hand. "I hope you do not mind me borrowing your dress for the evening. I had a whim to wear something different tonight. And the usual way of doing my hair did not suit it at all."

Iris shook her head drowsily, as if she could scarcely follow what her sister had said. Lily ran a hand over her damp, tousled hair in a caress that was almost maternal. This situation was such a reversal for the two of them. For once Iris was not the vigorous, active twin, but the half-forgotten invalid. A wave of pity for her sister washed over Lily, followed by one for her younger self.

"The party was not the same without you," she murmured as Iris's eyelids drifted shut again. "Everyone asked after you and hopes you will get well soon. Captain Turner spoke of you often. He is most eager to do anything he can to speed your recovery."

All that was perfectly true. Lily savored the relief of being able to speak with complete sincerity after an evening of omissions, half-truths and outright deception. She'd told herself it was all in the service of a good cause, but that did not silence her exacting conscience.

Now it protested again. Aaron Turner had expressed concern for the ailing Crawford sister in the mistaken belief that she was Lily, not Iris.

What did that signify? Lily brushed the nagging qualm away. No doubt the gallant captain would have been even more sympathetic if he knew Iris was the sufferer.

With obvious effort, Iris opened her eyes again. Her lips moved, but no sound emerged from her inflamed throat. Still, Lily could make out her intended question. *Lord Uvedale?*

"I believe he missed your company this evening as well." Lily slipped back into evasion with a pang of guilt. "Fortunately he managed to amuse himself with Miss Delany. She was obliged to be polite to him because of her position in his sister's household, but I believe she likes Rory Fitzwalter much better."

"Lord Gabriel and Miss Brennan only had eyes for one another," she continued in a gossipy vein quite unlike her usual conversation. "I wish I could be certain he cares for *her* more than he does for her fortune. I wonder if he will propose to her before the house party is over. No doubt that would please Lady Killoran. She would be able to boast at least one match made between a nobleman and an heiress."

Lily glanced down at her sister only to find her sound asleep again.

"I vow," she promised Iris in a vehement whisper, "*you* will not be ensnared in such a mercenary arrangement, even if it means I have to perjure myself to a fare-thee-well!"

"Is your sister feeling any better today?" Aaron asked Miss Crawford the following afternoon as they strolled through the gardens of Beckwith Abbey, accompanied by the other ladies of the party.

Off in the distance, the quiet country air was disturbed by the crack of gunfire. Lord Killoran and the other gentlemen were busy slaughtering game birds by the dozens. They had been aghast when Aaron declined to join them in the day's *sport*.

"I am sorry to disappoint you, gentlemen" he'd replied with a wry chuckle and a covert wink at Iris Crawford. "But I am not as bloodthirsty as you might expect of a pirate."

"Please yourself." Lord Killoran shook his head as if he could not fathom any man being reluctant to stand out in the damp cold for hours on end, firing at coveys of partridge or pheasants that had been flushed out by the dogs.

Lord Uvedale muttered darkly about blood sports not being bloodthirsty, but Rory and Lord Gabriel cast longing glances at the ladies. Aaron suspected they would have been quite happy to follow his lead. Now, as he walked and chatted with Iris Crawford, unhindered by the presence of his rival, Aaron congratulated himself for defying convention.

Miss Crawford hesitated before answering his question about her sister, which brought him a swift pang of concern for Lily.

But when she found her voice at last, her reply soothed his fears. "My sister sleeps a great deal and can scarcely coax a word out. But she seemed less feverish when I looked in on her this morning. I wish I could have sat with her this afternoon, but the woman taking care of her would not hear of it. Then my sister waved me away in quite an imperious manner. I could not defy them both."

Aaron grinned at the thought of Lily Crawford acting imperious. No doubt she wanted Iris to spend more time in his company. Ill as she might be, his loyal ally had not forgotten her promise to assist him.

"I pity Miss Lily for losing the pleasure of your companionship." He dropped his voice so as not to be overheard by Lady Killoran and Mrs. Henderson. Both ladies clearly disapproved of his refusal to join the shoot. "It was kind of her to allow me the enjoyment of your company at her expense. I owe her a considerable debt."

Miss Crawford looked away and appeared to blush. Or was it only the nip of January air that turned her cheeks such a pretty pink? As he became better acquainted with the lady, Aaron had discovered unexpected reticence and vulnerability beneath her vivacious confidence, just as he'd uncovered warm sympathy beneath her sister's aloofness. Was it because they were twins that each sought to distinguish herself from the other and deny their points of similarity? If so it was a shame, for the traits they tried to conceal endeared them to him even more.

"I am certain my sister would deny any obligation, Captain," Iris Crawford insisted. "No doubt she would rather have peace and quiet to speed her recovery than me nattering away at her."

Aaron shook his head. "You could not *natter* if you tried, my dear Miss Crawford. Your lively conversation is one of your greatest charms. As for your sister, she may be accustomed to solitude when she is ill. That does not mean it is best for her or what she wishes for in her heart of hearts."

A sudden catch in the lady's breath made Aaron wonder if his remark had affected her in a manner he did not intend. "I vow, Captain, you sound as if you know my sister better than I do. Perhaps better than she knows herself."

"Forgive me, Miss Crawford!" He hoped he had not squandered the opportunity Miss Lily had procured for him by offending her sister. "I did not mean to presume any such thing. I must admit, I valued the privilege of a closer acquaintance with your sister than she permits most people. I believe if she could overcome her bashfulness in company a little more, she would be as eagerly sought after by a certain type of gentleman as you are by your many admirers."

"Indeed?" Iris Crawford blushed — Aaron was certain of it this time. "Pray, what *type of gentleman* do you suppose would be drawn to my sister? Those with mounting debts and empty pockets?"

"No!" Aaron's features tensed into a scowl his crew had grown to fear. "I am surprised you would imply such a slight to your own sister, Miss Crawford. The two of you may be as different as chalk and cheese, but that does not mean one is altogether inferior to the other. Little wonder Miss Lily lacks confidence in herself if she enjoys so little consideration from those closest to her!"

Iris Crawford's pretty lips fell slack in an expression of shock, as if she had never before heard a word of reproach. Was it possible she never had, while Lily had endured enough for both of them?

"But ... but ..." she sputtered.

Discretion and desire both chided Aaron for not holding his tongue. Now they urged him to make a swift, abject apology, but his vocal organs turned stubbornly mute. He was not accustomed to eating his words and begging pardon, even when he'd been mistaken in a rush to judgment. That was not the case now. How could he retract what he'd said when he believed it with all his heart?

"If you will excuse me, Miss Crawford." He gave a stiff-necked bow and kept his gaze averted from her face, for fear the dismayed beauty he would glimpse might undo his resolve. "I just remembered an urgent errand I must attend to at once."

Without waiting for a reply, he strode off to the Killorans' stables, ordered his horse saddled and rode off toward the nearby town of Guildford.

Had she ruined her plan entirely by venting her long-held self-doubts?

As Lily dressed for dinner that evening, she recalled with sickening clarity the sight of Captain Turner stalking away and the tone of his voice, harsh as a lash, when he'd denounced her. The approving nod she'd received from Aunt Althea did nothing to ease her dismay.

And yet, in spite of the sting of the captain's rebuke and her fear that she had spoiled any chance of him marrying her sister, Lily could not stifle a ridiculous flicker of satisfaction. Such kind, perceptive things he had said about her. For the first time in her life, she felt as if someone truly *saw* and understood her a little.

Captain Turner had been correct that solitude was not what she craved. It was a state to which she'd become accustomed, one in which she was comfortable. Perhaps not *comfortable* but less uncomfortable than she felt in tiresome or judgmental company. So much of London Society tended to combine the worst of both faults.

Her new maid's voice broke in on Lily's brooding. "Does my way of dressing your hair not suit you, Miss Crawford?"

"Quite the contrary!" Lily strove to mold her features into the more cheerful cast of her sister's. "It looks very well. If I seem preoccupied, it is only because I had a quarrel with … one of the gentlemen earlier. I fear he may never speak to me again."

That prospect lowered her spirits to a depth she could scarcely bear. Yet when Lily reflected on how the captain had taken her part against the lady of whom he was so deeply enamored, it made her almost giddy.

Hannah Jackson rolled her eyes. "Don't fret on that account, Miss. Men get their noses out of joint over nothing and say a great many things they regret before they finish speaking. Mark my words, your gentleman will come groveling before you know it. If you are willing to forgive him, don't be too quick about it. Make him win his way back into favor and he will be bound to you tighter than ever."

In spite of all her misgivings Lily could not keep from laughing. "Why, Miss Jackson, you sound for all the world like my aunt! Between the two of you, I shall not lack for advice about managing suitors."

Somehow she could not picture Aaron Turner grovelling

to anyone for any reason. Besides, she was not at all certain she wanted him to recant the things he'd said about Lily. He might have been besotted with Iris, but his actions suggested the captain felt something deeper for her shy sister. Perhaps it was only friendship or pity, her sense of self-preservation insisted — nothing to threaten her plans for him and Iris.

His reaction this afternoon represented a much greater danger to those plans. Lily feared he might have left Beckwith Abbey never to return.

Striving to suppress her misgivings, she rose from her dressing table. "You have accomplished wonders once again, Miss Jackson. Now, I must hurry if I am to look in on my sister before I go down to dinner."

"Very good, Miss." Hannah Jackson looked pleased with her handiwork. "From what I hear in the servants' hall, both she and Miss Ingledew are on the mend, though the doctor's drafts will make them sleepy for a while."

Lily nodded. She was grateful that Iris was not in full possession of her wits. Otherwise she might be suspicious of why Lily was suddenly borrowing her gowns and wearing her hair in the style Iris favored.

When Lily entered the sick room, she found Iris dozing. But her sister roused when Lily conferred in whispers with the servant who was caring for her. She seemed more aware of her surroundings than the previous day.

"Good evening, dearest," said Lily, careful not to speak her sister's name in front of the Killorans' servant.

As she approached the bed, a basket on the night table caught her eye. "My goodness, what is all this?"

The caretaker replied on behalf of her mute patient. "Did I not tell you, Miss? 'Tis fine fruit Captain Turner fetched from Guildford for your sister, with his compliments and wishes for her speedy recovery. I cannot think what it must have cost him."

"I should say." Lily cast an appreciative glance over the plump red grapes, ripe oranges and delicate pears to marvel at the special luxuries of hothouse strawberries and an exotic pineapple. "Have you seen these, dearest? Was it not thoughtful of the captain to send you such a gift? It is a mark of the warm, constant feelings he has for you."

Not for Iris, a stubborn voice within her protested. This generous gift was a token of his feelings for *Lily*. Would a man go to such trouble and expense on account of mere friendship?

Iris looked over at the captain's gift with greater alertness and pleasure than she had shown since falling ill. She answered Lily's question with an emphatic nod and a pensive smile.

"Very kind," she spoke in a raspy whisper. "Thank him for me."

"I will, indeed. Dear me, look at the time! I must go or I shall be late for dinner again. Rest well, dearest, and try to eat as much as you can. If you finish all your broth, you can have some grapes or an orange. They will tempt your appetite, I am certain."

Lily dropped a kiss on her sister's forehead then hurried away. She told herself she ought to be encouraged by Iris's reaction to Captain Turner's thoughtful gift. It was precisely the change of heart she had hoped for.

Then why did it make her so uneasy?

Chapter Eight

DINNER THAT EVENING was perfect agony for Aaron. He had hoped for a private word with Iris Crawford before the meal. Though he was the first guest to arrive in the drawing room and watched anxiously for the lady, she did not appear until after all the others had assembled. No sooner had she joined them than Lady Killoran whisked the party into the dining room with Miss Crawford on Lord Uvedale's arm.

The table talk was all about the day's shooting — the total bag of birds, each gentleman's tally, a minor argument over which made the best eating, partridge or pheasant. Aaron had nothing to add to the conversation which might have allowed him to address a word down the table to Iris Crawford.

He stared at her, hoping to catch her eye, but she studiously ignored him. His only comfort was that she did not pay Viscount Uvedale much attention either. Miss Crawford seemed quite preoccupied, not her usual bright vivacious self. Was she so offended by his earlier outburst that she could not enjoy the party? Or had Miss Lily taken a turn for the worse, leaving her sister downcast with worry? Neither possibility calmed Aaron's mind.

It was worse still when the ladies withdrew. Aaron bolted his brandy then sat in sullen silence, letting the tiresome litany of shooting, racing, drinking and gambling stories wash over him like so much chatter in a foreign language. The instant Lord Killoran suggested they should consider rejoining the rest of the party Aaron shot to his feet and marched away.

He found Lady Killoran, Mrs. Henderson and Miss

Brennan engaged in animated conversation about a Twelfth Night ball being hosted at a neighboring estate. Apparently their entire party had been invited.

Aaron ignored them. Instead he approached Miss Crawford and Miss Delany, who sat at the pianoforte playing a duet. It surprised him to see the two ladies on such friendly terms. Until this evening Iris Crawford had paid neither Kitty Delany nor Moira Brennan much notice. When the gentlemen were not present, she seemed to prefer the company of her aunt and the countess.

When the duet concluded, Aaron applauded their performance more vigorously than it might have merited. "Well done, ladies! I enjoyed your playing a great deal."

"That is kind of you, Captain," Kitty Delany replied in a bantering tone that sounded more like Miss Crawford's, "considering you cannot have heard us for more than a minute. Perhaps it is the brevity of which you approve."

Iris Crawford joined in her companion's laughter, though she sounded self-conscious and avoided looking at Aaron.

"Or perhaps ..." Miss Delany continued with an impudent grin that made Aaron wonder what had come over her. "It is the performers you admire more than the performance ... one in particular."

Iris Crawford blushed as if she had never been an object of admiration in her life, while Aaron stammered like a school boy. "I ... er ... that is ... I did not have to hear you play for very long to recognize your skill, Miss Delany. Now if I might trouble Miss Crawford for a private word."

Miss Delany began to play a well-known Irish air. "If she has no objections I certainly do not."

Iris Crawford rose abruptly and fled to the far end of the room, where they had enjoyed such a pleasant conversation last evening. Aaron wondered whether he had lost whatever progress he'd made with her. Lily might have paid a painful price to give him that opportunity to woo her sister. She would not thank him for spoiling it, even to defend her.

As he approached Miss Crawford, Aaron inhaled a deep breath, readying himself to say as much as possible before she bid him to hold his tongue.

He was not able to get a word out before she launched into a most emphatic speech of her own. "Captain, before you say anything please allow me to thank you for your gift to my sister. We both appreciate your kind gesture. I am certain it will hasten her recovery."

"Nothing would please me more," replied Aaron, momentarily surprised out of his well-rehearsed apology. He had expected condemnation, not thanks. "I hope you will excuse my earlier rudeness on account of my concern for Miss Lily. I had no business making such ill-natured comments about your feelings toward your sister."

As he spoke Iris Crawford shook her head vigorously, making Aaron lose heart. The lady might appreciate his gift to her ailing sister, but that did not guarantee her forgiveness.

"Please, Captain," she cried when he paused to take a breath, "you are quite mistaken if you believe I am offended by what you said! On the contrary, you were right to correct me. I spoke without thinking, repeating something I have often heard Lily say about her marriage prospects. I did not mean it as a slight on her, but I realize that is how it must have sounded to you. I commend you for defending Lily so gallantly, even at the risk of contradicting me."

"Y-you do?" Aaron tried to marshal his slack features into a sensible expression. "You *can* forgive me?"

Miss Crawford's incomparable lips spread into a luminous smile that reassured him even more than her words. "I could indeed, Captain, if there was anything in your conduct that required forgiveness. I do not believe there was."

Sweet relief bubbled up in Aaron, like the head on a mug of fine ale. He swept Iris Crawford a deep bow to acknowledge her graciousness. "You are far less severe upon me than I was upon myself, and considerably less than I deserve. I feared you might never speak to me again after the way I behaved."

Her smile twisted into a warm grin, as if she regarded his admission as both amusing and endearing. "I was afraid you were so infuriated with me that you had left Beckwith Abbey, never to return."

"And the prospect dismayed you?" Aaron felt like a drowning man who had been plucked from the angry waves against all expectation. The world around him seemed to sparkle bright and new.

Miss Crawford caught her full lower lip between her teeth. A look of gentle melancholy settled briefly over her features, rendering them even lovelier than her usual vibrant smile.

"The thought of being parted from you grieved me more than I can say," she whispered so softly that Aaron wondered whether he had only imagined it.

Yet when their eyes met, the distress he glimpsed in hers persuaded him that he had heard correctly after all.

So deeply captivated was he that he failed notice her aunt bearing down on them.

"Come, Iris." Mrs. Henderson latched onto her niece's arm. "You must not be unsociable like your sister. This is a house *party*, remember?"

She shot Aaron a venomous glare. "If you will excuse us, Captain."

Without waiting for him to respond, she dragged Miss Crawford back toward the other guests, chattering about the upcoming ball.

Undeterred, Aaron followed the ladies. If Iris Crawford was not done with him, it would take a great deal more than the combined exertions of Mrs. Henderson and Viscount Uvedale to discourage his renewed pursuit of her.

If she had not been afraid of rousing her aunt's suspicion, Lily would have devoted every moment of that evening to Captain Turner. His earnest apology had endeared him to her more than ever.

For as long as she could recall, she had sought to avoid the slightest difference of opinion with her loved ones, fearing it might estrange them from her entirely. The possibility that an attachment could survive conflict was a foreign one to her. Did she dare trust it on the basis of her recent experiences with Aaron Turner?

Perhaps.

The captain was such a unique man in so many respects — all of which appealed to her. He possessed confidence, ambition and tenacity. Yet those manly virtues did not detract from the softer aspects of his nature. Lily admired the protective, loving attachment he had freely admitted for his delicate little sister. It was difficult not to envy Ella Turner the steadfast devotion of her brother.

The most endearing way Captain Turner differed from others was in his clear partiality for the Crawford sister no one else favored. Concern for *Lily* had led him to quarrel with the lady he believed to be Iris. Then he had ridden off in search of a gift of fine fruit for the invalid. Never in her life could Lily recall another person showing so much concern for her when she was ill.

Was it possible she had been wrong to assume no man could want her for anything except her fortune? Certainly the captain had nothing to gain from a connection with her that he could not get from marrying Iris. His actions today suggested that, given a choice between the Crawford sisters, he cared more for Lily.

And how did she feel about him?

Lily gazed past the handsome but tiresome viscount to the pianoforte, where Captain Turner pretended to listen as Miss Delany played. Whenever Lily stole a glance in their direction, she met the captain's rapt gaze. It never failed to ignite a blaze of heat in her cheeks and elsewhere. As she cast secret smiles at Aaron Turner and basked in the bright warmth of his regard, Lily questioned old, tyrannical certainties and challenged deep-rooted fears.

She had been drawn to the captain even before they were introduced. Ever since she glimpsed him in the courtyard of Beckwith Abbey, she'd been compelled to behave in ways quite contrary to her cautious nature — taking liberties, running risks, letting down her guard.

Could that be the true motive behind this audacious scheme to impersonate her sister? Not because she wanted to promote a match between Iris and the captain, but because she yearned to have him look at her the way he was doing this very moment. Had she wanted him to court her, confide in her and perhaps come to feel for her what she felt for him?

"What do you say to that, Miss Crawford?" The sharp tone of Lord Uvedale's sudden question jolted Lily from her hopeful reverie.

"I beg your pardon, sir?" She struggled to recall what he'd been talking about.

His lordship's upper lip curled in a scornful sneer. "Perhaps if you paid proper attention to a gentleman's addresses rather than making sheep's eyes at another, you might not lose the thread of conversation so easily."

Lord Uvedale had a point, Lily was compelled to admit. But the arrogance of his rebuke vexed her in a way Captain Turner's honest anger had not. It goaded her to assert herself in a manner her self-confident sister might.

"Conversation?" Lily raised her eyebrows and returned his haughty glare. "Is that was we were having? I assumed it must be a monologue, for you have not given me the opportunity to utter a single word in at least a quarter of an hour."

The gentleman's pale grey eyes bulged in a most unattractive way. Clearly he was not accustomed to having *his* behaviour questioned.

"That ... that is what I was trying to do just now," he sputtered.

"Nonsense." Lily gave a dismissive chuckle. "You were trying to catch me out so you could chide me for not hanging on your every word."

She fluttered her fan in a manner she hoped would look imperious, but was actually an attempt to disguise her trembling hand. "In future, if you wish to engage a lady's undivided attention, I suggest you make an effort to be more amusing."

Fearing she could not keep up the pretence of assurance any longer, Lily bobbed a barely civil curtsey then swept away. She cast a nervous glance toward the card table where her aunt was playing whist. Fortunately Rory Fitzwalter was leaning over Aunt Althea's chair, distracting her with a comical story. She seemed completely oblivious to her niece's behavior.

Captain Turner was far more observant. Excusing himself from Miss Delany, he strode to Lily's side at once.

"What on earth did you say to his lordship, just now?" The captain's dark eyes twinkled with irrepressible merriment. "You appear to have left him at a loss for words and that is no small feat."

Lily could not suppress a soft chuckle as she told him of her exchange with the viscount.

"Well done!" The captain subtly guided her to a spot in the room where her aunt could not see them unless she turned completely around. "It is high time someone gave that swaggering puppy a lesson in manners. Mind you, I could say the same about myself. May I ask why he received a reprimand while I was shown undeserved clemency?"

His approval of her assertiveness fuelled Lily's confidence. Not the sort she had borrowed by imitating her sister, but a genuine sense of her own worth and abilities.

"To begin with, *you* were right," she admitted. "Besides, I could not have been half as severe upon you as you were upon yourself. There is something quite disarming about a person who is willing to recognize and own his mistakes."

Unlike the viscount, Captain Turner truly listened to her. "That is an insightful observation, Miss Crawford. I hope you will not be offended if I suggest it reminds me of the sort of thing your sister might say."

"Why should that offend me?" Happiness bubbled up in Lily from some secret source that had never been tapped until now. "I will be the first to admit my sister notices things about people that others often miss. Perhaps it comes from observing others more than joining in with them."

It felt odd, discussing her behaviour at a remove like this. Yet it brought Lily a sense of clarity about herself that she had not expected.

"Another cogent insight, Miss Crawford." The captain's deep, resonant voice warmed. "The better acquainted we become, the more I find to admire about you."

Lily's heart fairly ached with joy. The aspects of her character he approved so sincerely were not her sister's traits which she strove to imitate, but parts of herself that no one had recognized until now. It was as if she had drifted through life like a forlorn ghost. Now someone could see her clearly, confirming that she was made of flesh and blood.

"I must admit," Aaron Turner continued when she was too overcome to reply, "Not all of your sister's observations about people are accurate."

"They aren't?" Lily tried to dismiss the subtle jab his words inflicted.

The captain shook his head with a fond smile that seemed to contradict his words. "For instance, that nonsense you repeated about gentlemen only caring for her fortune. Where did she get such a ridiculous idea?"

Was it ridiculous? Not long ago, Lily would have denied that as dangerous blasphemy. Suddenly she found herself more inclined to believe Aaron Turner than the harsh voice of past experience.

The unfamiliar sense of trust he inspired overcame her usual guardedness. "I believe my sister frequently heard such pronouncements from the servants during our younger years, when she was often ill and kept at home. Children can be sensitive to the harsh opinions of others and far too easily take them to heart."

"Why would anyone speak so unkindly of an ailing child?" The captain's rugged features darkened like a thunderhead.

His sudden severity might have frightened Lily, if she had not sensed his protective indignation was on her behalf. Until that moment, she had never questioned *why* she'd been ignored and ill-treated as a child. Instead she had tried to forget that part of her life, refusing to consider how much it might have shaped her present views and behavior.

"I —" She caught herself about to say *Iris* then remembered that the captain believed she was Iris. "*I* had high spirits and a knack for making myself agreeable to our father and the household. Lily was timid and quiet, which some people mistook for a sullen disposition."

"Blinkered fools!" Captain Turner muttered through clenched teeth. "If even one had taken the time to show her a little kindness, it might have made a world of difference to Lily. I trust you've made certain she is being well treated here, while she is ill."

It sounded as if he did not trust even Iris to do enough for her. "Your sister may pretend otherwise, but I fear she is lonely. I should pay her a little visit and do what I can to cheer her."

"No!" The word burst out louder than Lily intended.

She pressed her fingers to her lips and glanced about in fear of drawing attention to herself. Fortunately, Miss Delany's playing had grown more *forte* than *piano* just then and the card players were laughing loudly over some quip of Rory Fitzwalter's.

The only one who seemed to notice her outcry was the captain. He regarded her with surprise and a hint of disapproval.

Lily scrambled to recover from her gaffe. "Of course I am not sparing any effort to see that my sister receives the best possible care."

In spite of her insistence, she could not suppress a qualm of shame. Had she truly shown Iris any more concern than she'd received as a child? Or had she been preoccupied with taking advantage of her sister's absence to indulge her fancy for Captain Turner?

"It is kind of you to be so concerned about her, Captain." Lily's gaze faltered before his forthright stare. "But Lady Killoran has given strict instructions about keeping my sister out of contact with her other guests. It has taken all my powers of persuasion to steal a few brief visits. I will tell her all the very kind compliments you have paid her. I am certain that will cheer her as much as a visit from you."

The captain gave a reluctant nod. "I would not want to put you out of favor with her ladyship or run the risk of you not being allowed to see Lily at all. Be certain to tell your sister how much I miss her company . . . especially at breakfast."

"Of course." Out of the corner of her eye, Lily glimpsed Aunt Althea beginning to look around the room. It was only a matter of time until she would spot her niece with Captain Turner. "I should be happy to take her place, if you would like."

"Like?" His dark features lit up with the joyful surprise of a child who had received an unexpected gift. "I would be delighted!"

"Excellent." Lily started toward the card table to avert her aunt's disapproval. "So would I."

Chapter Nine

AARON BOUNDED OUT of bed the next morning before anyone else in Beckwith Abbey was stirring, except the servants.

He discovered his window well frosted, but he could make out the silver sickle of a waning moon in the clear, dark sky over Compton Hill. Outside, the world seemed still and cold after many mild days. While others in the party might be anxious about the weather and how it would affect their leisure pursuits, Aaron would not have been troubled by anything less than a hurricane. As long as he could enjoy the company of Iris Crawford, his world would be a warm, sunny place.

Though it was far too early for breakfast, Aaron began to prepare. He washed, shaved and dressed with the sort of elaborate care other gentlemen might reserve for a ball or presentation at court. As far as he was concerned, the morning ahead would be more important than either of those.

He would have the opportunity to spend time with Iris Crawford in the closest thing to privacy available at a country house party. No disapproving aunt to watch their every move and drag Iris away if their conversation threatened to grow intimate. No viscount lurking about, monopolizing the lady's company as if she belonged to him by right. With luck there might be no other guests about, to intrude on their time together.

As he groomed and dressed for the morning, Aaron reflected on the events of the previous evening with satisfaction and gratitude. He'd feared the chance of winning Iris

Crawford might be lost forever, only to discover his prospects were better than ever. Much of that, perhaps all, he owed to Lily.

His affection for her seemed to have created a bond between Iris and him. Aaron was not certain that anything else would have worked as well. Concern for her ailing sister seemed to bring out a more approachable, sympathetic side to Iris's nature. The things she had told him about her sister's childhood made Aaron more fiercely determined to protect Lily once he became her brother-in-law.

With that objective in mind, he marched down to the breakfast room, where he found the earl and Lord Gabriel Stanford. He bid them a civil good morning, while silently hoping they would eat quickly and leave. The earl obliged him within five minutes, but Lord Gabriel lingered at the table, even after Iris Crawford joined them. The trio made stilted conversation until the duke's son finally understood the pointed looks Aaron was giving him and excused himself.

"That's better." Aaron heaved a sigh of relief then smiled at Iris. "I was afraid we might be stuck with him until luncheon!"

"Would that have been a problem?" Iris Crawford arched one tawny brow and gave a droll little grin to show she was in jest. "I think Lord Gabriel is quite an agreeable gentleman. He does not put on intolerable airs because his father is a duke."

Was she comparing Stanford's conduct to Lord Uvedale's? Aaron approved of anyone who cast the viscount in an unfavorable light.

"I have only one thing against him." Aaron pushed a sausage around his plate without taking a bite. He wanted this breakfast to last as long as possible. "He should have shown more interest in Miss Lily. I am certain the countess hoped they would make a match."

"So you said." Iris grew flustered, for reasons that were not clear to Aaron. "I mean, Lily told me you had worked out which couples Lady Killoran wished to pair off."

Did she expect him to be annoyed that she and Lily had

discussed that? On the contrary, he would have been grateful if Lily had repeated every word of their conversations to her sister. Once again it pained Aaron to recall how he had reproached Lily for not doing enough to assist him. Here was further proof of her exertions on his behalf.

Before he had a chance to reply, Iris rallied her composure. "Do not trouble yourself too much on my sister's account. I doubt she gave poor Lord Gabriel much encouragement. He and Miss Brennan seem a good deal better suited. Her fortune may have been what first attracted him, but I believe he has become quite attached to the lady for her own sake."

"You sound like Lily," Aaron chuckled, "thinking every suitor must be a fortune hunter."

His quip did not amuse Iris. She seemed positively alarmed. Perhaps she was, at the thought of how close she had come to falling into the clutches of a real fortune hunter.

"You may find it amusing," she murmured, lowering her gaze to her breakfast plate, "but every woman who has money of her own would be wise to be on guard against men of that ilk."

"I suppose so, in the case of women who have nothing else to recommend them." Aaron gathered his thoughts as he took a drink of coffee, which was rapidly growing cold. "But you and your sister have beauty, wit and accomplishments that any man of taste would be bound to admire, even if you had no fortune at all."

Iris Crawford's divine eyes sparkled with pleasure at his praise. "You are very gallant, captain. More than I would have expected from ..."

"A pirate?" Aaron completed her thought ... or so he assumed.

But Iris shook her head. "I was going to say, more than I would have expected from someone who spent so many years exclusively in the company of other men."

"Ah!" Aaron lifted his coffee cup, as if in a toast to her. "Well done, Miss Crawford. I suppose that proves we all have our sensitive spots. It is not always easy to understand another person's until we know what past experiences have shaped their character."

He might not have spent as much time as he would have liked in the company of the fair sex, yet Aaron knew this was hardly the sort of banter a lady might expect when she was being courted. Iris Crawford did not seem to object.

She leaned forward, her eyes wide and her lips slightly parted. "What past experiences formed your sensitive spots, Captain?"

Her question ambushed Aaron. It was a breath-taking threat wrapped inside the most appealing invitation. Both made his heart hammer against his ribs. But how could he refuse anything his dearest one asked of him, especially when she looked so eager to hear his answer.

He shrugged. "As your sister may have told you, I am not much given to reflection. I can tell you a little about my past, make of it what you will."

"I should like to learn more about you." Her lips arched in an encouraging smile. "Not only your adventures and triumphs, but your struggles and sorrows. You may be certain of a sympathetic hearing."

Aaron had no doubt of that. Yet it felt as if parts of his past were locked securely away and he could not recall where he had put the key.

"I gather you were quite young when your father died." Iris prompted him. "Do you have any memories of him? Or your mother?"

Aaron gave a halting nod. The key to his past slid into the lock and turned. "I was twelve years old when we received word of my father's death, but I do not have many memories of him. He was a captain in the Royal Navy and often away at sea for years at a time. My mother was my whole world. She was like you — lively and lovely. She had been the belle of Hampshire in her youth, with her pick of wealthy and titled suitors. She spurned them all for a dashing young naval officer who had neither fortune nor lofty connections."

Was he trying to follow in his father's footsteps by winning the most desirable prize? Aaron did not care to think too deeply about that. In one matter he promised himself he would not follow his father's example.

"I do not believe my mother ever regretted her choice on account of those things, at least not for her own sake. But she had no idea how much his duties would keep them apart, nor of the danger that would part them forever."

Iris Crawford did not speak but urged him to continue with her rapt gaze.

"After Father was killed and she found herself with two children to support, my mother married one of her old suitors. My stepfather was a viscount with a comfortable fortune. He had two sons from his first marriage. They resented my mother and were the bane of my existence."

Both his stepbrothers had come to bad ends, which did not surprise Aaron.

"We managed well enough until my mother died. On her deathbed, she made our stepfather promised he would look after Ella and me. He kept his word, I'll say that for him. But I could not bear to live on his charity. I knew if any ill befell him, his sons would take great delight in turning my sister out without a penny."

"And that is why you joined the crew of a privateer," Iris murmured, as if many things about him now made sense to her.

Aaron was not certain he could say the same. In hindsight he wondered whether becoming a privateer had been the *only* way he could have provided for his sister. Had part of its appeal been the embarrassment his career would cause his painfully respectable stepfamily? If he had not been so determined to take his revenge, might he have been able to find employment capable of supporting his sister without taking him so far away from her?

He had never imagined Iris Crawford would be the sort of

woman to make him ponder such uncomfortable questions. Clearly she had more in common with her sister than they, or anyone else, believed.

———◆◆———

Aaron Turner might not have designs upon her sister's fortune, Lily reflected as she glanced down the table at him that evening. That did not mean he wanted to wed Iris for love alone.

Love her? Lily stifled a derisive chuckle. Aaron scarcely knew her sister.

He had admired Iris from a distance and been rebuffed when he'd tried to get close to her. She represented the sort of challenge he could not resist. She was the glittering, desirable prize he yearned to snatch out of the hands of despised noblemen, just as his father had done. But what would happen after that delirious rush of triumph wore off, as it was bound to? Would he be happy with a wife who was all but a stranger to him?

Aaron looked up from his dinner just then and his gaze captured Lily's. Though he did not realize it, the fondness that glowed in his dark eyes belonged to her, not Iris. For the past few days, she had successfully projected her sister's confident vivacity. But when she and Aaron were together, she had spoken and behaved more like herself than Iris. So much so, that Lily sometimes wondered if he suspected the truth.

So absorbed was she in such thoughts, that the dinner conversation swirled around her, scarcely noticed. Then a remark of Rory Fitzwalter's to the countess caught her attention.

"You have been quite mysterious about what sort of entertainment you have planned for us this evening, my dear Regina. Put us out of our suspense, I beg you."

If his sister-in-law detected a nip of sarcasm in Rory's lilting voice she chose to ignore it. "What do you say to making shades? Would that not be an amusing change from card-playing and dancing?"

Rory chuckled. "You underestimate my appetite for card play, even when there are no high wagers to be won."

"Or lost," muttered Lord Killoran, barely loud enough for Lily to hear.

She wondered how the earl's brother managed to pay his gambling debts, other than with the sort of personal favors he had bartered to Aaron. If Lord Killoran regularly rescued him from debt, no wonder the countess was anxious to find Rory a wealthy wife ... or at least one capable of reforming his rakish habits. Miss Brennan might have been up to the challenge but Rory ignored her as steadfastly as Iris had ignored Aaron Turner.

"I should very much enjoy making shades," Aaron addressed their hostess but did not take his eyes off Lily. "Especially if I can prevail upon Miss Crawford to sit for me. I am not certain I can do justice to her fine profile, but I shall try my best."

The countess stiffened, as if offended by the captain's eager approval of her plan. "Surely we can agree on partners after—"

"Thank you, Captain," Lily hastened to accept his invitation before anyone else could interfere. "If it turns out well, we can make a gift of it to my sister. I am certain she would like that."

Taking their cue, other members of the party proceeded to pair up, to Lady Killoran's visible annoyance.

The countess was not the only one vexed over the arrangements.

When the ladies retreated to the drawing room after dinner, Lily's aunt confronted her, fan fluttering furiously. "Whatever possessed you to accept Captain Turner's impudent request to draw your shade, Iris? I declare, I do not know what has gotten into you lately."

"It sounded quite civil to me." Lily tried to affect her sister's headstrong confidence. "Besides, I told you, Auntie. I am only trying to —"

"Make Lord Uvedale jealous?" her aunt concluded in

a tone of biting irony. "What you fail to realize is that the suitor in question must witness his rival's progress. Whatever *encouragement* you give Captain Turner behind the screen will only serve to increase his impudence. It will have no effect on Lord Uvedale but to make him flirt with that Delany girl out of boredom. Keep it up and you may lose his interest altogether."

Fortunately her aunt had no opportunity to sniff about further, for the gentlemen trooped in just then, sooner than they usually rejoined the ladies.

Captain Turner strode directly toward Lily with an eager smile that held an endearing hint of anxiety. "Shall we get to work at once, Miss Crawford? I hope you have not changed your mind about making shades with me?"

Before Lily could reply, Viscount Uvedale interrupted. She had not noticed how closely he'd followed the captain. "I hope the lady *has* changed her mind, as is her prerogative. Or at least come to her senses."

Lily cocked her eyebrow in an imperious expression she had sometimes seen her sister affect. "Are you questioning the soundness of my judgement, Lord Uvedale?"

"Not in general." He backed off quickly, no doubt stung by the sharpness of her tone. "Only in your sudden change of favor."

Aunt Althea shot a warning look as if to say this was what she feared. Lily knew she must tread carefully — if anyone guessed her ruse, there would be the devil to pay.

"Rest assured my favors have not *changed*, sir." She forced a smile at the viscount. Her words were quite true. She detested him as much as ever. "I only suppose it is agreeable to have a little variety in the acquaintance we keep."

Captain Turner gave an emphatic nod. "Quite true, Miss Crawford. A life of unvaried society is surely in danger of growing stale."

"Indeed, Captain!" Lily's lips needed no forcing to smile for him. "It is pleasant now and then to have the company of someone who judges us wise rather than foolish."

Taking the arm he offered her, she nodded toward a darkened corner of the room, blocked off by a tall ornamental screen. "Let us not delay. We must show our hostess that we value her effort to keep us amused."

Tingly warmth spread through Lily's hand where she clung to Aaron's sleeve. She sensed the firm strength of his arm beneath the layers of wool and linen. It made her feel safe in a way she could not recall experiencing before. After the things he had confessed to her about his past, Lily imagined she could confide in him without reserve on any subject. *Almost* any subject.

They slipped behind the screen where a clever device of lenses and mirrors cast a bright beam of light from a candle onto a large sheet of paper affixed to an easel. Between the light box and the easel was a chair for the sitter.

"Let us get to work, then." With a decisive sweep of his hand, Aaron invited Lily to be seated. "I only hope I can begin to capture the beauty of your profile and create a gift half worthy of your sister."

"You need have no fear on that score, Captain. My sister will approve of anything you do." Lily released his arm with a quiver of regret. "She thinks you are altogether superior to any man she has ever met."

"I could say the same about her." Aaron picked up one of the sketching pencils that lay on the lip of the easel and began to trace her profile. "Miss Lily is clever, kind and loyal. If she would only let her guard down, I have no doubt she could make a very fine man sincerely attached to her."

His heartfelt words of praise touched Lily so deeply that tears threatened to well up in her eyes. She blinked furiously to hold them back. She dared not speak for fear her voice would betray her.

Fortunately, Aaron did not seem to expect a reply. Perhaps he thought she was staying mute to hold her head still as he traced.

"If Lord Gabriel Stanford had a little more sense," he

continued, "he would not have been so easily put off by her stiffness. Though I believe it is just as well for Lily that he took up with Miss Brennan. She deserves better."

Did she detect an edge of jealousy in his voice that Lord Gabriel might have had some claim on her? The growing conviction that Aaron might care for her taxed Lily's composure beyond what she could conceal.

"Miss Crawford? Is something the matter?" Aaron flew from the easel to kneel before her.

The gaze he lifted to hers held a mixture of tender concern and something else. Lily thought it might be desire, for it answered that overpowering feeling within her.

Without any conscious intention of doing it, she leaned forward. Her lips whispered over his brow.

That seemed to be a signal for which he had been waiting with tightly-bound anticipation. Dropping the sketching pencil, he raised his strong, deft hands to cup her face and tilt it to the proper angle.

His lips found hers in a kiss of passionate certainty. Lily could think of nothing else. Indeed, she could not think at all. For a blissful instant, she was transformed into a creature of sense and instinct. She tasted the hot, brandied flavour of his mouth, felt its rousing fusion of strength and softness, heard the furious gallop of her pulse pounding in her ears.

Then she heard something else.

From beyond the screen, Aunt Althea's voice shattered their moment of stolen intimacy. "Iris, will you and Captain Turner be finished soon? There are others in our party who would like to take their turn at making shades."

Lily gave a guilty start as her slumbering conscience woke and reproached her scandalous impulses.

"We will not be much longer, Aunt Althea," she called back in a breathless, high-pitched voice. "Captain Turner is very meticulous."

Aaron scrambled to recover the pencil he had let fall on the carpet.

"I make no apologies," he cried with a forced chuckle. "Proper care must be taken in tracing such a fine profile."

Belying his words, he quickly set about to finish the work he had started.

Lily's shadow betrayed the powerful emotions swirling within her.

"You are trembling," Aaron whispered.

"I am not!" she lied in a hushed but insistent tone.

"You must stay still in the same position, or I shall never get done."

Aaron put down his pencil and strode to the chair, this time standing behind Lily. He grasped her shoulders and guided them to match his half-finished sketch. Hard as she tried to supress it, a quiver ran through her flesh that he could not miss. What would he make of it?

He placed two fingers under her chin, gently cupping the back of her head with his other hand. As he guided her into the proper position, Aaron leaned forward and whispered in her ear. "You have no reason to fear me, Miss Crawford. I will not take advantage of an unguarded moment. Our actions cannot always be ruled by propriety when passions are roused."

"I do not fear *you*, Captain," Lily murmured. "I know you an honorable man. It is myself I do not trust to do what is right."

———•◆•———

Iris Crawford could not trust herself around him? Aaron took that as a most encouraging sign.

Even after her aunt descended upon them and practically dragged her away, Aaron could not stop smiling. How could his lips do anything else when the imprint of their stolen kisses lingered there?

The moment her lips had grazed his forehead, his banked passion flared as if dosed with aromatic oil. Then his lips found hers in a kiss more wondrous than he had ever experienced. It was as if he had discovered some new tropical fruit — warm, smooth and succulent. He could have feasted for hours and never been sated!

He'd barely had a chance to whet his appetite when her aunt's suspicious query shattered the moment. Now he looked forward to their next kiss with a sense of urgent anticipation.

If Iris did not trust herself, it was clear her aunt did not trust either of them. Mrs. Henderson hovered around her niece for the rest of the evening, continually pushing her toward Viscount Uvedale. Whenever Aaron made the slightest move in their direction, Iris's aunt glared daggers at him. So determined was the lady to guard her niece from his attentions that she even turned down an invitation from Rory Fitzwalter to trace her shade.

Rory consoled himself by asking Miss Delany, who agreed on the condition that he must sit for her to draw in return.

Meanwhile Aaron bided his time. He recalled Lily's counsel about how her sister tended to resist what was forced upon her. Let Mrs. Henderson and Lord Uvedale try to pressure Iris all they liked. It would only make the lady rebel by turning to him.

Gratitude and affection for Lily warmed Aaron's heart in places that had been cold and barren for years — neglected corners that even his blazing passion for Iris had not quite managed to reach. How he wished he'd been more patient and appreciative when he had the opportunity to tell her how much he valued her faithful support.

With that thought in mind, he worked diligently to complete his gift for her. He cut out his tracing of Iris's profile with the meticulous care it deserved then darkened it with black paint so it looked like her shadow. Once the paint was dry, he glued the shade into a background of heavier white paper.

His gift for Lily gave him one final opportunity for a word with her sister before the evening was over. Even Mrs. Henderson could not object when he approached Iris to entrust her with its delivery.

His fingers managed to brush Iris's as he handed her the finished product. "Give this to Miss Lily with my very warmest regards."

He lowered his voice so that his next words might not carry to the ears of her aunt. "Tell Miss Lily I shall be sorry if she is not well enough to attend the ball tomorrow night at Compton Court. I wish I might have had the opportunity to dance with both the lovely Crawford sisters. I hope you will agree to serve as her proxy and save me all the dances I would have claimed from her, as well as those I will request from you."

Iris responded to his request with a shimmering yet oddly shy smile, as if she were both flattered and self-conscious. "I shall be delighted to dance with you as often as you ask me, Captain. I am certain my sister might soon forget her dread of such events if she had your company to divert her."

"Come, Iris." Mrs. Henderson shot one parting glare at Aaron. "We must get our sleep so that we will be fresh for the ball tomorrow."

Aaron bid them goodnight then joined Rory, his brother and Mr. Brennan in a hand of whist before he headed off to bed.

He had not gone far when he heard Miss Delany's voice coming from the small sitting room where he had kissed Lily.

"Please, sir, you must excuse me. I should check if your sister requires my assistance." So the lady was speaking to Lord Uvedale. That might explain why she sounded anxious.

Aaron paused to listen. Eavesdropping might not be gentlemanly conduct, but neither was slinking away when a lady might need his assistance.

"Regina can manage without you for one night, surely," the viscount drawled in a way that seemed to cajole yet subtly threaten. "Besides, my sister would want you to keep me ... entertained, rather than pining over Rory Fitzwalter."

"I am doing no such thing!" Miss Delany protested.

Lord Uvedale paid her no heed. "You two were as thick

as thieves when we were young. You may still fancy him, but Rory's taste in women has *matured* since then. He only wants the pleasure of feminine company without the responsibility. You have neither the age nor the fortune to attract him now. Fortunately, I prefer a woman of precisely your youth and beauty."

"But *not* my fortune." A note of irritation crept into the lady's voice. "Surely I cannot compete with Miss Crawford for your favour. Or have you abandoned your pursuit of her now that she is so clearly smitten with Captain Turner?"

Miss Delany's words acted to Aaron's spirits like a blast of warm air into a balloon.

The viscount gave a derisive snicker. "Iris Crawford is no more smitten with that oaf than I am with her wet goose of a sister. She is only toying with him to make me jealous and hasten my proposal."

A sharp arrow pierced Aaron's balloon and sent it plummeting. His fists clenched, itching to wet themselves with Lord Uvedale's blood. He could not decide which enraged him more — the slight to him or the one to Miss Lily.

"Indeed?" Kitty Delany replied. "Then Miss Crawford must be a fine actress, for she had me quite convinced of her fancy for the captain."

A rush of gratitude to the lady swept through Aaron. He would be a fool to heed Uvedale's opinion over hers. If only his lordship's aspersions did not echo his own doubts. Miss Crawford had behaved oddly in recent days, her behavior toward him running hot and cold for no reason he could fathom. This very evening he had heard her assure the viscount that her favours had not changed. Was he an arrogant fool to imagine he possessed the qualities to attract a woman who could have her pick of suitors?

Lord Uvedale laughed outright — a caustic sound that corroded Aaron's assurance. "When it comes to courting, all women are the equal of Mrs. Siddons. I have it directly from her aunt that Miss Crawford confided her true preference.

Depend upon it — I shall be betrothed to her before this party is over."

"Then why have you sought me out," Miss Delany demanded, "if you intend to marry Miss Crawford?"

The viscount's voice lost its derisive edge and turned almost fawning. "Because, my dear Kitty, marriage to an heiress will furnish me with the fortune to afford a charming and accomplished mistress — one a good deal better bred than my trade-tarnished wife."

Aaron's pulse pounded in his ears. It might have drowned out the voices from the sitting room, but those fell silent briefly.

Then Miss Delany replied with icy contempt. "In that case, I suggest you look elsewhere. My circumstances may be far reduced from what they once were, but my self-respect is not. I would never conspire to humiliate another woman by living off her fortune while usurping the affections of her husband."

"Dash it, Kitty, don't be such a prude!" The viscount sounded astonished that she would refuse his offer. "You must know I've fancied you from the moment I first took notice of the fair sex. I would wed you in a trice if either of us had any money. Surely what I propose is the next best thing. We can live in style and still be together. And if any harm should befall my bride, I promise I will make an honest woman of you."

Aaron could scarcely believe his ears. How any man could so callously plan to betray a woman like Iris Crawford beggared his imagination. The viscount's reference to some harm befalling her sounded positively sinister!

It must have seemed that way to Miss Delany as well, for she responded in a tone of horror. "I have never heard anything so despicable! I will not listen to another word!"

Aaron expected to see her storm out of the room. Instead he heard Lord Uvedale implore, "Please, Kitty, do not be so unkind!"

A fierce jumble of grunts and gasps followed, then Miss Delany cried out, "Let go of me!"

Her frantic plea released Aaron from the bewildered

outrage that had paralysed him. This was what he had feared from the moment he overheard their first words. Reproaching himself for not intervening sooner, he charged into the room and wrenched the viscount away from Miss Delany.

He seized the scoundrel by the scruff of the neck and shook him soundly. "Are you deaf or just wicked? The lady told you to let her go!"

"How dare you lay hands on me, you ill-bred cur?" Lord Uvedale struggled to free himself from Aaron's iron grip.

"It takes more than breeding to make a gentleman," Aaron growled.

His fist would have tasted the blood it craved if Kitty Delany had not seized his arm with surprising strength. "That is enough, Captain, I beg you! I fear you misunderstood. I was in no danger from his lordship."

Surely she did not believe that. Yet how could Aaron dispute her claim without betraying his own offense of listening to so much of their conversation?

"He was taking liberties," Aaron protested but his grip on the viscount eased.

"Only in jest." Miss Delany infuriated him by seeking to excuse the blackguard. "We are old friends. Lord Uvedale would never impose upon me."

"Are you certain?" Aaron's tone betrayed his disbelief, even as he released the viscount abruptly, causing him to stagger.

"Of course she's certain!" Uvedale snarled. "I shall inform my sister about this vicious attack. You will be barred from every gathering of respectable society."

The threat jolted Aaron worse than any physical blow. How could he win Iris Crawford if he was expelled from the Killorans' house party in disgrace? It would leave the field open for this miserable scoundrel to triumph by default. That would doom Iris to the kind of marriage no woman deserved. And what would become of Lily with no other male relative to protect her from her grasping brother-in-law?

"Surely there is no need to mention this to her ladyship,"

Miss Delany implored the viscount. "Captain Turner believed I was in need of assistance. We should not spoil your sister's party on account of such a trivial misunderstanding."

Aaron doubted Lord Uvedale would heed her pleas. The fellow had despised him almost on sight and clearly resented having him as a rival for Iris Crawford.

To his surprise, the viscount grew calmer. "I suppose you have a point."

Was he afraid Miss Delany might report their conversation to the countess or Iris Crawford?

"Consider the matter forgotten," Uvedale muttered, though his dark scowl made it plain he never would.

Aaron made a stiff, shallow bow that threatened to crack his spine. "*If* I misunderstood your intentions toward the lady, I apologize for my actions, sir."

The words nearly choked him, yet he spit them out. If a brief truce, no matter how insincere, would buy him time to rescue the Crawford sisters from Lord Uvedale's clutches, he was prepared to swallow worse humiliation than this.

"I beg your pardon as well, Miss Delany," he added with true feeling, "for any distress I caused you."

Aaron stood in stubborn silence as she bid them good night then fled the room. Once he was certain she'd had time to reach safety, he strode away deep in thought.

If it was true that Iris Crawford had only flirted with him to encourage Lord Uvedale, how could he save her from her own folly by persuading her to accept his proposal instead?

Never in his career as a privateer had Aaron Turner contemplated a battle where the stakes were so high ... and the outcome in such perilous doubt.

Chapter Ten

*C*OULD SHE TRUST herself with Aaron Turner?

The question haunted Lily the rest of that evening and still more after she retired for the night. She tried to pacify her conscience by insisting she had only kissed the captain to seal his devotion to Iris. Yet she did not have to examine her feelings in any great depth to realize that was simply not true.

When he had praised her with such warm sincerity, not as Iris but as Lily, his admiration overpowered her usual reserve. And when their lips met, his kiss ignited desire that had no reference to her sister whatsoever. How could she trust any part of herself that had lost all touch with propriety and consequences?

She hoped her visit with Iris the next day would help her sort out her hopelessly tangled feelings. Fortunately the doctor had declared her sister on the mend and allowed to have a visit from her.

"A ball?" Iris rasped tossing aside the pretty shade on which Aaron had worked so hard. "I want to go. I am feeling ever so much better than yesterday and the doctor says I'm no longer contagious. I feel certain a nice outing will do me far less harm than languishing here on my own. I shall expire of boredom soon if I cannot have some amusement or exchange a few words of stimulating conversation."

"I *could* ask the doctor." Lily strove to keep an edge of panic from her voice. "But I know what he will say. You must not jeopardize your recovery by overtaxing your strength too soon."

The sentiment was perfectly true, yet it was not what made her throat constrict and her palms grow moist. Even if Iris *was* fully recovered, Lily knew she could not bear to have her sister attend the ball and divert Aaron Turner's attention from her.

"As for the agonies of boredom," she continued. "I can fetch you some books from the earl's library. Reading provided me with no end of amusement and instruction when I was bedridden."

"Books?" Iris wrinkled her nose as if her sister had suggested a dose of brimstone and treacle. "I suspect all that reading is what made you ill in the first place, or at least prevented you from getting better."

"Nonsense!" Lily snapped — something she hardly ever did to her sister or anyone else. "Reading did me more good than any of the apothecary's vile potions or the physician's purging and blistering. It is a wonder I survived their efforts to cure me."

Years later, the mere mention of those torments made Lily queasy. She had learned never to complain for fear of inviting the painful attention of her so-called healers. Instead she had suffered most of her symptoms in silence, escaping the discomfort by retreating into her books.

"Poor dear!" Iris's petulance eased. She held out her hand to Lily. "I never understood what you must have suffered until now. I should have written you more often and come home to visit whenever I could."

A powerful surge of affection for her sister overcame the other emotions seething in Lily's heart. For a moment it even eclipsed her passionate fancy for Aaron Turner.

She perched on the edge of her sister's bed and grasped Iris's cold hand in hers. "Do not talk such foolishness, dearest! Your letters were always so full of color and life. They were my favourite reading material. I only regret I had nothing amusing to write in return. You must have saved my letter until bedtime to lull you to sleep."

"Not at all." Iris shook her head vigorously, yet Lily sensed she was not being altogether truthful. "You had a way with words that made even commonplace events seem interesting. I vow I will make it up to you, Sis. Once I am married with a home of my own, I shall take you travelling and introduce you to legions of fine gentlemen until you find one who catches your fancy."

She had already found one. Lily yearned to confide in her sister, but long habit made her hold her tongue. That and the fear she might be mistaken about Aaron's feelings for her. How could he possibly prefer dull, mousey Lily to captivating Iris? No one of their acquaintance ever had. Entertaining such a notion was surely the siren song of wishful thinking. It would wreck her carefully laid plans and cause no end of grief if she let it sweep her away.

When Lily did not reply right away, Iris settled back onto her pillows with a sigh of wistful resignation. "All those years you were kept at home, you never complained of what you were missing. I suppose turn-about is only fair. But if I cannot go to the ball, you must represent our family and show the other guests we are their equals, even if we have no titles."

Iris's words reminded Lily of what Aaron had said about dancing with her twice as often to compensate for her sister's absence. She tried to ignore the qualm of guilt that intrusive thought provoked. Instead she concentrated on something that might amuse Iris. "Aunt Althea has been doing a splendid job of representing our family. Unless I am very much mistaken, she has made an aristocratic conquest."

"Who is her admirer?" Iris's eyes sparkled with some of their accustomed vivacity. "It cannot be Mr. Brennan, for he is as common as we are. The earl is married, which only leaves the four gentlemen who are considerably her junior."

Lily nodded, relieved to steer the conversation away from subjects that would remind her of Aaron Turner. "I gather the earl's brother *prefers* ladies of more mature years."

Iris chuckled. "I thought Mr. Fitzwalter was being more attentive than courtesy demanded. I assumed he was trying to get into my good graces through Aunt Althea."

"I thought so too," said Lily, "until you were taken ill and his attentions only increased."

"How I have missed my ration of gossip!" It was clear from her tone that Iris was only half in jest. "Have you any other toothsome morsels to impart?"

Never had Lily felt such closeness with the twin who was her opposite in so many ways. For the first time, she savoured a tantalizing taste of the connection they might have shared if her illnesses had not kept them apart for so many years.

She obliged Iris with another scrap of tattle. "Speaking of Rory Fitzwalter, I believe Miss Delany fancies him. But he treats her more like a sister than a sweetheart."

"What about Lord Uvedale and Captain Turner?" demanded Iris. "Have they become friends since I have not been present to fuel their rivalry?"

Though the question was as light-hearted as her previous remarks, it altered the whole tone of their conversation for Lily.

Her old self-consciousness returned. "Well ... the gentlemen do not seem to like each other any better than before. Lord Uvedale flirts with Miss Delany, to no avail that I can see. The Captain shows no interest in anyone but ... you. He asks after you at every opportunity. If the doctor had not forbidden it, I believe he would have come to visit you by now."

"Thank goodness he did not! I could not bear to be seen by any gentleman in such a sorry state." Iris gave a shudder of mock horror then her features took on a pensive cast. "Yet I might have been so pathetically grateful for his company, who knows what I might have done? Perhaps even let him propose to me."

Lily tried to laugh along with her sister, but the false merriment caught in her throat, threatening to choke her.

That night a light fall of snow cast a soft white mantle over the Surrey countryside.

Aaron watched the grey sky with apprehension the next day in case it should begin to snow again, causing the ball to be cancelled. Every hour that went by without the appearance of more flurries let him breathe easier.

At the same time, the sluggish passing of the hours fed a mounting sense of impatience within him. He wished Iris would appear, so he could tell her everything he had overheard the previous night. But she and the other ladies seemed to require the whole day to prepare for the ball. Aaron had no doubt the result would be well worth the effort in her case. Yet he would have preferred to see her somewhat less entrancing this evening, in exchange for the pleasure of her company now.

Fortunately, Lord Uvedale made himself as scarce as the ladies, though for what reason Aaron had no idea. Was the viscount worried Miss Delany might report his lascivious behavior to the earl and countess? Or did he fear Aaron might have a change of heart and decide to thrash him after all? Whatever kept him away, Aaron was grateful for it. In his present agitated state, he was not certain he could hold his temper if the viscount baited him.

"For pity sake quit pacing, Turner," Rory Fitzwalter called from the card table. "You'll exhaust yourself for dancing this evening."

"You are not the only one who misses the company of the ladies," Lord Gabriel added, in a show of perception that surprised Aaron. "Peering out the window every five minutes will not make this evening come any quicker."

The other men at the card table chuckled, though their laughter seemed to ring with a note of tolerant sympathy.

"Have a drink of something to calm you." Rory beckoned Aaron to join them.

Mr. Brennan rose from his place at the table. "Play a few hands to occupy your mind, though I wish you better luck than I have had."

"The captain's luck is far too good for my liking," Rory quipped. "All my present winnings will no doubt end up in his pocket before it is time to dress for the ball."

"That is too tempting a prospect to resist." Aaron flashed a predatory grin as he slipped into the chair Mr. Brennan had vacated. "Only be careful what favors you wager once your purse is empty."

A footman fetched Aaron a cup of mulled wine while Lord Gabriel dealt the cards. Soon Aaron's competitive instincts roused and his thoughts were occupied with suits, trumps and wagers.

"I reckon that should be our last hand," Rory announced awhile later, raking his winnings toward him with an air of relief that he was still a few guineas ahead. "We fellows may not require hours of primping like the ladies, but we should make an effort to do old Beckwith Abbey credit this evening."

"So we should," Lord Gabriel agreed, casting a look of chagrin at the meagre number of coins before him.

If the duke's son managed to secure Miss Brennan's hand, all his money worries would be over. Aaron did not despise Lord Gabriel for pursuing an heiress, as he did Viscount Uvedale, since it was clear the young couple had sincere feelings for one another. Moira Brennan's fortune would make it possible for them to act upon those feelings. Lord Gabriel would never think of using his wife's money to support a mistress.

"Thank you for the diversion, gentlemen." Aaron made an effort not to gloat as he collected his winnings. Perhaps he should contrive to lose a little money to Rory and Lord Gabriel the next time they played. If only he could subdue his competitive spirit.

He had no intention of curbing it tonight, he reflected as he strode off to his room and dressed to achieve the most pleasing appearance. Once he had satisfied himself on that score, he hurried back to the entry hall, anxious to offer Iris Crawford and her aunt a seat in his carriage for the drive to

Compton Court.

The Killorans' butler shook his head when Aaron inquired after the ladies. "Mrs. Henderson and Miss Crawford just departed, sir, with Mr. Brennan and his daughter."

Aaron barely stifled a curse. It could have been worse, he supposed. At least Iris had not gone with Lord Uvedale.

The viscount appeared a moment later and received the same reply when he asked about Iris. Uvedale scowled at Aaron as if his rival had deliberately spoiled his plans. Aaron responded with a bland smile that held the faintest touch of mockery.

"Are you travelling with Captain Turner, Sidney?" the countess asked her brother when she appeared a moment later, accompanied by her husband and Miss Delany.

"No indeed." The viscount's tone proclaimed his distaste for the idea. "I hoped there might be room for me in your carriage."

"Why, of course," Lady Killoran replied.

Only Aaron seemed to notice Miss Delany turn pale. He wished he could offer her an escape from travelling with Lord Uvedale. But since it looked as though he would be going with Rory Fitzwalter and Lord Gabriel, it would not be proper for an unchaperoned lady to share a carriage with three gentlemen. Aaron consoled himself that the viscount would hardly dare impose upon her while in the company of Lord and Lady Killoran.

Besides, he had enough to worry about, trying to protect the Crawford sisters from Lord Uvedale.

The earl addressed Aaron. "If you would be so good as to bring my brother and Lord Gabriel with you, our party should all reach Compton Court with a minimum of inconvenience."

"I shall be happy to oblige you, sir," Aaron assured his host, though he would have been happier still if Rory and Lord Gabriel were ready to leave immediately.

Instead he was forced to watch Viscount Uvedale depart for Compton Court ahead of him, then cool his heels for a quarter of an hour until his travelling companions appeared.

He tried to hurry them along but Rory dismissed his efforts with infuriating nonchalance. "These affairs never truly get going until after midnight you know. One must know how to pace oneself."

All the way to the ball, Aaron listened to the two friends' good-natured banter with mounting exasperation. How many dances would his rival claim from Iris Crawford before he ever set foot in the ballroom? What if the unscrupulous viscount used his head start to make the lady an offer of marriage?

As Rory and Lord Gabriel laughed over some ridiculous jest, Aaron could barely resist the temptation to knock their heads together!

Fortunately both gentlemen reached Compton Court with their aristocratic skulls intact. But Aaron was far too anxious to indulge in the tiresome ritual of the receiving line. With the assistance of an obliging footman, he managed to avoid the slow-moving queue and slip into the ballroom through a side entrance.

There he discovered Mrs. Henderson, dressed like the belle of the ball and drinking punch in the company of Mr. Brennan and his daughter. Iris's aunt seemed unusually pleased to see Aaron. He understood why when she asked after his companions. Miss Brennan looked equally interested in his answer.

"Mr. Fitzwalter and Lord Gabriel did come in my carriage," he replied. "They cannot be far behind me. Would you know where I might find Miss Crawford? There is a matter I wish to discuss with her."

Mrs. Henderson's expression chilled. She raised her voice to carry over the music. "A formal ball is hardly the place for a *discussion*, Captain. Surely, merriment is the order of the evening."

She gestured toward the dance floor with her folded fan. "There is my niece, taking a turn with Viscount Uvedale. He has been most attentive to her since he arrived. What a fine looking couple they make! I do hope nothing will interfere with Iris contracting such a brilliant match."

Though she spoke in a tone of general conversation, Iris's aunt fixed Aaron with a look that made it clear he was the target of her remark.

Her observation seemed to demand agreement, but Aaron stubbornly refused to utter a bald lie. Instead he watched Iris Crawford, as she performed the dance steps with an air of grave concentration. This was not how she had looked when he'd seen her at several assemblies in London. Then, her smile had flashed often and there had been a spirited bounce in her step, as if dancing was what she'd been born to do.

Why did she appear so subdued now? Did Lord Uvedale's company dampen her spirits? Was she torn between a natural impulse to please her aunt by making such a *brilliant match* and her personal distaste for the viscount? Or did she regret the need to lead Aaron on in order to secure the husband she wanted? There was only one way to find out, though Aaron shrank from the possibility that it might be the latter.

Mrs. Henderson's voice interrupted his musings. "Surely anyone who claims to care for my niece would want to see her happy."

That, Aaron could answer truthfully. "I quite agree, ma'am. But, tell me, does Miss Crawford look happy to you just now?"

The lady gave a sharp intake of breath, as if he had uttered a scandalous blasphemy. Fortunately, before she could recover her voice and take him to task, the music concluded.

Aaron plowed through the crowd like a warship through a throng of rowboats. He did not care how many dark glares or mutters of outrage followed him. All that mattered was Iris Crawford. She was his lodestar, more powerfully attractive than he had ever seen her.

Many of the other ladies favored the conventional fashion of pure white ball gowns. A bold few wore jewel-toned colors of the season — ruby red or emerald green. Iris Crawford had brought a breath of springtime to the evening in a delicate floral print of pinks and blues. She wore her hair differently than the rest as well. In contrast to their tight, severe plaits or thick tube ringlets, her honey-gold curls were swept up in a loose pile, while a few soft tendrils framed her face. Aaron recalled the delightful fragrance of her hair — like a cottage garden full of roses, lavender and lilies.

Iris started when Aaron appeared in front of her. Her lips blossomed into a delighted smile but her blue-violet eyes betrayed wariness. Which expressed her true feelings?

Aaron quelled a flicker of doubt the way he would have trodden on a stray ember that landed on the deck of his ship. He was not about to let anything scuttle his plans.

He executed a bow as graceful as that of any blueblood, or so he fancied. "My dear Miss Crawford, I beg your pardon for being so tardy to arrive. I hope you have not promised away all your dances for the evening. If you recall, I have a prior claim which I intend to press."

The lady's gaze faltered before his blatantly admiring stare and she blushed to a shade that nearly matched the tiny flowers on her dress. "I have not forgotten my pledge to you, Captain Turner. I believe my sister would wish me to honor it."

At that moment it seemed to Aaron as if he and Iris Crawford were quite alone in the ballroom. The other guests faded into a hazy blur. The music and conversation muted as his ears attended to a single voice.

Then a harsh cough shattered Aaron's illusion of privacy.

Lord Uvedale's voice intruded. "Your company has not been missed, sir, I assure you. Miss Crawford has favored me with two dances already. Now she is fatigued and we are about to enjoy some refreshment before we take the floor again."

Was this what Iris Crawford wanted — the viscount's devoted attention with the assurance of a marriage proposal to crown the evening? Had she only encouraged Aaron to make herself a more attractive prize to his rival? Did she not realize her charms needed no enhancement to a man with any taste?

Aaron did not take his eyes off the enchanting object of his affections, but addressed himself to the viscount. "If the lady is too tired for another dance at present, I shall be content to wait. What do you say, Miss Crawford?"

He steeled himself for a polite dismissal.

Instead the lady met his gaze and answered with quiet resolve. "I believe I could manage one more dance, Captain. This music sounds slower than the last."

She reached out a delicate gloved hand, which Aaron took most eagerly. "If you will excuse us, Lord Uvedale."

Aaron could not resist flashing a triumphant grin at his rival as he led Iris Crawford to join a group of dancers.

The viscount glared back, his face almost purple with fury.

Just as the dance was about to begin, Aaron's partner leaned toward him and murmured, "Thank you for rescuing me!"

Did she have any idea of the true peril from which he was determined to rescue her and her sister?

The dance turned out to be a sedate one and Aaron was quite familiar with its steps. That left him sufficient breath and concentration to converse with his partner.

"You do not need to keep up the charade, Miss Crawford. It was good of you to dance with me, as you promised. But I assure you Lord Uvedale needs no further encouragement to propose. I have served my purpose and may be discarded."

If any of the surrounding dancers overheard his remark, they politely pretended otherwise. Most seemed too caught up in their own flirtations to notice anyone else's.

Iris Crawford certainly heard him. His words must have flustered her, for she put her foot the wrong way and stepped on his. She gasped an apology and stumbled back. She might have lost her balance if Aaron had not tightened his grip on her hand.

A moment later she had recovered enough to venture a reply. "You puzzle me exceedingly, Captain. I cannot think what you mean."

Her first reaction had told quite a different story — one Aaron was more inclined to believe. "Come, Miss Crawford, do not play me for more of a fool than you have already. I know what you have been up to. I overheard Lord Uvedale telling ... one of the other guests. He claimed to have been informed by your aunt that you were only encouraging me to make his lordship jealous. If the gentleman is aware of your ploy, surely it cannot have the effect you desire."

Hard as Aaron tried to keep from betraying his distress over her cavalier treatment, he could not quite manage it.

Iris Crawford tightened her grip on his hand. "Please believe me, Captain. Betrothal to Lord Uvedale is the last thing in the world I desire! I confess, I did tell my aunt what she repeated to his lordship. But that was only to keep her from nagging me and intruding upon my time with you."

The lady had no reason to lie to him now, yet Aaron found himself reluctant to believe her. "Are you saying you prefer a jumped-up privateer to a viscount, Miss Crawford?"

She hesitated a moment then gave a teasing answer suffused with barely suppressed mirth. "Not *any* jumped-up privateer, Captain Turner. Only one."

Iris Crawford gave his hand a playful squeeze to signify what Aaron already guessed — he was that fortunate one.

The music concluded, allowing Aaron the liberty to lean close and murmur in her ear. "I hope that is true, dear lady, for I could not bear to be deceived about your feelings."

If he had not been so very near to her, he might have missed the sharp little gasp his warning provoked.

Now if only he could work out what it meant.

Chapter Eleven

THANK HEAVEN THE dance was over!

As Aaron Turner escorted Lily toward one of the tables spread with refreshments, she found herself hard-pressed to *walk* without tripping over her own feet. All the noise of the crowded ballroom seemed to reach her from a great distance, while Aaron's last words echoed in her mind.

He would not forgive her if she deceived him.

That was what he had said and she knew better than to doubt such a determined man. As a penniless boy, he had resolved to make his fortune to provide for his ailing sister. In spite of all the obstacles and hardships he'd encountered, Aaron Turner had succeeded. More recently he had made up his mind to win the toast of the *Little Season* — Iris Crawford. How could she have been so foolish as to imagine he would settle for anything less?

She had come to the ball at Compton Court with a half-formed notion to tell Aaron Turner the truth — that it was not Iris but Lily he had wooed for the past several days, Lily he had confided in, Lily he had kissed. In all that time, he had not been able to tell the difference. So why could he not be satisfied with the sister who loved him rather than the one who had her sights set elsewhere? Even if she had not taken her sister's place and Aaron *had* persuaded Iris to accept his proposal, she could never care for him as Lily did.

Now Lily realized such a revelation was impossible. Aaron Turner would never understand why she had deceived him and he would never forgive her for doing it. She could bear anything but that.

Anything?

"Miss Crawford?" Those two words emerged from the surrounding babble of conversation to catch Lily's attention.

Aaron sounded concerned — even alarmed, which made her suspect this was not the first time he had called her name.

"Forgive me," he continued. "I fear I should have heeded Lord Uvedale and let you rest before I wearied you with another dance. I placed my own wishes ahead of your welfare and that is inexcusable."

It was all Lily could do to keep from flinching. By impersonating Iris, she had put her own selfish desires ahead of Aaron's and her sister's, the two people she claimed to care for most in the world.

She shook her head. "You are too severe on yourself, Captain. It was my choice to accept your invitation. You did not compel me. But in my eagerness to dance with you, I may have misjudged my endurance. I find myself rather lightheaded at the moment."

Part of Lily congratulated herself on contriving such a plausible excuse for her sudden confusion. Another part cringed to hear the falsehood fall from her lips with so little effort. The worst thing about deception was how quickly it begat further deception. If she kept on, she might soon be unable to speak a single true word without bringing down a whole tower of past lies upon her head.

"Lightheaded?" Aaron seized that pretext to wrap his arm around her waist. "Then we must find you a seat at once."

If only he knew, the warm strength of his touch made Lily truly dizzy.

He helped her through the milling crowd to a quieter corner of the grand ballroom. When another guest vacated her chair to accept a dance invitation, Aaron was quick to settle Lily on it. "Can you manage on your own long enough for me to fetch you a cup of punch?"

"Yes, of course." That was true at least.

She did not mention that his brief absence would be a relief, giving her time to compose herself and quiet the harsh inquisition of her conscience.

Aaron looked torn by the need to leave her, no matter how briefly. "I shall only be a moment. Do not stir from here in the meantime, I beg you."

Lily shook her head. "You have my word."

What should she do now? Lily watched Aaron stride away, heedless of other guests who stood between him and the nearest refreshment table. Revealing her true identity was clearly out of the question. But continuing with her original plan no longer seemed like a good idea either. Aaron had mistaken her for Iris under unusual circumstances. Once both twins were together again to compare, surely he would recognize that Iris was not the lady he had courted for the past several days.

How could she have failed to see the many flaws in her ridiculous plan to bring her sister and Captain Turner together? Lily asked herself just as Aaron reappeared bearing a cup of punch in each hand.

He placed one in her hands, which trembled in spite of her determined effort to still them. "Drink up, Miss Crawford. This should revive you."

Perhaps it was his air of authority, or her mounting alarm that made Lily drain the cup in one deep draft. The punch burned a potent trail down her throat, making her eyes water. She had never imbibed a drink so strong.

"Poor Miss Crawford!" The captain dropped to one knee beside her chair. He fairly radiated affectionate concern. "You must be parched."

Taking her empty cup, he pressed a full one into her hand. "Have mine too. I insist. I can fetch more. No wonder you felt lightheaded."

"I believe that had more to do with your presence than my thirst." A spasm of horror gripped Lily when she heard what should have been a private thought spoken aloud.

To prevent herself from saying anything worse, she drank

the second cup of punch nearly as quickly as the first. This time, it did not burn so painfully on the way down, though it did kindle a fire in her belly.

Aaron Turner's anxious frown turned into a wide, warm smile. "My dear Miss Crawford, you could not have said anything to make me happier! I must admit, I often feel weak in the knees when I am around you. The closer we are, the more pronounced the sensation."

He believed he was addressing Iris, Lily's sense of caution warned her. Yet the effect of his words was as stimulating as the potent punch she had drunk so quickly. It made her heart race and her flesh tingle from head to toe.

"Nothing could make me happier than to inspire that same sensation in you, Captain." Lily might have blushed at her shocking boldness, but her cheeks were already glowing from the exertion of dancing and the effect of the punch.

Aaron's gaze searched hers, insistent yet strangely wary. What he was seeking Lily could not guess. Yet she sensed he had found it when he thrust the empty cups beneath her chair then grasped her hands in his.

He fixed her with a stare of such blazing ardor Lily feared it might blind her if she looked too long. "If that is true, then you have it in your power to make us the most blissful couple at this ball."

"I ... I do?" The words squeaked out of her constricted throat.

The restrained power of his touch promised things Lily had never realized she wanted so desperately.

Aaron gave an emphatic nod, ruffling his thick dark hair. "If you consent to marry me, I shall be the happiest man in the county, if not the whole kingdom. And if my joy pleases you as much as you claim, we shall both be quite rapturous."

Marry him? The thought elated Lily beyond anything she could imagine only to cast her down even deeper.

Aaron Turner did not want to wed *her* and never would. His heart was set on Iris. She could not accept a marriage proposal on her sister's behalf and expect Iris to honor such a promise.

"I ... I ..." In spite of everything, her heart yearned with irrational eagerness to accept. "Believe me, Captain, there is nothing I would like more. Any woman would count herself blessed to secure a husband with so many wonderful qualities."

Her words kindled an expression of such unaffected delight on Aaron's rugged features that Lily could not bear to extinguish it. But what else could she do? Any joy gained from the answer he desired would be fleeting and false.

Lily forced out the most difficult words she had ever spoken. "In spite of that, I fear what you ask is not possible. Please forgive me for making you hope otherwise."

As she had expected, her answer dashed the expectant smile from Aaron's lips and quenched the hopeful glow in his eyes. In their place, she glimpsed a flash of indignant anger, which terrified her to the depths of her timid heart.

Yet something else in his gaze troubled Lily even more — the steely determination to make her change her mind.

———◆———

Victory had been within his grasp. Never had Aaron been more certain of it.

Everything he'd seen and heard this evening had quelled his foolish doubts. Iris Crawford was not toying with his feelings or using him to secure another man. She was as much in love with him as he was with her. His happiness mattered more to her than anything. The actual proposal would be a mere formality. Of course she would marry him and he would be the envy of every bachelor in London.

Her halting refusal took the wind out of his sails. Worse than that — it was as if a friendly vessel had approached his ship then suddenly hoisted the skull-and-crossbones while opening fire.

His first instinct was to launch a counterattack, but the

stricken look in Iris's eyes prevented him. This refusal was not her wish — quite the contrary. Something or someone was standing in the way of what they both wanted. He must discover the obstacle and overcome it by whatever means necessary!

"You led me to hope," he reminded her. "I do not believe you are the sort of woman to encourage a suitor she has no intention of accepting."

Iris shook her head. "You seemed to think otherwise not so long ago."

She was right, dash it. "I cannot deny Lord Uvedale's boast gave me doubts. But when you explained, I knew you were telling me the truth. I do not believe the answer you gave me just now reflects your true feelings. If there is something that prevents you from following your heart, you must tell me what it is so we can find a way around it, for both our sakes."

For an instant, Aaron hoped she might do as he asked, but then her tempting lips compressed into a stubborn line. "It cannot be gotten around ... I mean there is nothing to get around. I cannot marry you and that is all there is to it!"

She wrenched her fingers from his, sprang from the chair and fled into the crowd. Aaron scrambled to his feet and set off after her. Iris's desperate denial had done nothing to dispel his conviction that something was keeping her from accepting his proposal. He must persuade her that together they could conquer anything. And he must make her see why it was so important that they prevail.

Iris nearly gave him the slip. He searched high and low for her with mounting desperation that abated slightly when he glimpsed Lord Uvedale dancing with someone else. After what he'd overheard the previous night, Aaron knew better than to hope the viscount might set his sights elsewhere. Uvedale would pursue Iris Crawford all the harder because she was proving elusive. His aristocratic pride would not tolerate losing her to a common privateer.

If, as Aaron suspected, Iris was being pressured by her

aunt to marry the viscount, he must warn her how high the cost of such a mistake could be for her and her sister.

He continued to search for her as he might have done for a member of his crew who'd been washed overboard. He did not care who he jostled in his haste or how many conversations he interrupted to ask after her.

At last Aaron glimpsed a flutter of springtime color out of the corner of his eye. A closer look revealed Iris Crawford, about to slip out the side door through which he had entered. She wore a short cloak, with its hood pulled up to cover her hair. Aaron knew he had no time to retrieve his hat and great-coat if he hoped to catch her. He left them behind to be collected later or not. At the moment he did not care in the least.

He managed to overtake Iris just as her carriage was pulling away. Wrenching the door open, he scrambled in most ungracefully.

"Who are you?" Iris demanded, shrinking back in her seat. "What is the meaning of this?"

"I beg your pardon for startling you." Aaron sank onto the seat opposite her. "It is I, Captain Turner. I mean you no harm, Miss Crawford, quite the opposite in fact."

When Iris mustered her composure to answer, she did not sound reassured by his words. "Why did you follow me, Captain? I gave you my answer. There is nothing more to be said."

Aaron shook his head though he doubted Iris could see him in the darkened carriage. "I disagree. I still have a great deal to say. I beg you to hear me out, if not for your own sake then for your sister's."

"My sister?" The lady sounded almost as surprised as when he'd leapt into the carriage. "What has she got to do with any of this?"

"A great deal." Aaron hunched forward, wishing he could take her hand. "Since the two of you have no close male relatives, Lily will come under the protection of the man you marry. You must choose wisely, for your husband will have considerable control over her fortune as well as yours."

"I know that." Iris Crawford sounded weary yet also wary. "My sister reminds me of the fact constantly. It is why she urged you upon me with such determination. She seems to trust you to have her best interests at heart. But I cannot wed only to please my sister. You must see that."

Was that why she had encouraged his attentions recently, to humor her ailing sister? Yet when it came to accepting an actual proposal, Iris Crawford could not let her head and her sister's inclination rule her heart.

"Perhaps not," he agreed grudgingly. "But I urge you to keep Lily's wellbeing in mind when you make your choice. For both your sakes, you must not wed Lord Uvedale."

"Set your mind at ease, Captain. The viscount has made me no offer."

"But he means to." Aaron inched further forward until his knees brushed against hers. It should not have been provocative contact between them, yet it stirred his long-simmering desire for her to a pitch of delicious discomfort. "I overheard Lord Uvedale say so only last night. And I learned more about his plans for you."

"You eavesdropped on his lordship?" An odd teasing note in Iris's voice acted upon Aaron as if she had grazed some sensitive part of his person with playful fingers.

"I did when I realized he was talking about you," he confessed. "There are far worse offenses I would commit to keep you from harm."

She gave a rustling chuckle quite at odds with her earlier alarm. Had those two swiftly consumed cups of punch made her tipsy? "I am touched that you value my welfare above your honor, Captain. But what harm could Lord Uvedale do by making me an offer of marriage?"

"A great deal if you make the mistake of accepting." Aaron fumbled for her hands and clasped them in his. "I heard him boast that he intends to use your fortune for his own pleasure ... including the support of a mistress."

Iris stiffened. "He would never …" she cried, but doubt quickly crept in. "That man is a worse scoundrel than I took him for!"

Her emphatic declaration puzzled Aaron. "I did not suppose you took him for a scoundrel at all. There were times I thought you liked him very well."

"I … I …" she stammered, clearly dismayed to be reminded of her folly. "What I mean is, my sister took him for a scoundrel and did her best to persuade me. I see now that I should have listened to her. She only suspected him of fortune-hunting. Now you tell me he is already planning to betray the woman to whom he has not yet even proposed!"

Aaron could scarcely imagine how humiliating such information must be to a woman who had so recently been the toast of London Society. Fond compassion tempered his desire as he gave her hands a comforting squeeze. "I am sorry to have been the bearer of such distressing news. Nothing could have compelled me to speak of it except the most earnest desire to prevent you and Miss Lily from falling into the clutches of such a rogue."

"I understand, Captain." Iris Crawford made no attempt to extract her hands from his grasp or to pull her knees away from his. "Was your proposal an attempt to protect us as well?"

"It was *one* motive," Aaron admitted, "though far from the only one. Surely it cannot have escaped your notice that I am desperately enamored of you!"

Would the intensity of his feelings frighten her, if she could not return them to the same degree? Aaron hoped not, but neither could he conceal them any longer. "I came to Beckwith Abbey expressly to court you and to propose if you gave me any encouragement at all. I must admit my heart has been storm-tossed as your manner toward me blew cold and hot and cold again. But the result has been to fan my desire from a bright flame to a blazing inferno that quite consumes me!"

Every word he uttered seemed to act like a bellows — blowing air into a forge. The darkness and privacy of the carriage box served to concentrate his passion further.

The carriage must have hit a rut in the road just then. It heaved like a ship struck by a sudden, powerful wave, pitching Iris Crawford toward Aaron. Instinctively, his arms opened to catch her and hold her safe. That protective clasp soon became a passionate embrace.

Iris raised her face to his. Her lips roved over his cheek in search of his mouth. Every particle of Aaron's skin that received her prodigally strewn kisses began to tingle like nothing he'd never experienced before. It inflamed his longing for her to a dangerous degree.

He parted his lips to meet and welcome hers. When the soft, ripe flesh of her mouth made contact with his at last, it unleashed a surge of pleasure Aaron could scarcely contain. The eager play of their lips seemed to pour the wine of passion from one to the other and return it distilled into the sweetest, strongest brandy imaginable. It coursed through Aaron's veins, driving out dry reason and cold propriety.

Iris's ardent response persuaded him beyond any doubt that she wanted him as much as he wanted her. No lady had ever kissed him with such delicious abandon. No wanton strumpet ever inspired him with feelings so intemperate yet so tender. Much as he longed to claim her sweet delights, he also yearned to give of himself until he had sated her every desire.

How could she desire him so as a man yet refuse him as a husband? The intoxicating nectar of her kisses made sober reflection impossible. Yet Aaron's mind throbbed with more than one sweet certainty. Iris Crawford loved him with a passion that matched his — perhaps even surpassed it. Whatever had compelled her to refuse his proposal ran contrary to the inclination of her heart.

Iris needed his guidance to see that for herself. She needed protection from Viscount Uvedale and every man like him, men who coveted her fortune for their own ends. Whereas he would care for her if she hadn't a farthing to her name.

Was that quite true? An earnest whisper from Aaron's

conscience was all but drowned out by the hectic gallop of his pulse and the tempestuous gusts of his breath. Would he have looked twice at Iris Crawford if she were poor and obscure, with a retiring manner that attracted no admiration?

Aaron strove to silence that vexing doubt with a firm denial, but found he could not. So he did the next best thing. He flung it into the deepest, darkest hold of his mind. Then he slid one hand beneath Iris Crawford's cloak to explore her enticing feminine curves. If they did not distract him from troublesome speculation, nothing on earth could hope to.

When he cupped her breast and gave it an admiring caress, Aaron heard and felt a sigh of exquisite pleasure quiver through her. If only she knew, this was but the first of many sensual delights with which he longed to acquaint her. Once Iris experienced the bliss Aaron was confident he could bring her, she could not possibly contemplate wedding anyone but him.

How right it felt to be in Aaron Turner's arms, kissing him with a fevered ardor she had never suspected herself of possessing!

Never in her life had Lily felt so free. Bonds of obedience and propriety, that had constrained her for as long as she could recall, had been shattered. Now she was at liberty to do whatever she pleased and nothing pleased her more than being in Aaron's arms.

Every part of her body, that made the slightest contact with his, seemed to hum with life. She had been shuffling and creeping through her existence in a sort of numb half-sleep. But now she was awake and hungry from a long fast. Aaron's kisses were precisely the nourishment she craved. Yet the touch of his hand upon her breast made her wonder if he could offer other sustenance which might satisfy her need even more.

Encouraged by his eager response, she cradled his face

in her gloved hands and pressed kiss after kiss upon his lips, each more urgent than the last. Though a winter wind whistled around the carriage, Lily had never felt warmer. Not simply warm — but positively feverish!

Then suddenly the carriage came to a halt. Lily might have fallen between the seats if Aaron had not held her so securely.

Bobbing lanterns and the sound of voices from outside warned her that they had reached Beckwith Abbey. Though it seemed like no time at all since she and Aaron had left the ball at Compton Court, their passionate interlude felt as if it had lasted much longer.

Fortunately for her reputation, Aaron was able to keep a cool head, even when his desires were aroused. Muttering an oath under his breath, he grasped Lily around the waist and deposited her on the seat beside him. She could barely contain her frustration that their tryst had ended so abruptly.

Aaron seemed to sense her thwarted desire, which perhaps echoed his.

"This is only interrupted, not ended," he whispered, "unless you wish it to be."

With that, he quickly adjusted his attire so as not to appear too obviously rumpled. Lily followed his example.

"No indeed, Captain Turner," she replied to his whispered suggestion in a conversational tone that anyone might overhear. "That is the very last thing I wish."

The footman who pulled open the carriage door gave a start when he saw two passengers. "Begging your pardon, sir. I thought Miss Crawford came away by herself."

"She did," Aaron replied with brisk authority as he alighted and offered Lily his hand. "I saw her leave and thought she should have an escort in case she felt unwell. I climbed aboard just as you were getting underway."

"Of course, sir." The footman bowed. "We must go back now to fetch some of the other ladies and gentlemen when they are ready to leave. Do you wish us to take you along?"

Aaron shook his head. "Thank you for the offer, but I have

had enough revelry for one night. Besides, I wish to see Miss Crawford properly settled."

He whisked Lily inside where they were greeted by another of the Killorans' footmen, who asked if he should summon Miss Crawford's maid to attend her.

"No thank you." Lily had to concentrate on speaking properly. Was that from the punch she had drunk so quickly, or had Aaron Turner's breathtaking kisses addled her wits? "Tell Miss Jackson she may go to bed and ask her not to wake me too early tomorrow."

If the servant thought her instructions unusual, he was far too well trained to give any sign of surprise or disapproval. "Very well, Miss. Good night to you and to you, Captain."

"Well done," Aaron murmured as they headed off. "One might think you were an expert in arranging secret assignations."

"But I am not!" Lily did not want him to think this was some sort of meaningless dalliance. "I never felt this way about any man until I met you."

She was concentrating so hard on her emphatic denial that she failed to pay attention to her feet. She wobbled slightly, brushing against Aaron, who strode along beside her.

"Careful now." He wrapped a steadying arm around her. "Do not pay any mind to my teasing. I know this is not the sort of thing you make a habit of."

He grasped her left hand and raised it to his lips. "You do me a great honor by welcoming my attentions. I mean to make certain you never regret your decision."

A giddy chuckle bubbled up from some untapped well within her. "How could I possibly regret the opportunity to be with you?"

With Aaron's arm around her and her hand in his, Lily wafted up the great staircase, scarcely aware of her feet touching the steps. Her only thought was to continue the amorous delights she had experienced in the darkened carriage.

It was as if a curtain had been drawn over the past. The future was veiled in shadows she had no desire to penetrate.

All that mattered was this one night, a space of time illuminated with a magical glow.

When they reached her door, Aaron cast a swift glance up and down the corridor, but Lily was past caring who saw them together. The timid, proper part of herself that she had banished from consciousness might fret about discovery, gossip and her reputation. This new, bolder Lily cared only about satisfying the cravings Aaron had whetted within her.

The moment the door of her room was safely closed behind them, she clasped her arms around Aaron's neck and drew his face toward hers to exchange more passionate kisses. The past several minutes faded from her mind, leaving a sense that they had never left the carriage. Or perhaps the carriage box had magically transmuted into her bedchamber.

Lily expected Aaron's attentions to gather fresh urgency, as hers had. She prepared for his lips to explore and plunder hers with ravishing intensity to which she would blissfully surrender. To her surprise, he grew more gentle and restrained.

"There is no need to rush now, my love," he murmured, gathering her into an embrace as affectionate as it was amorous. "We have a whole night ahead of us and many more to come if I have my way. I promise you it will only be better if we take our time and savor every moment."

As if to prove his point, Aaron slowly unfastened her cloak and eased it off her shoulders. Lily felt it fall to the floor around her feet. Then he lifted each of her arms in turn and peeled off her gloves. Once both her hands were bare, he raised the left and grazed each of her fingertips with his smooth, warm lips. Compared to his earlier caresses, the gesture was almost chaste. Yet it communicated a provocative sensuality that sent ripples of delight through Lily's flesh.

Like a charge of black powder lit from afar, the sensations raced through her veins to ignite muted explosions in distant parts of her body. Nowhere were those more intense than in her bosom and between her thighs.

Lily heaved sigh of pleasure and desire.

"Like that, do you?" Mellow with fond amusement and satisfaction, Aaron's voice caressed her ears. "Then be warned, for I have scarcely begun. I shall coax more than sighs from you before I am finished."

The only light in the room came from the banked embers in the hearth. Their ruddy glow reflected in Aaron's dark eyes, which seemed to shimmer with heat, like the coals.

His words and gaze sent a shiver of anticipation through Lily. "I can hardly wait."

"You shall have to." Aaron gave a low chuckle. "But I promise you will be all the more delighted for having your pleasure ... drawn out."

He untied her bonnet with a deft touch then immersed his fingers in her hair as if he would caress and admire every strand. "Threads of silk are nothing to this."

"Nor to yours, I'm sure." Lily raised her hand to stroke his thick dark hair. "The only thing I have ever felt that compares to it is a pelt of the finest fur."

"Is that so?" He purred in a way Lily fancied a tiger might if it were almost tamed. Would Aaron Turner ever be domesticated? Or would there always be a streak of the reckless pirate in him?

"I am flattered by your approval," he continued. "Keep on like this and you shall twist me around your delicate little finger."

Did her good opinion matter so much to him? The notion was a heady one to Lily — having such a strong man in her power. A teasing chuckle bubbled up from deep within her. "I shall try not to twist you too tightly. But that may be difficult to avoid, since I find so very much to admire about you."

"As do I about you, my lovely Iris." He leaned in close, nuzzling her hair as he inhaled an appreciative breath. "You are as fragrant and beautiful as the flower you were named for."

A sickening ball of bile rose in Lily's throat. Fortunately Aaron was not looking her in the eye, or he might have glimpsed a flicker of anxiety that could betray her.

Instead he grazed her cheek with his. A light stubble of whisker created provocative friction that set her flesh aquiver. Then his lips trailed down her bare neck, leaving her breathless.

All troubling thoughts melted away like icicles falling into a blazing fire. It did not matter what name Aaron called her as long as he kept up his delicious seduction!

Chapter Twelve

Since he'd grown to manhood, Aaron Turner had seldom lacked for female company. A tolerably handsome face, genial manner and free-spending ways had all helped him get whichever woman he fancied — usually the prettiest. None had ever been the least unwilling. Quite the contrary.

Yet never had he encountered a partner as delightfully eager as Iris Crawford. It surprised him a little considering her earlier frosty manner toward him. Perhaps she was accustomed to being worshipped by her suitors and took pleasure in toying with them. Yet secretly she'd yearned for a man who possessed the strength of will to be master.

For his part Aaron fancied himself strong and confident enough to want a lover who could match his passion without fear or false prudery. Innocent but not missish, enthusiastic but not coarse — Iris Crawford was the woman he had been waiting for.

Her ardent response banished any troublesome scruples over what he was about to do. Even by the relaxed moral standards of a privateer, his intentions were less than honorable. He planned to compromise a lady's virtue so she would be obliged to marry him.

Every time a qualm of guilt threatened to intrude upon his pleasure, Aaron reminded himself that his motives were virtuous. He had no designs on the Crawford sisters' fortune. He only wanted to protect them from a more unscrupulous suitor, who would think nothing of robbing and humiliating Iris and perhaps even breaking her heart.

That was something he would never do, Aaron vowed as his lips feasted on the smooth, soft flesh of her neck. Her skin was still chilled from their drive through the winter night but Aaron had every intention of warming it with his ardor.

Were there other parts of her that needed to be warmed as well?

He interrupted his attentions long enough to inquire.

"I do not feel the slightest chill." Iris's curls fluttered over his cheek when she shook her head. "In fact, I do not think I have ever felt so warm."

Her mellow teasing tone turned suddenly concerned. "But what of you, Aaron? You came away from the ball on a cold night without your hat and greatcoat. You must be half-frozen."

There could be no mistaking her earnest concern for his welfare. That warmed Aaron's heart more than a roaring fire. Hearing her call him by name in a caressing tone banished the chill of doubt about what he intended to do.

"I would have frozen quite happily with you in my arms," he replied. "However there might be a part or two of me that would benefit from the application of a warm touch . . . if you would be willing to oblige me."

"More than willing." Iris pressed against him in a manner that spurred his desire to new heights.

For the first time, Aaron feared he might not be able to contain his yearning.

"Nor would I consider it an obligation," she added stroking his cheek with the back of her fingers, "but a most sincere pleasure."

"In that case . . ." He led her toward the bed, torn between the urgency of his desire and his aim to win Iris with his skill as a lover. ". . . let us make ourselves more comfortable, shall we? Then you can find where I am cold and proceed to warm me."

Iris gave a chuckle that sounded rather tipsy. Did she have her wits about her enough to know what she was doing?

Of course she did, Aaron insisted to his bothersome

conscience as he removed his coat and waistcoat. After all, she'd had the presence of mind to leave instructions so they would not be disturbed by her maid.

"Your feet must be cold, for mine are." Iris perched on the edge of the bed and kicked off her slippers.

His feet were not parts of his body that Aaron had ever associated with seduction. But he must admit the lady was correct — his were freezing.

Iris patted the bed beside her. "Come lie down and I shall chafe them for you."

"On one condition ..." Aaron kissed her then crawled onto the bed. "... that you allow me to return the favor."

He guided her into position, with her head on the pillows and his near the foot of the bed. Then he proceeded to rub her feet while she rubbed his.

It did not take Aaron long to realize that he had been blind to the amorous potential of such attentions. After all, Iris Crawford's feet were attached to a pair of the daintiest ankles he had ever encountered. It was not long before he ventured to caress them through her stockings. This inevitably led to an investigation of her shapely calves and delicate knees.

Aaron admired a fine pair of breasts as well as any man, but the fashions of the day left quite an expanse of a lady's bosom visible to the whole world. Her legs and backside, on the other hand, were usually well concealed with only the glimpse of a well-turned ankle or the beguiling suggestion of ripe roundness beneath skirts. To view such treasures, a man must make the most intimate acquaintance of a fair one.

Now as he pushed Iris's skirts higher, revealing a pair of the most thoroughly delectable legs, Aaron found himself as much aroused as he might have been by the more customary prelude of lips, neck and breasts. That arousal was further heightened by the play of her hands over his feet and legs.

To compensate for her lack of experience, Iris was clever enough to follow his lead. When he rubbed her feet, she returned the favor. When he slid his palm over her calf in an admiring caress, she did the same for him. To think he had begun this encounter with the plan of showing Iris how happy he could make her. She had neatly turned the tables, making him want her more than ever — not as a single conquest, but as a partner for life.

So it continued, give and take, his hands straying continually upward to her splendid thighs, where he encountered the ribbons of her stockings. He untied them with the deliberate anticipation he might have unwrapped a precious gift. She returned the favor, though her fingers fumbled a little, assuring Aaron that the thrill of his touch distracted her.

A delicious shiver went through her when he rolled each stocking down and removed them one by one. And when he ran his hands back up her bare legs, Iris's breath raced until his fingertips brushed against sensitive flesh between her thighs.

"Oh, my word!"

"I trust that feels pleasant," Aaron inquired as he continued to pet her. Her warm slick wetness provided the answer, yet he needed to hear it as well, so there could be no question she wanted this as much as he did.

"More than pleasant." She chuckled, perhaps at the absurdity that there could be any doubt. "I had no idea anything could feel like that. If I had words to describe it, you have driven them out of my head entirely."

"Did no one tell you what to expect between a man and a woman?" he asked, because her innocence intrigued him and also to distract her a little. He sensed she was too close to release and he did not want her first such pleasure to be over too quickly. "Your aunt, perhaps?"

"Aunt Althea never mentioned a word about it. Perhaps she was afraid it would encourage us in wanton behavior if we knew what we were missing." A gurgle of saucy mirth followed her jest. It was too infectious for Aaron to resist echoing.

"Surely there could be no danger with your sister." He quipped. "I cannot imagine anything inducing Miss Lily to behave in a wanton manner."

To his surprise, Iris did not laugh at his teasing observa-tion. "Lily might just surprise you, Captain. There is a good deal more to her than you know."

She sounded almost offended by his reference to her sister, though Aaron could not guess why. Surely she did not want him to regard a timid wallflower like Lily as wanton? Whatever was the matter, he feared it might chill her ardor beyond his power to rekindle.

As he searched for the words to smooth over his blunder and put Iris back in a receptive spirit, she suddenly tugged at the buttons of his breeches. "Will it feel as pleasant to you if I touch *you* there?"

Clearly he had misjudged her mood!

Aaron gave a vague murmur of agreement that he hoped she would understand, but he could manage no more. Her frankly curious but gentle explorations left him incapable of coherent speech.

Had he intended to go slowly, making this one encounter last the whole night? At this rate, Iris might push *him* over the edge before he could accomplish his goal of claiming her virginity.

One thing he did know without a doubt. Iris might not be certain of her feelings, but her eager passion and tender desire to please him proved that she cared far more for him than she realized. Once they were finished with one another tonight, her acceptance of his proposal would be assured.

———◆◆◆———

She would show Aaron Turner who could behave wantonly!

Though her spirit smarted from his unwitting slight, Lily refused to surrender to her fears. She wanted this man and the delights his touch promised more than she could recall wanting anything. She was not about to be thwarted now, least of all by her own self-doubt. It had held her prisoner far too long. For this one night, she refused to be ruled by it.

On that note of reckless resolve, she fumbled with the buttons of Aaron's breeches and reached in to caress him. He probably thought Lily too naive to know that men were made differently from women down below.

In fact, she had seen enough Classical paintings and sculpture to have a fair idea of the differences. What was more, she'd been clever enough to guess that if one set of organs stuck out while the other sank inward, the two must be meant to connect somehow. The part she had never imagined was that the union might result in such sensations of pleasure, especially for the woman.

When her fingertips brushed over his male part, it quivered at her touch, spreading into a great shudder that convulsed his whole body. Her attentions wrung a cry from him that sounded almost painful. Or perhaps quite the opposite ...

The intensity of his reaction surprised Lily, as did the size and firmness of him. She tried to tug down his breeches for a better look.

Before she got very far, Aaron twisted about until he loomed over her.

"Enough of that," he commanded in a husky murmur that sounded more like a plea than an order, "otherwise I may be spent before I can have my way with you."

Somehow his admission made Lily feel very much mistress of the situation. That was not an outlook to which she was accustomed, yet she found it very agreeable.

"We cannot have that, can we?" she teased him in a pert whisper calculated to solicit a kiss.

She succeeded admirably. Aaron pressed his lips to hers and nudged them apart with the tip of his tongue. Then he kissed her deeply as if savoring the texture and flavor of her mouth like fine wine.

One hand cupped her breast through the bodice of her gown, treating it to a series of admiring caresses. Somehow those delicious attentions provoked a sweet, yearning ache in her loins. She could hardly wait for him to explore her further.

He did, but not before he had driven her almost mad with desire.

Lily squirmed and whimpered. Finally she wrenching her lips free of his long enough to gasp, "Please!" Though she had little idea what she was begging for so desperately.

As if that word was the signal for which he'd been waiting, Aaron pushed his breeches down over his hips. An instant later Lily gasped again — with pleasure this time — when his fingertip probed between her lower lips, tapping a spring of warm, slick moisture. With the lightest of strokes, he spread it over the exquisitely sensitive flesh.

Did lovers ever die of delight? Lily could not imagine how it was possible to contain such potently distilled bliss without bursting. Just as she seemed about to discover, another part of Aaron took the place of his coaxing finger. It was larger and smoother ... Lily knew what it must be and guessed what was about to happen.

He pressed between her thighs, into the hot, wet passage that awaited him. There was a sensation of pressure that might have been painful if it had not been overpowered by waves of searing ecstasy.

Lily lost control of her body. Her hips heaved, meeting his thrusts. Her heart galloped, beating rhythmic thunder in her ears. She vaguely sensed Aaron's struggle to master a tempest within him and treat her as gently as possible. But he was soon overcome by the same waves of pleasure that had drowned her in delight.

His thrusting stilled, yet Lily could feel a series of pulses deep within her. His breath gusted in her ear like a North Sea gale. A deep clap of thunder rumbled through his chest then the storm passed.

Aaron rolled onto his side, clasping one hand over her bottom to keep them joined. Then he held her and stroked her hair as he whispered endearments and praise of her instinctive perfection in the arts of love.

"Just wait until we have been wed a while and you have

more practice." He gave a sensuous chuckle. "It would soon make me hard again just to think of it."

Lazing in the warm shoals of satiation, Lily smiled tenderly at the thought.

It was only hours later that she awoke to the cold, bitter reality. She and Aaron would never experience another night like this. In her selfish folly, she had made certain of that.

———◆———

Iris's bedchamber was cold and completely dark when Aaron woke some while later. Yet the languid warmth of her embrace warded off any chill. How he wished he dared linger in her bed, savoring the sweet rustle of her breathing until it came time to kiss her awake.

But he was not such a rogue as some of the Killorans' other guests believed him. He would not return the earl's hospitality by creating a scandal that might attach to Beckwith Abbey. Nor would he jeopardize Iris's reputation on any account.

His feelings toward her had begun as attraction and admiration. Lately they had ripened into something much deeper and more enduring. He'd discovered aspects of her character that he'd never suspected, but which delighted him. Beneath the vivacious charm which made her such an appealing sweetheart, lay a wealth of bold passion and warm sympathy that would make her a priceless wife. Any man fortunate enough to wake up beside her, every morning for the rest of his life, would be selfish to desire any other blessing.

She had done him an immense honor by taking him into her bed without the benefit of proper wedding vows. It showed that she considered him a true gentleman at heart. Aaron would rather have lost every penny of his fortune than betray the precious faith Iris Crawford placed in him.

Still, it was a struggle to abandon the paradise of her embrace — one that required every scrap of his willpower to accomplish. In the end, he mastered his formidable desire to linger in her bed. Carefully detaching himself from the soft arms he longed to clasp, he slid away by slow degrees so as not to disturb her peaceful slumber.

But he could not resist the temptation to pause and lean over her, inhaling her intoxicating scent one more time and bestowing a feather-light kiss on her forehead.

That nearly undid his resolve. If she had stirred or sighed in her sleep, Aaron might have been lured back into bed with her and hang the consequences. But when she continued to doze in trusting tranquility, he mustered his scruples and groped silently for his clothes.

He recovered all but one stocking, which he feared must be buried in the bedclothes. He did not dare search for it, for fear of waking Iris. So he stuffed the one he had found into the pocket of his coat, which he donned along with his waistcoat. Draping his neck linen over his shoulder and carrying his shoes in one hand, he crept to the door with soft, hesitant steps, anxious not to trip or knock anything over.

At last he reached the door, eased it open and slipped out into the hallway. He prayed it was not yet time for the servants to be up laying the morning fires.

To his relief, he found the passage empty with only a single stub of a candle burning low in its wall sconce. The wary tension in his body ebbed as he closed Iris's door softly behind him.

At that instant, the door across the hall swung open.

Aaron froze. He knew there was no chance of escaping unseen. A dozen improbable explanations for his presence in this wing of the house flashed through his mind. His dangling neck linen and the shoes in his hand made a mockery of them all.

Then Rory Fitzwalter emerged from the opposite room, looking every bit as rumpled as Aaron knew he must.

The earl's brother gave a violent start at the sight of him.

"Dash it all, Turner!" he hissed as he shut the door behind him. "You near frightened the life out of me."

"I could say the same," Aaron replied once he'd caught his breath.

Clearly Rory was no stranger to such late night stealth for he soon recovered his composure. With a roguish grin, he cast a shrewd glance at the door through which Aaron had just come. "So that's how it is. Well, well ..."

Aaron scowled. "Breathe a word of this to anyone and I shall thrash you within an inch of your life."

"I?" Rory looked wounded by Aaron's suggestion. "I am nothing if not the soul of discretion." He nodded toward the door behind him. "And I am hardly in a position to cast stones. If we can each agree to turn a blind eye, I reckon I can get us back to our own rooms with no one the wiser."

"Gladly," Aaron breathed, taking back every uncharitable thought he'd ever had about Rory. "Lead on."

The earl's brother did not need to be asked twice. With catlike stealth he headed down the corridor in the opposite direction to the one Aaron would have taken.

"If we are discovered," he whispered, "we must give one another an alibi. We can say we sat up late drinking then in our sorry condition we lost our way to bed."

Aaron replied with a grim nod.

Fortunately their scoundrel's pact was never put to the test. After a bewildering expedition up and down servant's stairs and along corridors, Rory delivered Aaron, as promised, to his own quarters.

"I intend to marry her, you know," Aaron felt compelled to inform Rory as they parted ways.

"Of course you do." Rory gave a jaunty shrug. "While I have no intention of marrying anyone. To each his own."

Once safely back in his chamber, Aaron was hard pressed to stagger to his bed. The bones in his legs seemed to have melted with relief and his bare feet were all but numb from their trek through the cold hallways.

How he wished Iris was there to warm them for him! The thought brought a welcome flicker of heat to his icy flesh. So did the thrill of his triumph. Soon Iris Crawford would be his and he would be the envy of every gentleman who had ever met her!

Chapter Thirteen

FOR A MOMENT when she first woke, Lily wondered if the previous night had been a dream. Being seduced by Aaron Turner and seducing him in turn was certainly the stuff of her sweetest fancies. Yet, in her innocence she could never have imagined how wonderful it would be!

Besides, she had a faint chafing in her loins as well as one of his stockings, which had gotten caught under her pillow.

In the wake of their encounter, Lily found herself more conflicted about Aaron Turner than ever. His gentle, playful lovemaking was not what she had expected from such a strong, forceful man. More than ever she was certain no other suitor would capture her heart as he had — not by force like a privateer, but inviting her to surrender with his tenderness.

Yet it was no use imagining they could ever be together. If she confessed her deception, it would only make him despise her and justly so. Lily might have been able to bear that. But she could not risk driving him away from Iris, leaving her prey to Viscount Uvedale. She had already done her sister a great wrong. She must not compound it by letting Iris throw herself away on that blue-blooded blackguard!

Hearing one of the maids quietly sweeping out her hearth to lay the morning fire, Lily peeked out through the bed curtains. She did not want to risk the girl seeing that she was still wearing her much-rumpled ball gown.

"Good morning," she called with feigned cheerfulness. "I don't suppose you would know if my sister is awake yet."

"For certain, Miss," the girl replied with a distinctive Irish lilt. "She's stirring and in as good cheer as yourself for such an early hour. Says she's not feeling ill at all and wants to be made ready to join the party today. Is that not good news?"

"The very best." Lily strove to sound sincere, but her thoughts flew like a flock of frightened birds. "I must go to her at once."

For the first time since she'd conceived this crack-brained ruse to impersonate her sister, Lily realized how impossible it would be to bring off in the way she'd imagined. Now that Iris could speak again, she would inform everyone that she — not Lily — had been ill. Then the whole deception would be exposed.

There was only one hope, and even that would be slim.

As soon as the maid had finished her work and moved on, Lily tore off her ball gown and tried not to recall the magical night she had enjoyed while wearing it. With a heavy, quaking heart she donned the drabbest of her own dresses and plaited her hair in a most severe style.

Then she went like an abject penitent to plead for her sister's forgiveness . . . and help.

Iris looked much better than she had in days. Her eyes had regained their accustomed sparkle and her smile its piquant charm.

Both faltered for a moment when she set eyes on Lily. "Oh, it's you. I thought it might be Miss Ingledew. If I am well enough to be out of bed, she should be too. I wish I had not let you persuade me to miss the ball last night. I don't believe it would have done me a bit of harm. You must tell me all about it."

As briefly as possible Lily told what she could remember of the ball at Compton Court, which was far too little to satisfy Iris. She followed with several questions while Lily grew increasingly anxious. Where was the bold adventuress who had matched her privateer lover passion for passion only hours ago? Her reckless behavior had landed her and her sister in deep trouble from which they might never recover. Lily's stern sense of discretion rebuked her fledgling courage.

At last Iris seemed to realize she would never get satisfactory answers from her preoccupied sister.

"I should never have let you talk me into staying behind." She repeated, heaving a tragic sigh. "At least I can rejoin the party for our last two days. Perhaps I can still revive my romance with Lord Uvedale ..."

Lily opened her mouth to protest.

Before she could speak Iris continued, "I am not certain I care to after the way he abandoned me during my illness. Perhaps there are more important things to consider than polish and a title when it comes to choosing a husband."

Her sister's sensible observation made Lily almost faint with relief. Perhaps their perilous situation might still be salvaged. "I believe you are right, dearest. Do not forget how thoughtful and constant Captain Turner has been during your illness. Scarcely a day went by that he did not inquire about you. Not to mention riding all the way to Guildford to fetch you that lovely basket of fruit."

"True." Iris gazed off into the distance. A mysterious little smile played across her lips. "The Captain is terribly handsome and wealthy in his own right."

Much as it pained Lily to hear her sister speak so admiringly of the man she loved, her conscience insisted it was Iris that Aaron Turner wanted. It was Iris he deserved. They both aimed to scale the heights of Society, something that held no appeal for Lily. With their combined wealth, looks, charm and confidence, no doors would be closed to such a golden couple.

"Most importantly ..." Lily struggled to keep her throat from constricting. "... Captain Turner is a good man — one you can trust. A fancy title is no guarantee of honorable intentions. There is something I must tell you about Lord Uvedale, though I fear it may distress you."

"That is precisely why you *should* tell me," Iris insisted. Her eyes glittered with wary curiosity. "Indeed you *must* or I am certain to imagine something far worse."

Lily doubted that, but there could be no going back now. Iris would have the secret out of her sooner or later. And it was something her sister should know, regardless of what a blow it might be to her pride.

"Very well, then." Lily inhaled a deep breath and forged ahead. "The other night as I was coming up to bed I overhead a conversation between Lord Uvedale and a certain lady. I did not mean to eavesdrop, but when your name was mentioned I felt obliged to listen, for your sake."

The intentional falsehood stung her conscience, but Lily did not dare tell her sister that Aaron had been the one who overheard Lord Uvedale's scandalous proposition to Kitty Delany. Iris might not believe Aaron, though Lily did without question.

She repeated his report, as near word-for-word as she could recall, resisting any temptation to embellish it. As Lily spoke, her sister's face turned an alarming shade of red and her hands clenched into tight little fists.

"The scoundrel!" she cried at last. "The miserable ... wretched ... vile ... abominable ..." Iris plundered her vocabulary for a sufficiently insulting description. "Of all the gall — planning to use *my* money to support his mistress! How could I have been such a fool? I should have seen him for the unscrupulous fortune hunter he is!"

She pounded the mattress until Lily feared it might burst. "I should have listened to you from the beginning. You never approved of Lord Uvedale, and with excellent reason. As you are my witness, Lily, I am done with lying, lecherous noblemen. There is nothing *noble* about them."

Iris's outrage finally seemed to spend itself, leaving behind a bitter residue of self-doubt. "Is that the only reason I have been sought after? Because of my fortune?"

She looked so bereft suddenly that Lily felt quite protective. "Of course not! There are plenty of women with money, myself included, who are not besieged with suitors as you are. And remember, not all your admirers are light of purse.

Captain Turner is rich enough that he can wed entirely to please himself, and the man is besotted with you."

A great lump of misery rose in her throat, cutting off any further conversation. It was true, though, Lily reminded herself. All Aaron's kindness, compliments, attention and lovemaking had been intended for Iris. She had stolen them and in doing so had betrayed the two people she cared for most in the world. Anything she suffered as a result was no more than she deserved. Yet she must try to atone. She must make certain neither Iris nor Aaron paid for *her* folly.

Iris grasped her sister's ice-cold hands. "Is it too late to encourage Captain Turner? I would not blame him if he became discouraged and took an interest in someone else. Perhaps he only inquired after me and sent that lovely fruit out of pity."

"No!" Lily forced out an adamant denial. "He cares for you as much as ever. More, in fact. I am certain of it."

"How can that be?" Iris's delicate brows knit in a doubtful frown. "And how can you be so certain if it is true?"

Lily's stomach contracted until it felt like a ball of lead. She wished she could sink through the floor and the room below and on down through the kitchen and cellars. At last the time had come to pay the price for her stolen delights. The currency would be bitter shame and perhaps rejection.

She forced herself to look Iris in the eye. She must not evade any of the reproach she deserved. "I *am* certain because Captain Turner has not been aware of your absence from the party. He believes he has been wooing you for the past several days."

Iris's frown deepened into bewilderment. "What sort of riddle are you talking, Lily? Have you fallen ill and gone delirious with fever?"

Lily shook her head. Her only sickness was guilt, for which she knew no cure. "There is something else I must tell you . . . something I must confess. I hope when you hear it you will not think as ill of me as you do of Viscount Uvedale."

"What have you done, Lily?" her sister demanded though she sounded less angry than anxious.

"When you fell ill," Lily began, "I wished it had been me instead. And I was certain everyone else in the party would feel the same."

For a moment Iris looked as if she meant to disagree then realized her sister was probably right.

"The Killorans' maid mistook me for you," Lily continued. "So I decided to pretend I was. It was a foolish impulse, but once I began, I could not stop or tell anyone the truth for fear they would think me mad."

Would they have been wrong? Reflecting on her reckless behavior, Lily wondered if she could have been in her right mind.

She expected Iris to suggest that as well, but something else seemed to preoccupy her sister. "You've pretended to be me all this time and no one suspected? Not even Aunt Althea?"

Lily gave a guilty shrug. "I tried not to spend too much time in her company. Besides, she was distracted by Rory Fitzwalter."

"What about Lord Uvedale?" Iris demanded. "No wonder he never asked after me or tried to steal a visit. He thought I was you. So did Captain Turner. That fruit was meant for you, not me!"

"Yes," Lily admitted, "but the way he behaved toward me, thinking I was you, proved just how much he cares for you. At the ball last night, he proposed."

"Proposed?" Iris repeated. It was difficult to tell whether she was flattered or enraged, perhaps a bit of both. "What answer did you give him? Don't tell me Captain Turner believes he is engaged to me!"

"Would that be so bad?" Lily could not imagine any sensible woman being dismayed at the prospect of marriage to a man like Aaron. "Only a few moments ago you were afraid it might be too late to encourage him. Besides, I did not accept."

That did nothing to pacify Iris. "So he thinks I refused

him? He will want nothing to do with me now!"

"I ... did not leave him entirely without hope." Lily's gaze faltered before her sister's livid glare.

"What is that supposed to mean?" Iris snapped. "There is something worse that you haven't told me. Out with it at once!"

"The punch at the ball was very strong," Lily began, though she knew very well it was not to blame for her behavior. She had been intoxicated with desire not spirits. "After the Captain proposed, I left the ball but he followed me. In the carriage ... we kissed and when we got back to Beckwith Abbey, we ... spent the night together."

"He took advantage of you ... of me?" Iris quivered with rage, as if she might explode at any moment.

"It was not like that." Lily clung to her sister's hands for fear Iris would box her ears if she let go. "I don't know what came over me, but I wanted him every bit as much as he did me. I didn't have a proper idea what was going to happen, but even if I had ..."

"Do you know what you've done?" Iris looked as if she might retch. "If this gets out both our reputations will be ruined. I will never be able to make a good marriage of any kind!"

"It will *not* get out if you help me," Lily pleaded. "Aaron ... Captain Turner will be delighted to marry you. If we change places and you tell him you have decided to accept his proposal after all, everything will work out as it should."

Iris grew calmer and thoughtful, giving Lily hope. But after a moment she seemed to dismiss the whole idea with an impatient flick of her hand. "Ridiculous! I barely know the man."

"You did not know Lord Uvedale any better," Lily reminded her. "Yet you were prepared to marry him. Besides, I do know the captain and I can assure you he will make you every bit as happy as Uvedale would have made you miserable."

Iris arched one eyebrow. "You *do* know the Captain, very

intimately. I am not certain I care to wed a man who has bedded my sister."

"I told you that was my doing." Lily clenched her hands in a beseeching gesture. "He has no idea it was me. Only you and I know. If I behave as if I have been ill instead of you, I am certain we will soon come to believe it ourselves."

It took more deliberation on Iris's part and more pleading on Lily's, but at last Iris agreed to do what her sister proposed. The twins stole back to their guest room and proceeded to trade places.

Lily slipped into bed while Iris strove to recover her appearance. She had made some headway when Miss Ingledew appeared. The maid still did not look well.

Iris gave a guilty start as if she had been caught stealing Lady Killoran's silver teaspoons. "Ingledew, are you certain you should be up and about yet?"

"I'll manage," Miss Ingledew insisted grimly. "I heard that Jackson chit bragging about how lovely she made you look for the ball. I was afraid I might lose my place."

"No need to fret on that account," Iris assured her.

"So I see." Miss Ingledew swept a critical eye over her mistress. "If this is her idea of grooming a lady, she has plenty still to learn."

Iris caught her lower lip between her teeth, perhaps to keep from laughing. Lily saw nothing amusing about their situation. They had made a narrow escape from disastrous scandal and they were not out of the woods yet by any means.

"I am happy to have you back, Ingledew," said Iris. "I do want to look my best for the final days of our visit."

"We'd better get busy, then." Miss Ingledew waved her mistress to a seat at the dressing table. "I cannot believe that silly girl did not wash your hair before a ball."

Clucking her tongue and muttering under her breath, the maid set to work. "What's Miss Lily doing back from the sick room?"

"I ... er ..." Lily stammered, flustered at being put on the spot when she would rather be an invisible observer.

"My sister is feeling better and wants to rejoin the party." Iris answered with easy conviction.

"I *did*," Lily piped up. Her sister's ability to keep a cool head and tell a convincing falsehood when necessary boded well for the success of their plan. "But coming back to our room tired me more than I expected. I believe I had better rest today after all. I doubt anyone will miss my presence at this point."

Iris nodded. "A very sensible idea, dear. You do not want to jeopardize your recovery."

For the other guests, and especially their aunt, to see the twins together might ruin their plans by raising awkward questions. If everyone saw only one of the Crawford sisters at a time, chances were much better that they would believe what they were told.

As Lily watched, Miss Ingledew worked her grooming magic on Iris until she looked quite her old self. No one would guess she'd been ill.

Iris clearly agreed. Smiling at her reflection in the glass she gave an approving nod. "Perfect. Now you must go back to bed, Ingledew. We cannot risk you having a relapse before we go back to London. "

Apparently satisfied that her position was not in jeopardy, the maid agreed and headed away.

Iris approached the bed, perching on the edge. For a moment Lily felt dizzy with the realization of how much alike they could look when they tried.

A doubtful frown twisted Iris's features. She clutched Lily's hands. "Will I be able to carry this off?"

"Of course you will." Lily gave her sister's fingers an encouraging squeeze. "I did and I was only pretending to have your confidence."

Iris shrugged. "I suspect most people who seem confident are only pretending. You underestimate yourself, Lily. Have the past days not proven that you can be every bit as popular as I, if you make the effort?"

Lily shook her head. "The past days have shown me the folly of trying to be someone I am not. Now go. Captain Turner will be anxious to see you."

Once Iris had gone, Lily sank back onto the pillows with a sigh of relief and regret so deep that it shook her whole body. Exhaustion and nausea gripped her as if she truly had been ill for the past several days.

Tears welled up in her eyes as she wondered how she would endure a lifetime of trying to conceal her feelings for her sister's husband. Part of her longed to bury her face in her pillows to stifle the sound of her weeping, as she had so often during her childhood.

She was not a child any more. Lily swallowed her unshed tears. She had no one else to blame for her misfortune. She had brought it upon herself and she would bear the consequences, whatever they might be.

———————•◦•——————

All the Killorans' guests were late rising the morning after the ball.

Aaron was the first one down. He ate a hearty breakfast while he waited for the others. As the minutes ticked by, he found it increasingly difficult to contain his restless anticipation. He could scarcely wait to celebrate Iris Crawford's formal acceptance of his proposal and savor his triumph over Viscount Uvedale. None of the victories he'd won during his lucrative career at sea had ever brought him such a heady sense of satisfaction.

He might have felt guilty over the less than honorable means he'd used to secure Iris, had she not surrendered to him so willingly and received such obvious pleasure from their lovemaking. On their wedding night, his beautiful bride would be able to enjoy his attentions even more, without the inconvenience of her virginity.

Gradually other guests began to join Aaron around the breakfast table. Was it his imagination or did he sense strange undercurrents between them?

Mr. Brennan and his daughter were the first to appear, followed shortly by Miss Delany. This was the first time Aaron had seen either lady at breakfast. He wondered why they had chosen this particular morning to alter their routine.

Mr. Brennan engaged Aaron in animated conversation about the previous night's festivities. The two ladies remained quiet. They seemed preoccupied with their own thoughts, which must have been very pleasant. If Aaron had been asked to describe their looks that morning, he would have said *radiant.*

Rory Fitzwalter seemed well-pleased with himself when he joined the others. Not a single guilty flush or sidelong look suggested he'd had a furtive encounter with Aaron outside two ladies' bedchambers.

Lord Uvedale came next. Much to Aaron's chagrin, the viscount appeared in excellent spirits. Did he have such a high opinion of himself that he still believed he could win Iris Crawford? No. It was something else, Aaron sensed. Uvedale seemed to be nursing a secret glee, as if he had gotten away with something or possessed a piece of information to his advantage.

Did the viscount know about his seduction of Iris Crawford and plan to use it against them? Aaron resolved to watch his back.

"Good morning, Lord Gabriel," Miss Brennan called when the young gentleman joined them.

Lord Gabriel started as if he had encountered a hungry tiger stalking the breakfast room. Of all of them, he looked the worst for the previous night's indulgence.

"Morning," he mumbled, shambling to a chair beside Aaron, when there was an empty place beside Moira Brennan.

Aaron had no opportunity to wonder at that for Iris Crawford and her aunt arrived just then. Mrs. Henderson immediately began chattering away about the ball, filling the awkward silence left by Lord Gabriel's taciturn entrance.

Iris looked more vibrant than ever as she took the seat next to Miss Brennan. Aaron scowled at Lord Gabriel for spoiling what might have been a very cozy arrangement. Then he caught Iris's eye and lavished her with a smile of fond admiration.

She lowered her gaze in a coy manner that surprised him after her daring behavior last night.

Then she turned to Moira Brennan. "What did you think of the ball, Miss Brennan?"

The Irish heiress fumbled her silverware. "I-I beg your pardon?"

"The ball," Iris repeated. "Did you enjoy yourself?"

"Of course." Moira Brennan's tone seemed at odds with her reply. "It was a delightful evening."

She cast a furtive glance at Lord Gabriel, who seemed too absorbed in his own suffering to notice.

"And you, Miss Delany?" Iris turned her attention elsewhere, clearly hoping to spark an actual conversation.

"I agree with Miss Brennan." The lady sounded more subdued than she had earlier. "What about you, Miss Crawford? I noticed you left early. Did a country ball disappoint you after the elegance of London?"

The questions and their subtle air of antagonism seemed to catch Iris by surprise, but her usual good-natured vivacity came to her rescue.

"No indeed." She chuckled as if Kitty Delany had teased her. "The arrangements would equal any in London. I thought the music especially fine. I was sorry not to stay longer, but I felt a bit ill and was afraid I might be coming down with my poor sister's ailment. Fortunately I am feeling perfectly well this morning."

Kitty Delany appeared to regret her earlier antagonism. "How is your sister recovering? Will she be able to rejoin us soon?"

The mention of Lily Crawford troubled Aaron. He had been so delightfully absorbed in wooing Iris. He had all but forgotten the dear friend who had done so much to promote his successful conquest.

Iris shook her head with a regretful air. "Lily is improving and will surely be able to travel in time for our departure. But she is not equal to the demands of too much activity at the moment."

Rory, Iris, Mrs. Henderson and Mr. Brennan began to talk of plans for how they would spend the final days of their visit. Iris seemed as vivacious as ever, yet Aaron knew her well enough to detect an air of uncertainty. Something troubled her, though she was doing her gallant best to hide it.

Was she worried that, having bedded her, he would refuse to renew his offer of marriage? It grieved him that she could believe him capable of such conduct. Yet he knew from experience that being in love could make the most confident person feel vulnerable without cause. He must reassure her of his honorable intentions at the earliest opportunity.

Lord Gabriel rose abruptly. "If you will excuse me, I must retire. I cannot bear the smell of food this morning."

"I do hope the poor gentleman has not contracted my niece's illness," said Mrs. Henderson as Lord Gabriel bolted from the room.

"Never fear," Rory quipped with heartless good humor. "My friend often succumbs to this ailment after a night of overindulgence. No doubt he is regretting his behavior in the cool light of day, as one often does."

Mrs. Henderson laughed. "Not you I hope, sir."

"Not in the slightest." Rory sipped his coffee. "What is the good of enjoying yourself if you mean to wallow in remorse afterward? I make it a policy never to regret anything I do."

Aaron was watching Iris for her reaction to Rory's rakish declaration . . . and because he could not take his eyes off her. He noticed Miss Delany shift in her seat, as if uncomfortable. Was she thinking of the proposition Lord Uvedale had made her? Had she been tempted to accept and now felt ashamed?

Moira Brennan rose from her chair. "I have … some letters to write if you will excuse me."

Her voice barely carried to Aaron's end of the table, yet he thought it nearly broke on the last words. The young lady hurried away as if she had some much more urgent reason for leaving than she'd claimed.

What had gotten into everyone this morning? Aaron wondered. Most of his fellow guests were behaving quite contrary to what he expected. Still he was not sorry when they all began to disperse on various pretexts.

"Who's for a hand or two of whist in the drawing room?" Rory suggested brightly.

Miss Delany murmured that she must attend Lady Killoran and excused herself. Mrs. Henderson, Mr. Brennan and Viscount Uvedale all expressed their willingness to play cards.

"What about you, Iris?" Mrs. Henderson asked her niece as the foursome headed off. "Will you join us?"

"As soon as I finish breakfast," Iris replied.

No one inquired about Aaron's plans, which suited him perfectly.

After the others had gone, Aaron flashed Iris a conspiratorial grin. "Once you finish, Miss Crawford, perhaps you might care to take a stroll with me to Lord Killoran's library. I have a fancy to read one of his books and I hoped you could recommend something that might suit me."

This bit of playacting was all for the benefit of a footman who hovered near the sideboard.

"I would be happy to oblige you, Captain." Iris took one last tiny bite of her buttered egg then placed her napkin beside her plate. "Though my sister knows far more about books than I."

Once they were out of earshot of the servant, Aaron leaned toward her and murmured, "My dearest Iris, I hope you know how much our night together meant to me. I was honored by such a warm demonstration of your feelings."

The lady's face turned a livid shade of red. "Thank you for trying to spare me any shame over my behavior, Captain. But we both know it was I who threw myself at you last night. I should not have drunk so very much when I have no head for spirits."

Drunk so much? Two cups of punch? Aaron was tempted to laugh until he sensed she was not in jest. And it was not true that she'd *thrown herself at him* after their first impetuous kiss in the carriage. In that moment of confusion, Aaron suddenly noticed a few subtle differences between the lovely lady beside him and the one he had wooed and bedded the previous night. Her delicate features appeared thinner. When her fierce blush subsided, the natural tone of her skin looked paler. Or did he only imagine it?

"If you did overindulge," he protested, "the fault is still mine for failing to curtail you after six cups. It is a wonder you are not in worse condition than Lord Gabriel this morning."

Much as his conscience reproached him for such blatant fishing, Aaron could not resist. He must know whether he was unjustly suspicious or the butt of a cruel hoax.

Iris — if indeed it was her — seemed to hesitate before replying. "I must admit, I do not feel as well as I might. But it was not your responsibility to keep me from drinking so much. I cannot think what got into me. I am usually more temperate."

By now they had reached the earl's library, which afforded greater privacy than the hallway.

Iris looked about the room, its tall shelves filled with many fine leather-bound volumes. Aaron could not escape the conviction that she was trying to avoid his gaze. He no longer felt guilty for trying to trick her. It set them even.

"Do not be too severe on yourself," he said. "Anyone would have been thirsty after so much dancing. There cannot have been many gentlemen present who missed the opportunity of taking a turn with you."

Again she did not attempt to contradict his false account. "My company is usually sought after at such events. But I assure you *yours* was the company I most enjoyed. Now that we are alone, was there a question you wished to ask me?"

She turned toward him but kept her eyes downcast. This was not out of modesty, Aaron sensed, but to avoid his scrutiny.

"There *is* a question I am anxious to ask you." Aaron tried to prevent his tone from giving away his growing suspicion. The element of surprise was surely his best chance of getting the truth from her.

"What is it, pray?" Though she continued to avoid his gaze, an expectant little smile hovered on her lips, threatening to bewitch him with its charm.

Aaron strove to resist her spell.

Clasping her hands in his so she could not easily turn away, he demanded, "Lily Crawford, why are you pretending to be your sister?"

His question startled her into glancing up. In her widened eyes, Aaron read the truth which she might later seek to deny.

She did with her next breath, but it was too late. "I cannot think what you mean, Captain. Lily is sick in bed. I am Iris."

She tried to pull away but Aaron held her fast. "Do not make this worse by continuing to lie once you have been caught! Iris would know she only drank two cups of punch last night and danced with nobody but me and Lord Uvedale."

His evidence stunned her silent for a moment.

Aaron took advantage of her hesitation to add, "All I wish to hear from you is a full confession of the truth and some explanation. I cannot imagine what would prompt you and your sister to deceive me this way."

His mind spun like a whirligig in a gale, trying to fathom the situation, but he could not. One thing was clear, however. Iris Crawford must not care about his feelings in the least. He was nothing more to her than a source of callous amusement.

Had Lily been a willing participant in the prank as well? Had the Crawford twins laughed behind his back? Somehow that thought struck Aaron an even harder blow.

"It is not what you think." She seemed anxious and

remorseful, now that her deception had been uncovered. But Aaron knew what persuasive actresses she and her sister could be.

"Indeed?" He released her hands abruptly, not trusting himself to have even the most innocent contact with her. "What is it, then?"

Of all the things in the world she might have said, the next words out of her mouth were the last he expected. "I am Iris Crawford. I swear! The woman you courted the past few days and bedded last night is the imposter — my sister, Lily."

Chapter Fourteen

Had Aaron Turner proposed to Iris yet? Lily wondered as the minutes dragged by and she had nothing to distract her from tormenting worries about the future and regrets about the past.

What had possessed her to impersonate Iris that first evening without proper forethought? And when she realized her feelings for Aaron had begun to grow dangerously romantic, why had she not confessed the truth when there was still a possibility he might have understood and forgiven her?

Now she could only hope Iris would charm Aaron into ignoring any inconsistencies between her usual behavior and the way Lily had acted in her place. On that score she had less to worry. Aaron was too besotted with Iris to care if she confused some detail of the past few days. Besides, he would want nothing to stand in the way of their betrothal. It would signify his triumph over Lord Uvedale and all the aristocrats from his past.

What would happen *after* her sister's engagement and actual wedding troubled Lily far more. Would she be able to listen to the man she loved declare his lifelong devotion to her sister? Could she bear to watch them make a home together and fill the nursery at suitable intervals?

Would it be worse to live with them, so close to the situation she craved, yet never close enough? Or might she decide to marry a man she could never love in order to escape that domestic torment? If she thought too hard about either prospect, Lily did not have to *pretend* to be ill. A bone-deep chill gripped her, while her stomach seethed with dread.

"Are you certain I cannot fetch you something to eat, Miss?" Hannah Jackson inquired with a worried frown. "You won't get well by starving yourself."

"Perhaps later," Lily murmured, trying to mimic the slight hoarseness that lingered in Iris's voice. "Just now I should like to rest."

The girl shook her head. "I heard you were ever so much better yesterday, eager to be off to the ball. Today you cannot get out of bed."

"I may have overtaxed my strength, yesterday," Lily suggested. "Or perhaps I am out of spirits from having missed the ball. I did not sleep well."

"That must have been a disappointment." The maid sank onto a chair by the fire and took up a bit of sewing. "I hear it was very elegant."

"It was." The words slipped out before Lily caught herself. "Or so I heard from my sister."

Tedious as it had been to pass the time alone, Lily found she preferred it to pretending there was nothing wrong except a lingering illness. "You need not stay here with me, Jackson. I shall be fine on my own."

"Are you sure, Miss?" The girl looked reluctant to go. "I don't mind and I'll not disturb you."

It went against the habit of many years for Lily to give priority to her own wishes before those of another person, even a servant. Perhaps walking in her sister's shoes for several days had given her a taste of Iris's assurance.

"I do not doubt that," she answered in a kind but firm tone, "but I would still prefer to be alone."

"Very well, Miss." The maid gathered up her sewing and headed off. "Ring for me if you need anything."

That had not been so hard after all, Lily reflected with a brief flicker of satisfaction before she fell to brooding again.

Even by her unreliable sense of time, it did not seem long before she heard footsteps out in the corridor and the door flew open.

"Jackson!" Lily cried, not bothering to curb her annoyance. "I told you I wish to be left alone."

She gasped when she saw it was not the Killorans' maid. Iris entered, looking deeply distressed. Aaron Turner stalked in behind her, his rugged features dark as a thundercloud.

"Aaron!" Lily cried, pulling the bedclothes up over her chest like a shield. "I mean … Captain Turner, what are you doing here?"

The moment the question left her mouth, she knew.

He strode to the bed and grasped her chin in his large, strong hand. "I am here to see for myself if what I suspect can be true."

"Stop it!" Lily struggled against his firm grip as he turned her face this way and that, examining her as if she were a very expensive animal he meant to purchase. "How dare you?"

His unyielding touch was as different as could be from last night's coaxing caresses. Yet part of Lily could not help thrilling to it, even as her sense of propriety reacted with outrage.

Her indignant question did not make him stop. Instead, he bent closer, until his nose nearly touched hers. For one mad instant, Lily wondered if he meant to kiss her. Her lips tingled expectantly.

Of course he had no such intention.

"How dare *I*?" he demanded. "How dare *you*? This is nothing to the way you and your sister have played me for a fool these past days. Was either of you truly ill, or was that all part of your game as well?"

His manner should have intimidated Lily into a quivering jelly, but instead it was Iris who retreated to the farthest corner of the room looking pale and shaken. Meanwhile Lily experienced an unexpected surge of spirit, as if she had absorbed some of Aaron's strength from his touch.

"There was no game." She stopped struggling and spoke with quiet firmness. "Iris *was* ill. I'm not certain she has fully recovered yet."

Her sudden calmness seemed to take the wind out of Aaron's sails. Releasing her chin, he straightened up and backed away from the bed. "I suppose the pair of you had a great laugh at how you fooled me and the others. Or was it just me? Was Lord Uvedale in on your prank as well? I shall be the laughing stock of every assembly and drawing room in London, I suppose!"

"You'll be nothing of the kind." Lily found she could not bear to sit there in bed. It made her feel too vulnerable — as if she were still a frightened, ailing child abandoned by her family.

She climbed out from under the covers, pulled on a dressing gown and faced Aaron Turner. "No one else knows anything about this, certainly not Lord Uvedale. Even Iris did not know what I'd done until a few hours ago. Do not blame her. She is entirely innocent. This was all my doing and I am sorrier than you can possibly imagine."

Some of the righteous wrath melted out of Aaron's scowl, leaving behind an air of injured bewilderment that grieved Lily far worse.

"What made you do it?" he asked in a tone that was less a demand than a plea.

For an instant Lily considered telling him the truth. But how could she? Bad enough he should think her a heartless minx who had led him on out of some selfish desire for amusement. Better that than to have him pity her as a lovelorn wallflower who would commit any kind of folly to steal the attentions he meant to give her sister.

"I wanted you and Iris together," Lily repeated the lie she had told herself in the beginning. If it fooled Aaron half as well as it had fooled her, perhaps the situation might still be salvaged. "When she fell ill, I was afraid you would turn your attention elsewhere and Iris would end up with Lord Uvedale. I never meant for it to go so far, but once I started I did not dare stop for fear of making matters ten times worse."

Aaron's gaze moved restlessly from Lily to Iris and back

again. "The two of you are so different in every other way, I never thought of you looking so much alike. I never suspected for an instant."

He lowered his voice and addressed Lily. "Does your sister know about ...?"

"Last night?" Lily gave a guilty nod. "I had to take her into my confidence, or you would have suspected at once. Not that it helped in the end. How did you know?"

"Give me a little credit." Aaron no longer sounded enraged. A colder, more enduring resentment seemed to have taken hold of him. "I may have mistaken a lady I'd admired from afar but seldom got close to. I was not quite so easy to fool after having made her intimate acquaintance ... or should I say *yours*. How could you have let it come to that?"

"I don't know!" The strain of this encounter, and the extreme emotions warring within her, were more than Lily could bear. She just wanted to be left alone with her shame and misery, not tormented with questions for which she had no answers. "Perhaps I became confused and forgot I wasn't Iris and that I wasn't in love with you. Perhaps I was curious about the doings of men and women and all the fuss over it. Perhaps I went a little mad. Take your pick of those reasons or come up with one of your own. What does it matter now? What's done is done and cannot be fixed any more than eggs can be unscrambled!"

Her outburst seemed to rock Aaron back on his heels. Lily feared he would respond with more reproaches or continue his interrogation.

Instead he shook his head as if no amount of explanation could make him understand her actions. "What have I done to deserve being manipulated and lied to? I only wanted the opportunity to show your sister that I could make her happy. I wanted to protect you both from Lord Uvedale."

Did Aaron believe she had impersonated Iris in order to *punish* him? Lily's shame over her behavior was nothing to the guilt she felt that Aaron might question whether he deserved such betrayal. She knew all too well how easy it was for a person to believe they had done something to justify being mistreated. The last thing she wanted was for such a fine man to feel that way because of her folly.

She longed to explain that he had done nothing to deserve being placed in this position. She'd been so preoccupied with her own needs and feelings that she had never stopped to properly consider how any of this might affect him. What kind of love was that?

Before she could articulate any of those painful thoughts, Iris spoke up with a question of her own. "What will you do, Captain? If this gets out, Lily and I will be ruined forever!"

Aaron flinched. "You do not have a very high opinion of me do you, Miss Crawford? If *this* gets out, I can assure you it will not be my doing."

Iris sank onto a nearby chair, clearly weak with relief. For Lily, the prospect of scandal and ruin scarcely signified. She would have accepted such punishment gladly if only it relieved Aaron's sense of injury.

"As for what I will do," he continued in a tone of bitter resignation, "that depends entirely upon your wishes ... and whether your sister is with child."

With child.

Those words had scarcely left Aaron's lips before Lily Crawford's mouth fell open and the color drained from her face. Her horrified astonishment suggested that such a possibility had never crossed her mind. Could a lady of marriageable years in this day and age truly be so innocent?

Lily Crawford had never known her mother nor had a step-mother, Aaron recalled. He remembered what she had said about her aunt keeping both sisters ignorant of such matters for fear of encouraging wanton behavior.

He did not relish being the one to impart such information,

but it seemed he had little choice — as he would have little choice about his future domestic arrangements. Lily Crawford had seen to that.

Still, some lingering protective feeling toward her compelled Aaron to soften his tone. "When a man and woman … lie together, she may conceive a child, though it does not happen every time."

Lily continued to stare in horror. Clearly this possible consequence of her foolish playacting had never occurred to her. Perhaps none of the others had either. That was cold comfort to Aaron at the moment.

"When … will I know?" she asked at last in a halting murmur.

It was a question Aaron could not answer, having never gotten a woman with child — at least not that he knew of. He had secretly cherished his relative ignorance on the subject.

Then Iris piped up from the corner to which she had retreated. To his chagrin, Aaron realized he had forgotten she was there.

"In a month or so," she informed her sister, "when your courses don't come on time. Then your belly will begin to swell. In nine or ten months, if all goes as it should, you'll be brought to bed and give birth."

Lily stared at her sister as if she was both amazed and appalled. "How do you know all that?"

Iris heaved an exasperated sigh. "I talk to other women. I ask discreet questions. Not everything worth learning is in your precious books."

Lily flinched at her sister's rebuke, once again rousing Aaron's reluctant pity. For an instant her lower lip trembled. Then she caught it between her teeth.

"Aunt Althea told me a thing or two as well," Iris added in a softer tone. "I suppose no one thought it their place to tell you. Or they might have believed you would not live long enough to require such information. I would have told you, but I thought you must know."

Then she addressed herself to Aaron. "So you will do right by Lily if she is with child, Captain? And if she is not — what then?"

She sounded pleasantly surprised by his intention to behave honorably, which offended Aaron.

He drew himself erect. "That will be for you and your sister to decide. I meant to propose to you, Miss Crawford, and I still wish to marry you if . . . circumstances permit and you will have me."

Strangely, something within him rebelled at that declaration. This was not the Iris Crawford to whom he had proposed. Yet neither was her sister, entirely. Was it possible the feminine ideal with whom he'd fallen in love existed more in his own imagination than in either of the Crawford sisters?

"What if I would rather not?" asked Iris. "Will you tell people what went on between you and my sister?"

For an instant Aaron was too incensed to speak.

Before he could regain his composure, Lily answered for him. "Did you not hear what the Captain said? He vowed that none of this would become public knowledge on his account."

"Of course I heard," Iris shot back, clearly not accustomed to being challenged by her timid twin, "but—"

"But you doubt his integrity?" Disbelief and indignation battled in Lily's tone. "You think he would blackmail you into a marriage you do not want? If you believe that, then you are the worst judge of character I have ever met!"

Could he marshal such sincere indignation on his own behalf? Aaron wondered. He had not seduced Iris . . . or Lily to blackmail her into marriage. But he had known it would make any other course of action unlikely. Was that so very different? He had put his own wishes ahead of hers, justifying his selfishness in the name of wanting to protect the Crawford sisters. He might not have designs on their fortunes, but was he any less self-serving than Viscount Uvedale?

Aaron expected proud, spirited Iris to bristle at her sister's rebuke, but she did not argue. Perhaps Lily's passionate defense had persuaded her, or perhaps she had been shocked into submission.

"I beg your pardon, Captain Turner." She addressed him with downcast eyes and a contrite air. "I fear I *have* misjudged you ... and others."

Aaron shook his head. "Not as much as you may suppose, Miss Crawford. I cannot take pride in my recent behavior. But I assure you I meant well. At least I believed I did. I promise you on my honor ... no, on something I hold truly sacred, the memory of my dear sister, that I will never speak a word of what took place last night. If you do not want to wed me, I shall accept your decision and wish you well in finding a better husband."

"That is very gracious of you, Captain." The real Iris Crawford regarded Aaron with greater esteem than she had ever shown him before. "I believe if circumstances prove favorable, I should be pleased to consider your proposal."

Was it possible that out of this disaster he might still triumph? Aaron scarcely dared hope.

Only one small obstacle might stand in his way.

Chapter Fifteen

THE NEXT THREE weeks were some of the longest Lily had ever endured.

As an ailing child with too little to occupy her, she had often found that time hung heavy on her hands. Back then at least she had not borne the additional burdens of a guilty conscience and a painfully divided mind.

From the moment she and Iris returned to London with their aunt, Lily had been haunted by regrets and torn between conflicting inclinations. One part of her longed to feel the familiar pangs of her monthly courses. That would set Aaron Turner free to propose to Iris and absolve the worst of her guilt over what she'd done.

At the same time, another stubborn, selfish part yearned to have Aaron and his child, even if it was only to satisfy honor. If they were obliged to wed and she did everything in her power to make it up to him, he might learn to care for her, in time.

Her conscience always had the same severe answer to such wishful thinking. She did not deserve to profit from her deception. More likely, if Aaron felt trapped into a marriage he did not want, he would always pine for Iris and grow to despise his unwanted wife.

Reason assured Lily that was the most likely outcome. Yet Aaron's behavior toward her since their return to London stirred the embers of her foolish hopes. He often called on her while Iris and Aunt Althea were busy preparing for the approaching Season. Sometimes he took her for drives in Hyde

Park, chaperoned by her new lady's maid, Hannah Jackson. They had visited a picture gallery and twice stopped at Mr. Lackington's bookstore in Finsbury Square to investigate the new volumes for sale. Sometimes, if the weather was cold and damp, they would stay in and play backgammon by the fire.

As if summoned by her thoughts, a knock sounded on the sitting room door and her maid announced Captain Turner.

"I did not expect you today." Lily's mildly scolding tone could not conceal her pleasure. "I hope you do not catch a chill being out in that cold rain. Sensible folks ought not to stir from their own hearths on such a day."

She called to her maid, "Miss Jackson, please fetch tea for the captain and me."

"Do not fuss," Aaron protested even as he strode to the fire and warmed his hands before it. "I was only in the rain long enough to climb in and out of my carriage. Save your sympathy for my coachman, though he has a good stout hat and greatcoat, and I pay him well for his pains."

Lily chuckled as she took a seat by the fire. Anyone listening might think they were a congenial old married couple. "I am certain he will find a warm welcome below stairs. Our cook has taken quite a fancy to him, I'm told."

Aaron's droll grin suggested this information was not news to him. "As for the weather keeping everyone at home, did I not meet your aunt's carriage just down the street?"

Lily nodded. "She and Iris had a fitting with the dressmaker. Such vital matters are too important to be postponed for anything less than a hurricane."

"Priorities, my dear Lily." Aaron laughed. "One must have proper priorities."

His *dear* Lily? Why must he call her that and encourage the foolish hopes she worked so hard to keep in check? Perhaps he had only come today hoping to find Iris at home. Yet he did not seem greatly disappointed by her absence.

"I do not understand why you call on me so often." Lily gave voice to a question that had puzzled her for some time, but which she had not mentioned for fear his visits might stop. "After all that happened, I would think you could not stand the sight of me. If you are anxious for news of my situation, I promise I shall not waste a moment sending you news that I am not in *an inconvenient condition.*"

All the levity deserted Aaron's bold features. "That is not why I visit. And I can stand the sight of you quite well, as it happens."

His assurances came as a relief, yet they did not answer her question.

Aaron must have realized that, for he continued. "If it does prove necessary for us to wed, we shall need to act quickly. I want to lay the groundwork for an engagement, so it will not cause speculation. Besides, after failing to win your sister, I find myself a figure of ridicule among a certain segment of Society. I much prefer your company to theirs."

On top of everything else, she had made him a laughing-stock among men not half his worth. Lily's throat tightened.

"If I had not acted so foolishly, you might be engaged to Iris now and everyone would envy you instead of making fun. You must hate me."

Hard as Lily tried to maintain her composure, a wretched sob burst out of her. The past few days, her emotions seemed to swing wildly from one extreme to another. No doubt it was the continued suspense over her future and his.

"I do not *hate* you." Aaron sank onto a nearby footstool and took out a handkerchief which he offered to Lily. "I know full well that I share the responsibility for what happened. But I fear I cannot trust you after you lied to me again and again. The hardest part of this situation is that it has made it impossible for me to freely choose my future. But I promise you, if it proves necessary, I will do everything in my power to be a good husband and father."

If he hoped to bring her comfort, his efforts failed. How could any man bear to have a wife he mistrusted and resented?

"I n-never intended it t-to end l-like this." Lily pressed

his handkerchief to her brimming eyes. "I only wanted what was b-best for you and Iris."

"Best in whose opinion?" Aaron muttered.

Somehow his remark changed her sorrow to indignation. "Was it not what you wanted, for you and my sister to be together? Did you consider Iris's choice when you believed you were bedding *her*?"

Her sudden show of spirit seemed to take Aaron as much by surprise as it did Lily.

"I fear you are right," he admitted ruefully. "But it only proves my point. We must let others make their own decisions and their own mistakes if necessary. Trying to manipulate events only leads to trouble ... like our present predicament."

He heaved a sigh that melted Lily's antagonism back into bitter regret.

Just then, Hannah Jackson bustled in with the tea tray.

Lily thrust the damp handkerchief back at Aaron who accepted it with obvious reluctance.

For the next hour, as her maid sat at the window sewing, Lily and Aaron made awkward conversation. Their earlier frank exchange lay between them like an insurmountable barrier. Was this how their marriage would be if he was forced to wed her? He claimed he did not hate her and that was a great relief. But clearly it was not enough to keep them both from being miserable. If he felt trapped and duped into marriage, what chance would she have to win his love?

She was responsible for this wretched situation, Lily reminded herself. It was up to her to make it right. If she gave Aaron back his freedom to choose, perhaps she might still have a chance to improve his opinion of her.

She surged up from her seat so abruptly, it caught Aaron by surprise. He scrambled to his feet.

"Forgive me, Captain," she said. "I suddenly feel unwell. Jackson, will you fetch the captain's hat and coat?"

"Yes, Miss." The maid dropped her sewing and hurried away.

"I am sorry you are ill." Aaron's brow creased in a frown of fond concern that touched Lily's heart. It made her more determined than ever to restore his lost freedom. "I hope it is not serious."

She shook her head. "Quite the opposite. I can now assure you there will be no need for us to wed."

"You ...? Oh!" Aaron's eyes widened. "Are you certain?"

The maid bustled back in with his coat and hat, making further conversation on the subject impossible, for which Lily was grateful.

"Entirely certain," she replied. "Thank you for calling, Captain. I am sorry to cut our visit short."

"Think no more of it," Aaron insisted as he pulled on his greatcoat. The tension of the past three weeks had eased from his face. He looked as if a weight had been lifted from his shoulders. "I hope I have not tired you. Get some rest and I hope you will feel better very soon."

To Lily's surprise, he grasped her hand and pressed it to his lips. Then he turned and strode away with a much lighter step than when he'd arrived.

"Well, well." Hannah Jackson gave Lily a knowing look. "I thought Captain Turner had a fancy for your sister when you were in Beckwith Abbey. Lately he seems to have taken a liking to you."

"I fear you are mistaken," said Lily, even as she raised the hand Aaron had kissed and pressed it to her cheek. "Iris and the captain will make a match of it yet, mark my words."

The maid did not seem convinced. "Forgive me, Miss. You said you felt unwell. Is there anything I can get for you? I hope it is not a return of that fever you had at Christmas."

"Nothing so serious." Lily headed for the door. "I believe a little rest will soon put me right."

It was true she did not feel well, Lily reflected as she climbed the stairs to her bedchamber. But it was not the familiar pangs of her monthly courses, which were late arriving. Rather her stomach seethed with a fitful spell of nausea.

———•—•———

A month later, Aaron stood on the edge of the dance floor at a Mayfair assembly slowly sipping his second cup of punch. This was the third such event he had attended with Iris that week and he could scarcely suppress a yawn. So many late nights did not agree with him. Besides, now that the challenge and novelty of gaining acceptance had worn off, he found the endless round of Society gatherings deadly tiresome.

More than once he'd recalled with longing a visit to the picture gallery with Lily or a quiet game of backgammon by the fire.

"Captain Turner, well met indeed." A familiar voice hailed Aaron. He turned to see Rory Fitzwalter, Lord Gabriel Stanford and another man. "May we introduce our friend Jack Warwick? The three of us share a townhouse on Bruton Street."

"What Rory means," Lord Gabriel amended, "is that Jack has a house and he lets us stay with him."

Aaron bowed to Mr. Warwick. "It is a pleasure to make the acquaintance of mutual friends, sir."

Jack Warwick returned his greeting. "Are you the fellow who won an invitation to Lord Killoran's Christmas party off Rory? Well done, Captain! I was invited but begged off when I heard the countess's peacock of a brother would be in attendance. I hope you enjoyed yourself better than I would have."

"I did, sir." Aaron took an immediate liking to Rory and Lord Gabriel's forthright friend. "In spite of Lord Uvedale's presence."

Rory slapped Aaron on the back, a gesture better suited to a casual gathering than a Society evening. "No need to be modest, old fellow. Jack will think all the better of you for poaching the heiress Uvedale had his eye on."

Lord Gabriel nodded. "Did I not read that you have won

the hand of the fair Miss Crawford at last? You must be the envy of every bachelor in the West End — beauty, charm *and* a fortune. Has a date for the happy event been set?"

Aaron shook his head. "Miss Crawford wishes to wait until the end of the Season, so we do not miss out on any amusements when we take our honeymoon."

Lord Gabriel was right about Aaron being the envy of every bachelor in Society. He had basked in that envy at first, but lately it had grown stale. Now that every door was open to him, he began to wonder whether any of them were worth the trouble to enter. He welcomed the company of Rory and his friends, for they were a good deal more interesting than anyone else he had spoken to in days.

"Speaking of happy events," he grinned at Lord Gabriel, "I would have wagered good money that another engagement might come out of Lady Killoran's house party. What of the fair Miss Brennan? Surely beauty, charm and fortune describe her as well. We could both be the envy of all our acquaintances."

"Envy? Hardly!" The young nobleman blushed to a painful shade. "It is all very well for you, Turner. You have a fortune of your own. If you marry an heiress, no one will accuse you of fortune-hunting! If I do, I will be an object of contempt."

Did the son of a duke care what anyone thought of him? The notion bewildered Aaron. He had assumed only upstarts like him set such store by the opinion of others.

"Rubbish!" Jack made a rather rude, dismissive gesture. "You are too sensitive, Gabriel. Nobody whose opinion matters will care in the least, except to wish you joy."

Aaron found himself nodding in agreement though he felt like a fraud for doing so. He might not fear Society's censure as Lord Gabriel did but he could not deny he had coveted its favor. Did either truly matter in the end?

The duke's son shrugged. "I am only saying a man of fortune is free to wed any lady he chooses and no one will think worse of him."

Had he made a free choice? Aaron wondered. Or had he

been compelled to pursue the lady everyone else wanted?

"There you are, Captain!" Iris Crawford approached the group and latched onto Aaron's arm. "Now that we are engaged, I hope you do not think that you no longer need to make an effort. A lady may change her mind, remember?"

Rory and his friends chuckled at her quip and regarded Iris with blatant admiration that had once gratified Aaron. Now it felt like one too many helpings of rich food. No matter how delicious, it eventually passed the point of satisfaction.

Aaron introduced Jack Warwick after which Iris entertained the gentlemen with the latest gossip. Then she practically dragged Aaron onto the dance floor.

She was a much more proficient dancer than her sister, yet Aaron could not recapture the pleasure of his dances with Lily at Beckwith Abbey and Compton Court. He had believed she was Iris at the time. Yet now when he looked back on their Christmas interlude, he thought of her as Lily.

Iris was in fine form tonight — dancing flawlessly, conversing with vivacious energy, drawing admiring eyes toward both of them.

This was what he'd wanted, Aaron reminded himself. Now that he had it in his grasp, it felt empty somehow.

Could that be because he'd begun to anticipate the far more rewarding challenge of fatherhood? Though he would never admit it to either of the Crawford sisters, Aaron had experienced an odd sense of disappointment after Lily's announcement that she was not with child. Without realizing it, he had begun to imagine himself as a father.

That was still possible with Iris, of course. Aaron tried to shake off the sense of restless discontent that had been growing in recent weeks. Indeed, it was almost inevitable that they would have a family.

"Enjoy this social whirl while you can," he teased his fiancée as he escorted her and her aunt home from the assembly later that night. "By the time the next Season rolls around, you may have domestic duties to occupy you."

"A child, you mean?" There was a distinct lack of enthusiasm in Iris's tone. "That is what wet nurses are for — so a lady need not ruin her figure and miss out on all the lovely diversions London has to offer."

Aaron expected her aunt to chide Iris for her indelicacy and lack of maternal feeling, but Mrs. Henderson seemed to have dozed off.

Though he knew his fiancée's comment might be nothing more than a high-spirited jest, it still did not sit well with Aaron. Not long ago he had blamed Lily for depriving him of the opportunity to choose his wife. Now he found himself questioning whether he had made the right choice.

Chapter Sixteen

WHAT WOULD SHE do now?

Lily swallowed convulsively in an effort to ride out a fresh wave of nausea. If she gave in to every qualm, she would soon waste away to nothing. While that was a fate she might deserve, her baby did not. What was more, once the child was born, the poor little creature would need a healthy mother to care for it.

Lately she had made it her mission to remedy her dangerous ignorance about matters pertaining to the breeding and bearing of infants. She needed to be discreet, of course, for fear her sister or Aaron hear of her unseemly curiosity and guess the reason. It had taken some doing, in a houseful of women, to simulate her monthly courses, but she had managed. She did not want that effort to be undone.

Fortunately her new maid came from a large family. Two of Hannah's sisters had recently given birth. A friendly inquiry about their health often led to the sharing of useful information which Lily added to her growing store.

She'd learned that queasiness like hers usually went away around the time her belly would begin to swell. Since that would be harder to conceal or explain away, Lily was prepared to accept the nausea and not wish it away too soon.

If only Iris and Aaron would hurry up and get married, it would not matter so much if her condition was discovered. Then it would be too late for Aaron to insist on satisfying honor by marrying the mother of his child. Now that he and Iris were engaged, her sister seemed in no hurry to seal their union. What if she continued to dally?

Hannah Jackson appeared just then to announce Aaron.

Lily's stomach heaved again. She barely managed to hold her gorge. Yet when he strode through the door and smiled at her, she thought she had never felt so well in her life.

"You are out of luck, Captain," she informed him. "Iris and Aunt Althea went out to pay a call not half an hour ago. She will be sorry to have missed you."

"Will she?" Aaron did not sound very certain, yet his doubt did not seem to trouble him. "You needn't take pity on me, Miss Lily, for it is you I came to see. Will you indulge me in a brief visit?"

"I-I suppose." Conflicting inclinations strove within her. Part of her wanted to send Aaron away with a flea in his ear so he would not return any time soon. Spending time with him made her yearn for things she might never have. It gave her an unpleasant idea of what the years ahead were likely to hold. Besides, caution warned her she would run the risk of Aaron discovering her secret. She could not permit that — could she?

Another part of her, more passionate than wise, longed for any opportunity to spend time with him, no matter what the risks.

"Forgive me, Captain." Lily took a seat and gestured for Aaron to do likewise. "I did not mean to be inhospitable. You are always welcome here."

"Shall I fetch tea, Miss?" Hannah Jackson inquired.

Though her stomach churned ominously at the mere mention of food, Lily nodded. A few minutes of unchaperoned time with Aaron was worth far greater discomfort than that.

"Now," she said when the door closed behind her maid, "tell me what truly brings you here today. You may not *need* a reason to call upon me when Iris is away, but I know you seldom do anything without a good one."

Aaron laughed, with just a hint of sheepishness. "You know me too well, Lily. Better than your sister does, I sometimes think."

Was that so strange? Lily wanted to ask. Unlike her sister, she was vitally interested in everything about him. Besides, she and Aaron had spent far more time in private conversation. Iris scarcely saw him with fewer than twenty other people present.

"The truth is," Aaron continued, "I am worried about you. You have not been out to a ball or assembly in weeks. I hope you are not still unwell."

He worried about her? He noticed her absence from an event when Iris was there? Though Lily tried to tell herself not to make too much of it, a flicker of hope quickened within her.

"You cannot possibly have missed my awkward dancing and self-conscious conversation," she teased, reluctant to tell him an outright falsehood.

She had far too many of those on her conscience.

Aaron shrugged. "There are plenty of ladies in this town who can perfectly execute the steps of any dance. Still more can spout enough gossip and small talk to make my ears bleed. But one who can give me a good game of backgammon, point out the particular merits of a painting or recommend a book I might enjoy, that is a rarity. I cannot deny I miss your company. What keeps you away?"

"Have you not answered your own question?" Lily's cheeks grew warm and her heart beat faster. "Balls are occasions for dancing and gossip, not backgammon or literary discussion. Besides, what need is there for me to venture out in Society, now that my sister has found herself a good, reliable husband?"

"The knot has yet to be tied," Aaron was quick to remind her. A little *too* quick, perhaps? "Iris could still break it off. Only the other night she reminded me that it is her prerogative."

He did not sound particularly troubled by the possibility.

"What do you say?" He entreated her with a smile Lily found almost impossible to deny. "Would you like to accompany me to the Royal Academy or Mr. Parker's Panorama? Perhaps you can suggest another destination of interest."

Difficult as she found it to say no to him, Lily shook her

head reluctantly. "We have tea coming, remember? Besides, I am not feeling quite up to an outing today."

"I knew it!" Aaron sprang from his chair to kneel beside hers. He pressed his hand to her forehead. "Do you have a fever? How long have you felt ill? Should I summon a physician?"

His concern seemed far greater than a man should feel for his future sister. Or was she hearing only what she wanted to hear?

"There is no need for a physician." Lily reached up to remove his hand, which lingered on her brow. "But you do not seem quite yourself, either. Are you happy, Aaron? I thought that being engaged to Iris would delight you."

For a moment, he seemed on the point of deflecting her earnest query with a quip or a denial. But instead he sighed. "I thought so, too. I was certain of it. Yet the more time I spend with your sister, the less I feel I know her. How is it possible I could have been so mistaken in my affections?"

"Not mistaken — *misled*." Lily hung her head. Still she clung to Aaron's hand, unable to let it go. "At the Christmas party, I tried to impersonate my sister. Yet I fear I encouraged you to see her in a way that is not true to her character. For that and so much else, I am sorry. What is worse, I destroyed your trust, so you would be justified in doubting my regret is sincere."

"Nonsense!" Aaron insisted. "You did not trick me into falling in love with Iris. If I was misled, it was by that fool I see in the mirror every morning. The moment I saw how your sister attracted such general admiration, my fancy made her over into my ideal woman. It refused to see or hear anything that did not conform to the image I had created of her."

What did Aaron mean and what would come of it if he confessed such feelings to Iris? The thought made Lily feel faint. Her sister was too accustomed to being adored to tolerate tepid affection from her fiancé. If Iris broke off her engagement, everything Lily had done would be in vain.

"Lately," Aaron continued, "I have begun to look forward to having a family. But I have reservations about what sort of mother Iris would make. Perhaps I have misjudged her. But if I have not, then marrying her would be a mistake for which others besides myself would pay the price."

She could not continue to keep Aaron ignorant of the child she was carrying, Lily realized. She had not let herself think beyond his and Iris's wedding, except to wonder if she might give them her baby to raise. Now that hope might be in peril. She could not bear to keep Aaron's child from him, but neither did she want to rob him of his choice again.

There might be a way out of her dilemma, but it ran the risk of making matters even worse. And it would leave her terrifyingly vulnerable.

"You look pale as a ghost." Aaron's brow furrowed. "Forgive me if I have upset you, talking this way. Ever since we met, I have felt you were someone in whom I could confide. I should have considered whether some confidences might not be agreeable for you to hear."

Lily shook her head. "How can you wish to confide in someone you cannot trust? Of all the consequences of my folly, that is the one I most regret — losing your trust."

"As do I," Aaron murmured.

He had not left the side of her chair. Though she feared what her maid might think if she returned to find him there, Lily could not bring herself to bid him away. Neither did she wish Hannah Jackson would hurry with her errand. In fact, the longer she stayed away, the better.

After a pensive pause Aaron continued. "It pains me to doubt you. At times I forget all that happened in the past. Then I feel I could tell you anything and believe anything you might tell me. But when I remember, the wary side of my nature berates me for a fool."

"You are not a fool!" Without thinking, Lily reached for his hand and clung to it. "You are a good man who wants to think well of others, even after they have disappointed you. One thing is true. I swear it by all I hold dear — I never meant to harm you with my deception, quite the opposite. But I have learned that one innocent falsehood prompted by the most generous motives soon needs another to prop it up, then another to cover the second. On it goes until one day you find you have dug yourself into a deep, dark pit, a teaspoon at a time."

The soft glow of sympathy in Aaron's eyes gave Lily courage. It was fear that had motivated her initial deception and her present one. When it came to matters of the heart in particular, she could see now that fear was a poor state from which to proceed.

Yet could she alter the habits of a lifetime, even for the man who meant so much to her? Aaron Turner deserved a woman as forthright and brave as he was. Harsh lessons from her childhood warned her that those were virtues she would never possess.

More recent experience reminded her that she had been able to behave in a confident manner even when she did not feel that way. She had been able to convince everyone that was her natural character, until at last she almost believed it herself. Could she practice other virtues until they too became natural?

If ever there was a time to try, surely this was it.

Lily took a deep breath and tried to ignore her queasy stomach. "I would do anything in my power to win back your trust, Aaron. There are two matters about which I have not been truthful. I mean to confess them both now and promise most solemnly that I will never speak a false word to you again. Nor will I mislead you by withholding the truth. That may not be enough to persuade you at once, but I hope as time goes by, you will believe that I mean what I say."

"Two *more* lies?" Aaron's expression darkened in a look of bitter disappointment.

A wave of panic engulfed Lily, urging her to deny it all. But she owed Aaron the truth no matter what he might think of her as a result.

"Please hear me out," she begged. "The truth is … I care for you in a way that is far more than sisterly. At first I pretended to be Iris so you would not lose interest in her. But the better acquainted we became, the more I grew to … love you. That was why I let you make love to me that night — because I wanted to be yours, if only for a few hours."

The look of astonishment with which he greeted her news made Lily's heart sink.

She kept talking to forestall his rejection. "I know I should have told you, but I was afraid it would drive you away or make you pity me. I could not bear either of those things."

"Why … are you telling me this now?" Aaron sounded as bewildered as he looked.

"Because I would rather have your pity or contempt than your mistrust. And because I want to become a better person — not by pretending to be someone I am not, but by doing my best to change who I am."

She tried to let go of his hand, but Aaron would not allow it. "Do not change too much, Lily. And do not be so severe on yourself. You are not the only one who has made mistakes."

Aaron could scarcely believe his ears when Lily spoke of her feelings for him.

He'd been certain that all her past actions were driven by her desire to have him marry her sister. Or had that been another lie he'd told himself to protect his goal of winning Iris?

Now there could be no doubting her sincerity. Knowing what he did of her love-starved childhood, he could guess what it must cost her to lay her heart before him with no expectation that he would want her love, let alone be prepared to return it. Instead she had been willing to settle for the more modest goal of regaining his trust, no matter what it cost her in pride. The gesture stirred Aaron's heart. It elevated and humbled his spirit at the same time, in ways that he felt certain would make him a better man.

Yet when he reviewed his own actions since they'd met, he wondered if it was a transformation great enough to make him worthy of the priceless gift she offered. Had Lily also made the mistake of falling in love with the man she imagined him to be — one who bore little resemblance to his true character? Much as he now realized he wanted her, he could not sell her a false bill of goods.

"Do not judge yourself too harshly," he begged her. If anyone else had tried to reproach Lily that way, he would have made them very sorry for it. "You are not the only one who has made mistakes. You may have misled me, but not half so much as I misled myself and you. Besides, your motives were a good deal more generous than mine."

Now it was Lily's turn to look bewildered. "I do not understand. How did you mislead yourself? Or me?"

Behind him Aaron heard the sitting room door swing open, followed by a muted gasp. No doubt her maid was surprised by his nearness to Lily and her hand clasped in his.

"Out!" he ordered over his shoulder. "And do not return until you are summoned."

To her credit, the maid showed more spirit than many of the crewmen who served under Aaron.

"Miss Lily?" she called. "Is that what *you* would like me to do?"

After a glance at Aaron, Lily nodded. "Yes, please, Jackson. There are important matters I need to discuss with Captain Turner."

"Very well, Miss." The girl did not sound anxious to leave her mistress unchaperoned a moment longer. "But I will stay near enough to hear if you call me."

The door shut forcefully behind her, shattering the tension between Aaron and Lily. They both sputtered with laughter.

"I had better mind my manners then, hadn't I?" Aaron quipped.

"I should say so." Lily pressed her lips together in an unsuccessful attempt to smother a grin. "Though not too much, I hope. It would be a shame if you lost that privateer's audacity altogether."

"Never fear." Aaron winked at her, enjoying this easy banter though he knew they must return to more serious subjects. "I shall always be a privateer at heart. I need to remember that. I need to take pride in who and what I am, rather than trying to prove myself to a set of folks whose opinion does not matter in the end."

"It is natural to desire the approval of others," Lily replied. "Though you may always be certain of mine ..."

Her gaze fell for an instant, recalling the sweet, shy lady he had first encountered at Beckwith Abbey. Then, she seemed to borrow some of her sister's confidence to look him in the eye and smile. "... no matter what mistakes you might make."

Aaron's heart swelled to contain an infusion of happiness greater than he had ever known. "I sensed that from very early in our acquaintance. It was something that did not change when you pretended to be Iris. I should have known it was you in spite of the superficial differences. And when I discovered the truth, I should have realized the admiration and affection you'd shown me was altogether sincere. I let my determination to win your sister blind me to any insights that might have threatened my foolish ambition."

Contemplating his recent folly made him shake his head. "Only when I achieved the goal I thought I wanted did I realize how hollow it was. The better I came to know your sister, the more I sensed it was you I had grown to love during our Christmas courtship. *You* are the woman I want to spend my life with, Lily Crawford."

Like a magic spell, his words seemed to transform her back into that woman — one who possessed all Lily's fine qualities, along with the zest and confidence she so deserved. Her eyes sparkled with playful delight while her smile glowed with warm felicity.

The next thing Aaron knew, her arms were around his neck and her soft lips pressed to his in a blaze of ardor that would have truly scandalized her maid. He returned her kiss eagerly and with more than a little relief. How miserable would they all have been if he'd gone ahead and married Iris?

For a time, they let their lips express the feelings of which they had not been able to speak.

Finally Aaron could not hold back the question that would settle their future to his perfect satisfaction. "I proposed to you once before, thinking you were Iris. You refused me then, quite properly. Will you have me now, Lily, knowing it is you I love and want for my wife?"

He expected a swift, enthusiastic acceptance. Instead Lily's smile faltered. "I meant what I said the first time you proposed. I want very much to marry you, Aaron Turner. But do not forget you are still betrothed to my sister. What will we do if Iris refuses to break your engagement? You will be humiliated enough if she appears to jilt you and you must settle for her wallflower of a sister. But if *you* try to break the engagement, you will be dishonored and shunned."

Hard as he tried Aaron could not keep his face from betraying his reluctance to endure such public disgrace.

Lily gave a wistful nod. Aaron sensed she did not blame him for his reaction. Rather she regretted the scorn he might endure and wished to spare him.

"You may not long to prove yourself as you once did," she reminded him gently. "But could you bear that kind of condemnation? I want you to be admired as you deserve."

Did it matter what anyone else thought of him, as long as he could respect himself and strive to be worthy of the admiration Lily bestowed so generously?

Clasping her to his heart, Aaron pressed his cheek to her hair with a sigh that gusted up from the depths of his heart. "There is only one person whose opinion matters to me now and that is the lady in my arms. During the past weeks, I have feasted on the acclaim of Society only to find how quickly it lost its flavor. I have no doubt public disgrace will lose its bitterness just as readily. But our happiness will endure and only sweeten with age. So accept my proposal and let Iris take care of herself."

"Very well." Lily nodded, her silken hair whispering against his face. "If you still wish to have me once I have confessed my second falsehood."

A chill went through Aaron. He had forgotten there was another. Might it have the power to snatch the happiness of a lifetime from his grasp at the last instant?

Reluctantly he released Lily from his embrace and drew back so he could see her face. "If you can find it in your kind, faithful heart to forgive my folly, I will gladly overlook any other falsehood you have told me, provided we can agree to be truthful with one another from now on."

He'd hoped Lily would agree without a great deal more persuasion, but when he finished speaking he sensed an air of reluctance from her.

"Do not offer such a generous bargain until you know what you will get in return," she advised him.

Could it be so bad that he would be tempted to cast away the joyous future he foresaw with her?

"Out with it then." The words came out gruffer than he intended.

Lily seemed to steel herself for an ordeal whose outcome she doubted. "I did not want to deceive you again. I was trying to undo the damage of my earlier deception and I could see no other way. I did not want to take away your choice but now that you have freely chosen ..."

She paused for breath or perhaps to seek the proper words. In that instant, Aaron knew. "You *are* with child."

Lily nodded. "I am so sorry to have kept it from you. I should have remembered how one lie leads to another and another. That was why I decided I must tell you. Can you forgive me? Can you still love me?"

Though it troubled him to think of what might have

happened if she had persisted in her deception, Aaron knew she had only done it to spare him, no matter what it might have cost her.

He took her hands in his and pressed them to his lips. "It would take more than that to change my feelings for you, my sweet Lily. Your news has made me a very happy man. The only thing that could make me happier is claiming you as my wife, if you are still agreeable."

"Agreeable?" The last shreds of her anxiety melted in a smile that assured Aaron there would be no more secrets between them. "I am far more than agreeable. If I had my way, Aaron Turner, I would bundle you into a carriage this minute and elope to Gretna Green!"

Epilogue

London, a year later

"LILY, YOU WILL never guess the news I just heard." Aaron strode into the nursery of their London townhouse only to be stopped short by the sight of Iris Crawford visiting his wife and little daughter. "Forgive me, my dear! I did not know you had company."

Though Iris had been quite as eager as Aaron to break their engagement, Lily knew her husband still felt guilty for the way he'd treated her sister. Iris knew it too, and teased him mercilessly. Lily had been relieved to know she had not injured her sister by marrying Aaron. She and Iris were closer than ever now, in spite of their different temperaments.

"I am hardly company, dear brother." Iris insisted on giving Aaron a peck on the cheek, which flustered him much to her amusement. "Lily assures me your door is always open so I may come by often to see my pretty little niece."

She cast a doting smile at the baby, who reposed contentedly in Lily's arms. "Really, she is such a good-natured creature that I am quite looking forward to having one of my own someday."

"That is a turnabout, indeed." Aaron circled past his sister-in-law to join Lily and the baby. Though he had not been gone long, he treated his wife to a fond kiss. "Does this mean one of your many admirers has secured you?"

Contrary to custom, Iris's broken engagement had not made her any less popular with the gentlemen. In fact there seemed to be heightened competition over who could succeed in getting the skittish belle down the aisle.

"Not yet," Iris chuckled, "though I do have a very agreeable baron and the son of an earl vying for my favors."

"I cannot imagine why you still hanker after an aristocratic beau," Lily teased her sister. "When you see how happy I am with my untitled husband."

Iris wagged her finger. "Now sister, I thought you'd learned your lesson about letting me make my own decisions. I may not find quite the gem of a man you have, but he will suit me all the same, title or no title."

"She is right, you know," Aaron whispered in Lily's ear.

Lily nodded and gave him the baby to hold.

She caught Iris in a warm embrace. "As long as you are truly happy, you may wed the King of the Cannibal Islands with my blessing."

Aaron laughed heartily. "Only do not invite us to dine with you!"

Iris returned her sister's embrace and made a face at Aaron. "No cannibals for me, I assure you, no matter how exalted their rank. Now I must fly. Aunt Althea and I are going to the theatre tonight. I am told our new Prince Regent is likely to be in attendance."

With a merry wave, she took her leave.

Lily turned back to her beloved husband and their darling daughter who smiled and cooed in his arms. "What were you saying when you came in, dearest? Some news you heard?"

"Ah, yes," said Aaron. "There is a rumor going around that an infant was left on the doorstep of the house Rory Fitzwalter and Lord Gabriel Stanford share with their friend, Jack Warwick. Apparently one of them is the child's father but no one knows which. I hear it is a little girl, the age of our dear Ella Rose."

"Oh, my!" Lily shook her head in astonishment. "If the baby belongs to Mr. Fitzwalter or Lord Gabriel, it must have been conceived over Christmas at Beckwith Abbey. Do you suppose Miss Brennan could be the mother?"

"It is possible." Aaron seemed rather pensive as he cradled their daughter. Was he thinking what might have become of her if he and Lily had not found their way to one another?

"The poor wee thing." Lily leaned against her husband, stroking their daughter's soft cheek. "Whoever she belongs to, I hope she will be properly cared for and loved."

Aaron nodded. "I heard that a widowed kinswoman of Jack Warwick's is helping to care for the baby until her mother can be found. As for love, if our own experience is anything to judge by, the Bachelors of Bruton Street will be as besotted with their little lady as we are with ours."

"Does this mean I have a rival for your affections?" Lily teased him.

"No need to worry on that score." Aaron leaned over to press a kiss upon her brow. "This little one is my princess, but you are the undisputed queen of my heart!"

The End

Dear Reader,

If you read my earlier novel, *Scandal on His Doorstep*, or any of the other works from the multi-author Regency series *A Most Peculiar Season*, thank you for your patience in waiting for *Scandal Takes a Holiday*. In nearly twenty years of publishing, none of my books has taken quite such a meandering path to completion!

Shortly after releasing *Scandal on His Doorstep*, I started work on a sequel featuring Lord Gabriel Stanford and Irish heiress Moira Brennan. But as I wrote, I realized I needed to know a lot more about the fateful house party at which they met, and where Baby Sarah may have been conceived. I decided to go back and write a prequel novella about the party, but was advised not to feature Gabriel and Moira as its main characters, since their love story would not be resolved at the end.

That's when the idea of mistaken twins occurred to me. I know from personal experience how confusingly similar identical twins can appear, while often being exact opposites in personality. My twin sons were like that for many years. One April Fool's Day, the boys changed places in school, fooling all their classmates and teachers!

In *Scandal Takes a Holiday* shy heiress Lily Crawford takes the place of her vivacious twin sister when Iris falls ill. Lily does not want Iris to wed the fortune-hunting aristocrat who has been wooing her. She would rather see her sister married to a responsible, resourceful man like Captain Aaron Turner. Aaron made his fortune as a privateer, but is now ready to settle down and gain acceptance from Society by winning the beautiful, sought-after Iris Crawford. When she rebuffs his advances, Aaron enlists her sister Lily to help him court the reluctant heiress during Lady Killoran's Christmas house party.

Fearing her sister's sudden illness could wreck their plans, Lily decides to take Iris's place and give Captain Turner the romantic encouragement he needs. Her playacting soon turns all too real as Lily begins to fall in love with the man who is determined to marry her sister. When the masquerade is discovered, scandal threatens all their futures. Can Lily overcome a lifetime of fear to step out of her sister's shadow and risk her heart? And can Aaron take a hard look at his motives for wanting Iris Crawford to realize that Lily may hold the key his happiness?

As I wrote Lily and Aaron's story, I discovered it was too big for a novella, especially with Gabriel, Rory and other characters busy in the background! When I got to the end, I found that a novel which began as a novella needed a *lot* of revising to make it work. I am so happy to finally share this story with my readers — I hope you will enjoy it. Now I can get back to working on Gabriel and Moira's story with a better understanding of its history.

To get news of my future books, previews of covers and excerpts, special giveaways and more, sign up for my newsletter: http://eepurl.com/F4RWX

Happy reading! Deborah

About the Author

Deborah's first novel won the Golden Heart award for Long Historical and was nominated for a RITA for Best First Book. Since then Deborah has written more than two dozen novels in the genres of historical romance, inspirational romance and otherworld fantasy. Her books have been translated into more than a dozen languages and sold millions of copies worldwide. Deborah invites you to visit her website for more information.

Website: www.deborahhale.com
Facebook: www.facebook.com/AuthorDeborahHale
Goodreads: http://www.goodreads.com/
author/show/133710.Deborah_Hale
Pinterest: http://pinterest.com/hrwdebhale/

"Hale's characters are so finely created they become real in her readers' minds and hearts."
— *syndicated romance reviewer, Sheryl Horst*

Also Available

Confessions of a Courtesan

In a Stranger's Arms

Snowbound with the Baronet

Scandal on His Doorstep

Made in the USA
Las Vegas, NV
07 August 2021

27757466R00132